A

Long

Love

Ago

Misty Jae Ogert

Dedication

To all my readers. This one is for you.

CONTENTS AND TRIGGER WARNINGS

Dear Reader,

This book is a work of fiction. Names, characters, places, and incidents are products of the author's imagination or are used factiously.
Any resemblance to actual events or locales or persons, living or dead is entirely coincidental.
For those of you that appreciate a heads-up about certain content in a book, this is for you. First of all, there is explicit sex and language in the contents of this book. If you don't want any spoilers, you may not want to read the rest of this warning. This book deals with cheating while it is with the main characters wanting to be together their significant others are being cheated on. There is also a death of a loved one that takes place in the book. I'm sorry if this is the end of your journey with this story. I hope you will check out my other work now or in the future. Take care, my friend. For those of you still wanting to take the plunge. Happy Reading!

Playlist:

Can't Help Falling in Love-Haley Reinhart

Lips of An Angel-Hinder

I've Had The Time of My Life-Bill Medley &
Jennifer Warnes

Surrender-Natalie Taylor

How Do I Say Goodbye-Dean Lewis

You Raise Me Up-Josh Groban

Shallow-Lady Gaga & Bradley Cooper

Higher-Creed

Love Me Like You Do-Ellie Goulding

I'm Yours-Brent Anderson

Table of Contents

Also by Misty Jae Ogert

See You Never

Amnesia at the Altar

ACKNOWLEDGMENTS

I want to thank the readers that stuck by me waiting patiently for my next book. Those of you that continue to encourage me on my writing adventures. Life has continuously found a way to interfere with my creativity. I feel like I'm finally on a roll so hang tight there is more to come. Courtney, my best friend, thank you for being there from the first book to hopefully the last. Trish, my work muse that has kept me on task, the fire under my butt to keep me moving forward. Both ladies are excellent alpha readers. To Julie for helping with the developmental edits. Ann-Marie for your instrumental suggestion I add the second point of view, I hadn't planned on it, but I feel it gave the book so much more depth. As always to my ever-supportive husband, Donny. He figured out the difficult task of formatting. Last but certainly not least to my super creative and talented daughter, Madison for the cover art. I love you both to the moon and back.

Chapter One

♥

     Kinsey's gaze in the mirror of the luxury hotel bathroom stares back at her accusingly. Her slim fingers grip the edges of the granite countertop. Steam is rising from the sink as the continuous stream of water flows out of the faucet and down the drain untouched. She is attempting to slow her breathing as her heart threatens to pound out of her chest. Puffing out her cheeks she releases a slow shaky breath her head ducking down. She peers down at her pretty bare feet. Her toes are painted a pale pink.

     Pushing away from the vanity, she paces on the heated marble floors her hands firmly on her hips. She is stalling for time, and she knows it. Kinsey has prepared for this. She has been professionally waxed, her hair blown out, and indulged in a deluxe manicure and pedicure purchased this week. There is another mirror on the back of the bathroom door. Rotating left and right she nods in approval at her forty-year-old body.

     How has she gotten herself into this predicament? On the other side of the door, two men are waiting for her to join them. She is a married woman, happily married for the past eighteen years. Turning off the water she unlocks the bathroom door and turns the knob…

Chapter Two

Kinsey Nineteen years earlier…

Kinsey is laughing hysterically with her friends. They are blowing off steam at the end of a long work week. Standing around at a tall pub-style table in the middle of a crowded Manhattan bar they are drinking to numb the pain of the crappy week. That's when he strides through the front door bringing a much-needed gust of wind to the overheated crowded room. Her breath hitches in her throat as she assesses his pilot's uniform, his hat tucked up under one arm. His eyes find hers immediately in the throng of strangers. The smile freezes on her lips and her airway seems to constrict.

Kinsey's friend Trish notices immediately and follows her gaze. Trish gives a low whistle. "I know, right?" Kinsey says out of the side of her mouth. The man nods his head in Kinsey's direction a warm smile on his face as he continues to fight his way through the patrons making it to the bar. Within ten minutes, their waiter brings over a round of drinks they hadn't ordered. "From the gentleman at the bar," he explains. Kinsey didn't have to look to know which "gentleman at the bar" but she can't help but peer in his direction.

The man lifts his drink when she spots him. She mimics his gesture in a silent toast to him. "You need to go over there," Trish tells her.

Kinsey looks down at her much shorter friend, "You think so?" She is certain she will head over there. She knew the second he walked in the door it would happen. She is biding her time. She doesn't wait for a response and her other two friends gasp as she heads straight for him.

He stands when she reaches him. Good, he has manners. He is taller than her even in her high heels which she finds an instant turn-on. His uniform also doesn't hurt, it fits him like a glove showing off a slender figure. "My name is Grayson Wells." He offers his hand, and she takes it finding it firm and warm.

"Hi, I'm Kinsey Marshall. Nice to meet you. Thank you for the drinks."

"Sure thing. Would you care to join me?"

She looks at her friends who are blatantly staring. He smiles and waves to them and they all giddily respond with waves and grins of their own. "I should get back…" she trails off because it is as if they are reading her lips. They shake their heads and even mouth no. Some of them even wave their hands in her direction as if telling her to stay away from them. A small laugh escapes her lips as she turns to face him, "I suppose I can join you for a while." He has the warmest smile that reaches his blue eyes, making her feet sweat.

A couple seated next to his barstool leave and she easily slides into place. He waits for her to make herself comfortable before following suit. "So, are you in town for business?" she asks taking a sip of her drink.

"I am. I live in San Diego."

"Wow, long way from home. When do you go back?"

"Tomorrow night."

"That's not too long of a layover. Do you fly out here often?"

"I just took a shift for a friend this isn't my normal stop."

"Where do you usually fly to?"

"All over, but mostly Hawaii."

"Well, this is a serious downgrade. It's the middle of February and we have a blizzard going on."

Grayson laughs and then says, "Not from where I'm sitting." She blushes. "That's enough about me. Tell me about yourself, Kinsey. Where are you from? What do you do for a living?"

"I was born and raised on the Upper East Side and work in finance like my dad."

"You look like a power suit." She looks down at herself and laughs at her Dolce and Gabbana, legit power suit.

"Thanks?"

"No, it's a compliment. Trust me you look great."

"Well thank you. I appreciate that. It's been a hellish week at work."

"Thank God it's Friday."

"Cheers to that," Kinsey clinks her wine glass to his beer bottle.

"Care to share?"

She sighs, "I'm sure you don't want to hear about corporate bullshit."

Grayson shrugs, "Try me."

She relates the most interesting details of the goings-on of her company. They move on to other topics and before they know it the bar is closing. Looking around they find themselves as some of the few customers left, it has thinned out quite a bit. Even her friends left hours earlier, texting her their goodbyes from afar rather than interrupting the pair.

Grayson settles the tab while she runs to the lady's room. Walking out onto the sidewalk together he asks, "Can I hail you a cab?" The streets are empty.

"No, I'm just around the corner. I'm going to walk home." Snow is falling gently covering the sidewalk. Piles of snow are plowed to the curb.

"May I walk you home?" Grayson asks.

Kinsey isn't nervous about her neighborhood, and she usually doesn't allow strangers to know where she lives but she feels at ease with Grayson, "Yes." He falls into step next to her. "Today was not the day to wear high heels," she observes.

He looks down at her struggling through the slush. "Here," he hands her his hat.

"What am I doing with this?"

He steps in front of her and bends his knees, "I'll give you a lift." His meaning dawns on her as she puts his captain's hat on and jumps on his back. He carries her with no problem. Kinsey laughs as she wraps her arms around his neck. Luckily, she isn't far, just a block and a half.

"Turn here," she instructs at the end of the block. When he reaches her apartment, he deposits her on the first step. Grayson turns and finds her eye level with him. "You look good in my hat."

"Why thank you, Captain." She takes the hat off and places it on his head. "You're hot," she declares, "I think you wear it much better than me."

"Agree to disagree." They take in each other for a minute, smiles on their faces. Her hands rest on his shoulders. Grayson takes a step closer his hands resting on her hips. Kinsey leans forward and he meets her, their lips touching. The kiss is sweet and tender.

When he pulls away, he asked, "Can I call you if I'm ever back in New York?"

"I'd like that." They exchanged numbers and share another longer kiss then he watches her make her way up the stairs and into her building.

Chapter Three

♥

A month later Kinsey is at work in a meeting when a text pings her phone. Grayson's number shows up. "I'm in town for the night. I'd love to take you out to dinner if you are free."

Delighted she responds immediately, "When and where?" He texts her the details for later.

Kinsey shows up in a sexy navy-blue dress. Grayson has picked a nice restaurant with white linen tablecloths, real candles on the tables, and servers dressed all in black. As the hostess walks her to their table, Grayson stands to greet her "Kinsey," his hand lightly touches her hip and he leans in for a chaste kiss on the cheek, "You look stunning." Blushing at his compliment, she slips into the chair he pulls out for her. She admires the grey suit he is dressed in as he sits opposite her. They share a romantic dinner. She has a roommate, so they go to his hotel.

Grayson takes her hand when they enter the hotel. They walk to the elevators, and he pushes the button to his floor. They ride up in silence. It's a long walk to the end of the corridor. Taking his key out of his pocket he swipes it into the reader, and they hear a soft click, and the light flashes green.

He opens the door for her, and she walks in ahead of him. It's a typical hotel room with a giant king-size bed in the middle. "Would you care for a drink?" Grayson walks to the mini-fridge and holds it open.

"I'm good, thanks." He closes the door without looking inside.

"Are you nervous?" he asks.

"No-yes. I've never done the one-night stand thing."

"Is that what you think this is?"

She shrugs, "I don't know. Isn't it?"

"Well, I guess anything is possible, but I do plan on seeing you again."

"I thought you didn't have this route?"

He smiles, "I gave up Hawaii."

"Seriously? For me?" She closes her eyes briefly she hadn't meant to ask but she wants to know.

"I find you fascinating. I wanted to see you again and after tonight I still want to see you." That takes her breath away.

She walks to him and takes his hand, "I want to see you again too."

"I'm glad we are on the same page." Kinsey lifts her head for him to kiss her. He does, "You know I'm not opposed to taking this slowly."

She visibly relaxes, "Really?"

"Of course. I'm going to be coming and going from your life in my line of work. You may decide this doesn't work for you. Let's get to know each other. Will you spend the night with me? We can talk and watch pay-per-view movies?" He is holding her hands.

Smiling she nods, "That sounds perfect."

"I may make out with you a bit too," he says slyly.

She grins, "Even better." He kisses the top of her knuckles.

"It's settled then. Should we order popcorn?"

Giggling she says, "I don't think they have popcorn on the room service menu."

"I'm sure if I called down to the front desk, I could get it. Any other special requests?"

She ponders the question seriously, pacing the room, one hand on her bent elbow, her finger tapping her lips, "Hmmm, what do I want? A diet soda."

Grayson walks to the fridge and opens it. He pulls a glass bottle of diet soda out and puts it on the stand in front of the TV, "Too easy Kinsey, give me a challenge."

"How about that candy that is rainbow-colored and has sugar on it?"

"Yes! That's the spirit." He picks up the phone to dial.

"Oh! Chocolate covered anything."

"That's my girl."

She blushes at the pet name he has for her. Is she his? It makes her heart race to think so. Turns out the concierge service isn't as full-service as Grayson would like. He is disappointed as he gets off the phone, and none of their demands are met.

"There is a bodega not far from here. I'm sure they will have all of this. If you want to go back out?" Kinsey offers.

"Great, let's do it." He looks at her for a second before asking, "Do you want to borrow my sneakers? They are probably way too big for your feet, but it might be a more comfortable walk."

His thoughtfulness is overwhelming. "That would be great, thank you."

He goes to the closet and produces his running shoes for her. Kinsey sits on the edge of the bed slipping out of one shoe and replacing it with the other. She has to tighten the laces to keep them on but they are considerably more comfortable than her heels.

When she stands, he smiles, "Wow, you've shrunk."

"Are you disappointed the illusion is gone? Thank God we didn't sleep together, might have ruined it for you in the morning."

"Never," he assures her leaning down for a kiss. They walk hand in hand down to the local bodega grocery store. When they reach the street the night air is cool. Grayson shrugs out of his suit coat and places it over her shoulders. She snuggles into the coat not only is it keeping the wind at bay, but it is warm from his body heat. His cologne grazes across her nose and she inhales deeply.

"Thank you," she murmurs looking up at him through her lashes a move she knows drives a man wild. She is not disappointed. He stops on the sidewalk his hands taking a hold of the lapels on his coat and pulls her to him. They kiss right there for all the world to see. Strangers walking around them. Her hands wrap around his waist, her fingertips sliding up his back, taking a step closer to him.

"You're beautiful," he tells her when he pulls away.

She laughs at herself, "I'm wearing a nice dress, men's sneakers, and a suit coat."

"My opinion stands." She kisses him again.

Inside the jam-packed store, Kinsey holds up a bag of white cheddar popcorn already popped in triumph. Grayson sneaks up on her in the aisle. His arms full, after raiding the candy at the register, not only did he have her requests but several more selections.

Back at the hotel room, they dump their haul on the bed including a bottle of wine he purchased when checking out. "I'll get the glasses," Grayson goes to the bathroom and brings back the water glasses from the sink. "These will have to do."

"Works for me," she tells him as she opens the bottle and pours them both a drink. He hands her one after she twists the top back sealing the wine and placing it on the nightstand.

"To getting to know each other," he offers as a way of a toast.

"I'll drink to that," she assures him as she clinks her glass to his. He hands her the remote. She walks around to the side closest to the window. Putting down her glass and the remote she uses her toe to pull off the heel of his sneaker and repeats the step for the other foot. Grayson kicks out of his shoes on the other side of the bed. She takes off his jacket placing it over the back of one of the chairs.

They climb onto the bed on top of the covers. She turns on the TV and goes through the list of movies sipping her wine. She gives him three options of what she would be willing to watch and he picks one. They purchase the movie as he opens the bag of popcorn.

"Do you want to slip into something a little more comfortable," he asks as he shovels popcorn into his mouth. She raises an eyebrow at him. "The hotel has terry-cloth robes in the closet."

"Yes, please. I'll be right back." Kinsey scoots off the bed and heads to the closet grabbing the robe before closing herself in the bathroom. She pulls the pins holding her hair up before shaking out her long locks. She wiggles out of her dress and removes her stockings. She debates for a full five minutes if she wants to remove her bra or not, her underwear is staying on. In the long run, she votes for comfort and removes her bra, tucking it under her dress.

When she returns, Kinsey sees that Grayson has changed as well. He is in navy sweatpants and a grey t-shirt. "I hope you don't mind."

"Not at all."

This time when crawling into bed she slips under the comforter. "I can stay on top of the sheets if it makes you more comfortable?"

"Don't be silly," Kinsey pulls the comforter back on his side and pats the bed. Grayson joins her. The movie is forgotten as they kiss sliding further down under the sheets until they are laying facing each other. They talk in between long kisses. Eventually, they fall asleep entangled together.

In the morning, Kinsey is woken with a kiss on the forehead. Stretching she opens her eyes and finds Grayson is already showered and dressed in his pilot's uniform. "You're leaving already?" She sits up in bed.

"I didn't want to wake you. You looked so peaceful. Stay if you like. Check-out is at noon. I left you the key. Feel free to order room service if you are hungry." Kinsey gets up on her knees straightening his already straight tie.

"Thank you for last night. I had a lot of fun."

He smiles, "You're welcome. I had a good time too. I'll call you when I land?"

"I'd like that. Have a good flight." Her hand wraps around his neck pulling him towards her. They kiss, then kiss again, more intensely. She finds herself falling back onto the bed, him on top of her. He settles in between her thighs.

"I have to go," he tells her.

"I know," she says beckoning him for another kiss which he gives her. She finally releases him and gently pushes him away.

"I'll be back in a couple of weeks. It's a Wednesday. I only have time for lunch if you are available?" She picks up her phone from the nightstand and puts it into her calendar.

"I will see you then." She follows him to the door where he gives her another kiss goodbye. When he leaves, she runs to the bed and jumps in. Holding a pillow over her face she screams kicking her legs in excitement.

Chapter Four

♥

In the two weeks since Grayson left, they call and text every day. They talk about work, music, family, goals, and dreams. When Wednesday arrives, Kinsey is exuberant. She has carefully planned her outfit, hair, and make-up.

She meets him at a small café near the airport. She sits at a black wrought iron table on the other side of a matching wrought iron fence. His face lights up when he sees her. She stands as he heads directly to her. The fence in between them, he reaches over and brings her lips to his. It is not a quick kiss, it is intense, long, and lingering. She smiles when they finally separate their lips, his hands still cup her face, and her hands are resting on his wrists. "Care to join me on this side of the fence?" Kinsey asks.

Grinning he kisses her again before jogging around the fence to join her. "Have you been waiting long?" He asks as he takes a seat opposite her.

"No, not long."

"Good."

They eat outside, before taking a stroll through a nearby park. "I've missed you," he tells her.

"I missed you too."

"I'll be in town in three and a half weeks for an overnight layover," Grayson said.

"Three and a half weeks?" It had been difficult for Kinsey the past two weeks waiting for him.

"I told you the schedule sucks," he sounds apologetic. "I need to get going. Did you want to take a ride to the airport with me or do you need to get back to work?"

She looks at her watch, she knows she should get back to work but instead tells him, "I have time." His grin is rewarding, and she knows she made the right decision.

Grayson hails a cab, and he holds the door open for her. He climbs in after her. "It's going to be a long three and a half weeks," she tells him as she scoots closer.

"Impossibly long," he murmurs as he looks down at her his arm slung over the backseat of the cab. She pulls his handsome face towards her. His lips met hers as they did at the restaurant, urgent and eager. Kinsey offers her own fire and heat to the kiss, moaning when she feels his hand slide under her thigh. Tongues mingle and hands roam their bodies swaying with the motion of the cab.

They only break apart when they hear a rapping on the plexiglass that separates them from the driver. She laughs as she realizes they have made out the entire way back to the airport. "I'll call you when I land. Thanks for meeting me for lunch."

"Of course. I'll see you when you get back."

Four days later Kinsey is in her apartment watching one of the late shows when she hears a knock on her door. Her roommate Bethany is spending the night with her boyfriend, so she goes to the door cautiously.

Kinsey looks through the peephole then quickly unlocks and removes the deadbolt before throwing the door open wide. "You're back!" she exclaims as she stands there in her PJs. Grayson is holding his hat, with his bag at his feet, and looks amazing in his uniform.

"I couldn't wait to see you. I traded some flights-"

Kinsey doesn't let him finish, she squeals and jumps in his arms. Grayson catches her easily and kisses her, twirling her around. "I only have six hours," he tells her.

"We better make it count." Kinsey pulls his carry-on bag inside and locks the door. He is behind her kissing her neck as she deadbolts the lock.

Turning he kisses her again and she starts to unbutton his collared shirt, his hat falling to the ground. Grayson is pulling the shirt from the confines of his pants.

They strip off each other's clothes as they kiss and head down the hallway to her bedroom. His shoes are in the living room, and his shirt is at the kitchen entrance. His belt is on the door handle of her roommate's door.

They fall into her bed removing the rest of their clothing. He fishes a condom out of his pocket and puts it on. He is inside her quickly and she gasps at the sensation her body adjusting to the feel of him. Kinsey cradles him between her thighs as he pushes inside her repeatedly. His chest is rubbing against her breasts his head is above hers. She holds on, her hands on his smooth back, her hips working in succession with his. Kinsey climaxes easily enough, the anticipation of this night brought on by the unexpectedness of seeing him before he was due to be back. Grayson's orgasm arrives shortly after hers and he collapses on top of her.

Their breathing is ragged as they hold each other. She is drawing lazy lines across his back. He kisses her collarbone before rolling off her. "Where is your bathroom?"

"Down the hall right before the kitchen."

"Thanks, I'll be right back."

Grayson rolls out of bed, and she admires his nice ass as he leaves the room. She hears him turn on the faucet down the hall and she stretches under the covers. Kinsey smiles at his secret visit.

When he comes back into the room, she pushes herself up onto her elbow. He has his pilot's hat over his private area. She giggles but her eyes widen as he raises his hands, and the hat stays in place. "Impressive."

"I was thinking about you on the way back to the room. Six hours is going to go by fast and I want to use every minute of it touching you."

"Aye, aye Captain!" she salutes him the bedsheet falling from her breasts. He tosses her the hat, and she catches it, putting it on her head. Taking the sheet, he flicks it off her. Crawling into bed his face sets up camp between her thighs. Grayson licks her and she moans holding the hat firmly to her head. His large hand fondles one breast as he uses his middle finger to slide in and out of her while his tongue continues to lap up her juices.

Grayson excels in this department. Kinsey's eyes roll into the back of her head her body arching off the bed. He is now using two fingers and his teeth intermingled with his tongue and lips. The hat is forgotten as she clutches her pillow for dear life. He brings her to the brink then backs off, over and over again until when she finally does climax it's huge. Enveloping her in waves of pleasure that seem to last.

He comes to lay next to her as she recovers, his hands roaming her still-writhing body. His head is propped on his hand as he watches her a satisfied grin on his face. "That was amazing," Kinsey finally musters some words. "Do you have more condoms?"

"Yes, ma'am."

"Good," she says kissing him, pushing him to his back as she crawls on top of him. They make love again. At two in the morning, she cooks them omelets. They have a few bites before they are at it again in the living room. They take a shower before collapsing back into her bed as the sun rises.

Chapter Five

♥

They hook up every time he comes into town. Four months into Kinsey and Grayson's relationship they are having a picnic in Central Park. His back is against a tree and her head is laying in his lap. He is playing with her hair. "I have a present for you," Grayson said.

"I love presents." She smiles up at him. He pulls an envelope out of the bottom of the picnic basket. Opening it she finds a ticket to San Diego. Squealing, she sits up to hug him. "I love you."

Grayson assesses her, this is the first time either has made this declaration. "I love you too."

Two weeks later she flies out to see him for an extended weekend. Grayson picks her up from the airport. He pulls into his driveway. The house is white with a flat roof and a red door. Grayson unlocks the entrance and holds it open for her. His house sits directly on the beach. It is gorgeous, floor to ceiling windows. Kinsey knows he makes decent money being a pilot, but it seems like he may be either overextended, living beyond his means, or has money from another source.

After watching the sunset on the balcony, they share a candlelight dinner. They make love in his coastal bedroom tangled in crisp white sheets. Grayson's balcony door is open, letting in the salty air and soothing sounds of the crashing waves. The moon is bright tonight illuminating the bedroom in a soft blue glow.

Sated she has her fingers linked over his chest staring up at him. She plays with a scar on the underside of his chin. He takes her hand and kisses her fingers. "Can I guess?" she asks referring to his scar.

He shrugs his shoulders, "Sure."

"Biking accident as a kid?"

"Nope."

"As an adult?"

"Try again."

"You got into a fight with your best friend over a girl."

Grayson laughed, "No. Do you just want me to tell you?"

She sits up wrapping the sheet around her naked body, "No." Kinsey ponders some more, "Car accident in the middle of the night. You were upside down and no one found you until morning?"

He chuckles, "You have quite the imagination. Don't give up now you will probably come up with the real story."

Kinsey cracks her knuckles now getting serious with her guessing game. "It was a sword fight. He got the first blow, but you won in the end?"

"Yes, that's what happened."

"It is not!"

"Why not?"

"Because it is not. Will you just tell me the story?"

"I thought you wanted to guess?" Grayson said.

"Did you get beaten up by a girl?"

"It was a plane crash."

"What? Are you serious?"

Grayson sits up in bed his back against his cushioned headboard. "I was a rookie co-pilot. The landing gear wouldn't engage. We managed to put the plane down, but it skidded off the runway. Everyone survived. It's why I have such a nice house. Everyone got a settlement from the crash. It was a mechanical error that should have been caught earlier."

That would explain the house. "I'm so glad. I can't imagine not meeting you."

He smiles cupping her head, he pulls her close, "I know now, you are the reason I survived." Kinsey kisses him straddling his hips.

"I love you so much," she tells him.

"I love you," he tucks her hair behind her ear, "I want you to meet my family." "Kinsey looks at him in surprise they hadn't discussed this before. He met her dad when he was in town for a Sunday brunch once but that had been it. Her dad had given his approval of Grayson and that had made her happy.

"When?" "he asks.

"Tomorrow, they are coming for a BBQ."

"Great."

The following afternoon his mother walks through the front door, no knocking, no ringing of the doorbell, just pushing her way inside. "Hello?" she calls. She is holding a dish with tortellini pesto pasta salad that Kinsey can't wait to try. Grayson is outside so Kinsey smiles tipping her head and walking cautiously toward this woman.

"Hi, I'm Kinsey." he sees a middle-aged man that looks a lot like Grayson closing the door behind his wife. They shake hands and make introductions. His parents are Fred and Rosemary. Kinsey takes the bowl from Rosemary, putting it in the fridge. Kinsey asks if they would like any refreshments and Fred requests a beer while Rosemary says she is good for now.

Outside Grayson's parents embrace their son. Kinsey has brought out the same beer to Grayson that his dad is drinking, and he thanks her his eyes sparkling when he looks at her. It causes her stomach to flutter. Rosemary helps Kinsey finish setting the long table with ten chairs. They are expecting Grayson's older sisters, and their spouses and each of them has a toddler in tow.

The rest of the crew show up moments later almost as if they had caravanned there. It is utter chaos, but Kinsey thrives on it, having only her and her dad most of the time. Each sister has a daughter of their own and they are precious. They are two and three years old with big ringlet curls that seem to run in the family on Rosemary's side.

Kinsey looks to Grayson. His hair is cut short, and she wonders if he were to grow it out if it would be curly too. They go down to the beach and watch the girls splash in the waves, their moms standing close by, their feet in the shallow water while the rest sit in beach chairs to watch. Grayson cooks steaks and chicken on the grill, while Kinsey boils corn on the cob. The sisters brought fruit salad and baked beans with brown sugar, bacon, and ground hamburger. The tortellini salad is as good as it looks. Kinsey asks Rosemary for the recipe, and she seems delighted to be asked.

"I'll write down the recipe before I go," Rosemary tells her resting her hand on her forearm.

After dinner and some playful interrogation from the family, they retire down to the beach where Grayson has built a bonfire. The girls, an endless ball of energy, finally settle down with their moms wrapped in a blanket and fall asleep.

Once everything is cleaned up and everyone has left Grayson and Kinsey lay in bed. "My family loves you."

"How do you know?"

"They told me."

"When? I want details."

Grayson chuckles, "When you went to the bathroom. They said you were beautiful and kind. Smart and funny. They all pretty much agreed I should marry you."

Kinsey's eyes widen. They have only been dating for five months and it seems sudden although she isn't sure why. They love each other, they never fight, and things are as close to perfect as she can make them.

"Don't worry this isn't a proposal," he teases her, and she relaxes. The rest of the weekend is magical, and she doesn't want to leave when he drops her off at the airport. New York feels cold even though it's a beautiful eighty degrees. She throws herself into work until Grayson visits again. He flies her out to San Diego to spend Christmas with him and his family and she feels bad for her dad. Even though he told her he was going upstate to visit his family and not to worry. She calls him Christmas Eve and Christmas morning.

Chapter Six

♥

A year after dating, Grayson puts in for a transfer to NYC. Bethany is getting married and moving out, so Grayson moves in with Kinsey.

A couple of months after unpacking, they decide to go ice skating in central park. It's a large rink, nearby lamp posts shine down on the ice at night and the tall buildings looming on the other side of the street are lit up giving off a romantic glow. After a few laps around the rink, snow starts gently falling. It's landing on Kinsey's hair and not melting. She holds out her hand cupping it in her mittens as she tries to catch the falling flakes.

Grayson goes down beside her, "Oh, no," she giggles as she easily circles back around. When she reaches him, he is down on one knee pulling a black jewelry box out of his coat pocket. Her mittens cover the lower half of her face as tears start to well up. Stopping easily in front of him she waits for his speech, "Kinsey Marshall, from the moment I laid eyes on you I knew I wanted you in my life. From our first kiss to our last you make me feel complete. You dazzle me with your presence, and I can't imagine my life without you. Will you do me the honor of becoming my wife?"

Kinsey's head has been nodding since Grayson started speaking, "Yes!" The crowd that has gathered around them begins clapping and cheering as Grayson stands up, kissing her and wrapping her up in his arms. "Oh my gosh, I can't believe this is happening."

Pulling back, he shows her the ring. "Do you like it? I had Trish help me pick it out."

The center diamond is pear-shaped, surrounded by round diamonds, and the band itself is a circle of diamonds. It's not what she would have picked out for herself, but it is beautiful, and she loves that her best friend and her fiancé had picked it out together. "I love it," Kinsey pulls her mitten off and Grayson removes it from the box slipping it onto her finger.

Kinsey plans her dream wedding. She had always wanted a wedding at the Plaza in June but after his proposal and the fact that they met in the middle of February, she changes her mind to a winter wedding, but still at the Plaza.

"Don't you think that is a little pricey?" Grayson asks her when she tells him of her plan.

"I'm Daddy's princess. He has been planning for this day my whole life."

"Well, you're my Queen."

Kinsey kisses him, "Awe, I get a promotion."

The wedding is beautiful and in the middle of a blizzard. Grayson's family had flown in ahead of time and her relatives have come down from upstate New York. Trish is her maid of honor and Chase one of Grayson's co-workers is his best man. The ceremony is elegant, and the reception is a blast.

Kinsey's dad, Pierce gives the couple a generous cash gift they use as a down payment on a townhouse on the Upper East Side. When they want to start a family, Kinsey has a hard time conceiving. Grayson takes on international flights for more money so they can afford IVF treatment. They have twin boys.

Grayson is a great father when he is home. His schedule is rotating from four days on to four days off. He makes the most out of family time when he is home. He teaches them to ride a bike and play catch in the park.

As a husband, she couldn't ask for better. Grayson still surprises her with flowers or a spontaneous night out. He would arrange a sitter for the boys and take her away for an overnight getaway. She thinks their love life is great. It isn't as frequent as when they were younger and before kids but it's still good.

He spices things up and buys her toys to use in the bedroom. He starts to talk dirty to her suggesting he let her sleep with another man. "I would let him do things to you while I watch."

They are in the middle of making love, "Oh yeah? Like what kind of things?"

"Like fucking you with his tongue," Grayson growls in her ear.

Kinsey pictures her favorite ripped actor between her thighs and has an instant orgasm at the thought of him doing that to her as Grayson watches. Afterward, they clean up in the bathroom before snuggling under the sheets again.

"So, what do you think?" Grayson asks her.

Kinsey is turning on the TV. "About what?"

He is rubbing her back. "Having sex with someone else." Kinsey laughs but sobers when he doesn't. Muting the TV, she turns to him.

"No, I'm not going to have sex with someone else."

"Why not?" he asks seriously, and she frowns at him.

"Because I'm married? To you. What kind of question is that?"

"I'm serious. What if we find some stranger? You can pick him up in a bar. Wouldn't that be exciting, to be able to kiss someone else for the first time? Someone different touching you. Fucking you."

Kinsey assesses him. "That's a ridiculously bad idea."

"What's the worst that could happen?"

"I could think of a whole slew of things. Wait." Kinsey sits up her hand on his chest. "Do you want to sleep with someone else? Is that what this is all about?"

Grayson sits up next to her, "No. Not at all. That's not what this is about. I just thought it might be fun to mix things up. I love pleasuring you and I thought you might be bored with me."

"What? I'm not bored with you."

"It was just a thought. I'm sorry if I upset you."

"You didn't upset me. I'm just a little surprised."

Grayson doesn't mention it again until about a month later. They have a more in-depth conversation about it. Kinsey holds him off telling him she needs to lose weight. She starts going to the gym, eating healthier, and making a difference. He doesn't mention it for a while, and she thinks that he has changed his mind. But he doesn't let it go and now a plan has been set into motion. Not wanting to move forward, but already agreeing to it, she wonders if she can have a workaround.

Chapter Seven

♥

At work, Trish comes into Kinsey's office and closes the door. "What is with you lately?" she asks. Kinsey looks at her friend perplexed.

"What are you talking about? I'm fine."

"No one that says, "they're fine," she puts her fingers in the air quoting her, "Is fine. You know that, right?"

"Is that a thing? I'm fine." Kinsey says shuffling papers on her desk.

Trish lets out a frustrated groan, "You know I love you right? And I've known you for a long time. Something is up. Now if you don't want to talk about it, I respect that, but you might not realize you are putting off a vibe."

Kinsey sinks in her desk chair, "Shit, am I?"

"Yes!" Trish assures her.

Kinsey assesses Trish wondering if she should tell her anything. Trish sits in one of the chairs facing her desk waiting silently. Kinsey takes a deep breath, "Promise you won't say anything?"

"Obviously."

"No, I mean it you can't even tell your pillow tonight," Kinsey demands.

Trish puts her hands in the air palms facing out, "Promise," she even does the airlock and key over her lips and pretends to throw it away over her shoulder.

"Grayson wants to watch me have sex with another man."

"What!?" Trish's response is explosive.

"Shhh…." Kinsey stands waving her hands at her.

Trish's hands clamp down over her mouth trying to control the giggles that are now escaping involuntarily. "Oh my God I'm sorry," she is regaining control over herself, "I just wasn't expecting that." Kinsey sinks back down as she waits for her confidant to pull it together.

"Are you going to do it?" she asks.

"I don't know. I feel like it's a bad idea?" Kinsey looks to her friend for confirmation.

"I wish Tom would let me sleep with someone else."

"Trish!"

"What? Aren't you bored? Don't get me wrong I love Tom, but his belly has gotten big, and we pretty much have sex the same way every time. It might be fun to mix it up. Especially if Grayson is on board?"

"It was his idea. At first, I thought we were just role-playing in bed, but he started bringing it up when we weren't having sex. I feel like this could ruin our marriage."

"Or be the best thing that has ever happened to it. Just think he is giving you a hall pass to sleep with someone else. The catch is he wants to watch all the dirty deeds."

"Do you think I should?"

"Hell yes."

"Wow, okay."

"What are you worried about?"

"Everything. What if I can't get a guy?"

"As if," Trish waves her hand up and down as if her appearance explains everything.

"What if it's not good?"

"Well, that could be a problem," Trish concedes.

"I don't want to have sex with another person. What if they have a disease?"

"Use protection," Trish interjects.

"What if they get attached?" Kinsey's eyes widen at the possibility and whispers, "What if I start to have feelings for this other person? What if I like it and want to continue to do it but he decides he has had his fix and wants me to stop? Or worse I hate it and he wants me to continue?"

Both women sit silently running all the scenarios in their heads. "What if you use a decoy?" Trish asks.

"What?"

"Hear me out." Trish holds her hands out scooting to the edge of the chair, "What if you could get someone to agree to this plan before it happens so that it removes some of the pressure off of you finding someone, getting them to agree, yadda, yadda, yadda."

"Who would I even ask?"

Trish looks up wide-eyed, "What about one of your exes? Someone you have already slept with, so you know if they are good or not. Make sure they know this is a one-time thing, they would be doing you a favor."

"My exes are my exes for a reason, Trish." Even as she says it, she is running through the list of them in her head. Nope, nope, definitely not-wait a fucking minute.

"What?" Trish asks, noticing the change on Kinsey's face she is trying to hide.

"I may have thought of someone."

"Really? Do tell."

Kinsey isn't paying attention to her friend as she thinks back to the day she met, Sam.

Chapter Eight

Twenty-one years earlier…

Kinsey is twenty-one and has a paid internship at a company her college has set her up with. The internship during her senior year takes the place of classes. They are starting in September. They will still have all school vacations including Christmas break. If she does well, which she fully expects, she will come back for the spring semester.

Kinsey is waiting in the lobby with nineteen other college students all just as eager to please as her. In walks a man in a navy suit and slicked-back black hair, he claps his hands together to get everyone's attention.

"Okay everyone, huddle up. I'm Roger Wilcox I will be your mentor for the next three months, if you last that long. Those of you that do will be asked to stay for an additional four months and at the end of that time will be let go or given a contract. Any questions?" Several hands go up, "No? Good. Follow me this way."

Someone bumps her shoulder as the crowd walks past her knocking her pen out of her hand and onto the floor. Bending down to pick it up someone has beaten her to it. Her hand is resting over another hand holding the pen. Standing, she glances over her shoulder to find the most adorable boy/man standing next to her.

"Thank you," she tells him with a smile.

"No problem. I hope you didn't have any questions. This guy seems like a real piece of work."

He releases the pen, and she clips it onto her incoming folder packet they were all given when they arrived. Kinsey has hers tucked close to her chest while his is down at his side. "I'm Sam Anderson." He holds out a hand for her to shake.

His hand envelopes hers and she loves his touch, "Kinsey Marshall," she says as sweetly as possible.

"I love your name," he tells her as they continue shaking hands. Neither realizes the group has left them in the lobby.

"Psst!" They look up and drop their hands as they become aware the last of the group is going through a door. A pretty blonde is holding it open for them. Laughing, they run to join her. The blonde rushes to catch up with the group. Sam and Kinsey are now the last two people in line but they take their time following the crowd. They don't pay much attention to their tour as they talk.

"You two in the back." Oh shit. They look up and everyone is watching them. Roger walks through the crowd and holds out a folder for them. Kinsey takes it.

"These are our biggest clients. I'm putting you two in charge. If you fuck it up, you will be the first two gone by the end of the week. Questions? No. Great." Turning he walks back to the front of the group and continues his tour. Kinsey notices a few wide eyes on some of the externs but even worse are the smirks on others hoping to slim down the pool of candidates.

"What are we going to do?" Kinsey asks nervously. "My dad helped get me this internship and if I screw it up on the first day, he is going to murder me."

Sam takes the folder from her and begins leafing through it as they walk to catch up with the group. "It's a bluff. This isn't their biggest client. They aren't going to screw themselves over like that. But we are going to treat them like their biggest clients and when we dazzle them, which we will, they will be begging us to stay an additional four months."

"You're pretty confident about that. I hope you're right."

"I am. Let's get lunch together and we can strategize."

"Okay."

They are taken upstairs and shown their desks. Down a corridor on the left is a row of offices and on the right is a wall of windows. In front of the windows is two rows of desks, half is close to the window and the other half is closer to the offices. There are nameplates on all the desks as they find their way down the row. Kinsey watches as Sam swipes a name badge off the desk in front of hers and replaces it with his own. Her mouth gapes open. "What if they find out?" she whispers.

He shrugs his shoulders and sits down. They are on the right side towards the window. His desk is first in their grouping. The other grouping is six feet away two rows facing toward them. Her desk and computer face him but turning in his chair he is easily facing her.

A guy across from Sam comes over, "I'm Gabe. That was my seat," he says as they shake hands.

"And?" Sam challenges.

"And I'm totally fine with it," he said his hands up in the air instantly on the defense, "I get it," he says in a whisper looking Kinsey's way who pretends she hasn't heard the whole exchange.

"I'm Fiona," Kinsey hears behind her. Turning in her seat she shakes hands and introduces herself to the pretty blonde that had warned them they were falling behind in the group.

"Hey thanks for the heads up earlier," Kinsey tells her.

"No problem." Fiona leans forward and whispers, "You seemed otherwise occupied." Kinsey's smile matches hers, conspiratorially. "Did you see the gym they have here?"

"No, did we walk by it on the tour?"

"Yes, we walked through it!" Fiona giggles at Kinsey's obvious lack of attention given to the tour as she was so enthralled with Sam.

Kinsey gives a forced fake smile, "Is that bad?"

Fiona nods and opens her folder. "It's all in here though," she pulls out one of the sheets and hands it to her. It has a picture of some of the equipment, the locker room, a steam room, and an indoor pool.

"Wow, the pool is a nice touch. It says here it's open before, during, and after work. That's convenient."

"And here I was thinking you might be getting your exercise somewhere else." Both women look to Sam who is standing in the aisle still talking to Gabe. Sam grins at Kinsey when he notices her eyes on him. She returns his smile before she swivels back to Fiona.

"I don't know where you would get that notion from."

"You're right. I'm not very perceptive," Fiona jokes in a deadpan voice.

"Absolutely blind," Kinsey reassures her before both women burst out laughing.

"What's so funny?" Gabe saddles up to Fiona's desk to join the conversation. Sam follows his hip resting casually against Kinsey's desk.

Both women restrain themselves but still hold a twinkle in their eyes. "I'm Fiona," she says instead holding out her hand for Gabe to shake. They make introductions all around.

"Sam, did you know they have a gym here?" Kinsey asks him.

"Of course, I did. It's in the packet."

"Do you remember seeing it? Today?" Kinsey asks pointedly.

His eyes narrow at her like this is a trick question. "Did we walk by it?" he asks slowly.

Gabe laughs, "Dude! We walked through it! People on machines, the smell of sweat in the air. You don't remember it was ten minutes ago?"

"Oh! Right! Kinsey," he turns towards her, "That's when we were strategizing on how we are going to take over this company one client at a time."

"Yes, that's what we were doing," she folds her fingers on Fiona's desk and looks to the other two to see if they bought it, which they don't but they leave it alone for now.

"I liked the napping pods they have here." Gabe offers up.

"Do you think we will be able to use them?" Fiona asks.

Sam shrugs, "Only one way to find out."

Roger claps his hands. He is now standing between the two groups. "Settle down. You will have time to talk to your co-workers later. Please, have a seat." He gestures toward the desks as people quickly find their way to their assigned seats.

"If you open your packet," he continues, "You will find a wide array of resources at your disposal. Please study this. Also, inside you will find a username and password that is individual to you. Do not share this with anyone. We are a financial institution, and we have sensitive information on these computers. You must log off anytime you leave your desk even if it is to grab a coffee or run to the restrooms. Do we understand?" There was a collective nod, and he moves on, "Use this time to get familiar with the computer program and go over the information provided in the packets. Any questions? No? Great. My office is the last one down on the right that is where I can be found."

Everyone spends the rest of the morning engrossed in their task. TVs line the walls with the stock market and the news going in the background. On the toolbar of their computers stocks also scroll across the screen. Sam has taken the folder with "their client" and is bent over the paperwork. Kinsey wonders if they are still going to lunch when at one o'clock, he turns to her and asks, "Are you ready for lunch?"

"Sure, where do you want to go?" Gabe and Fiona had headed out with others at noon. More left at twelve-thirty. They had been told anytime between 12 and 2 was acceptable for a one-hour lunch.

"We can go down to the cafeteria if you want or find something close by?"

"It's up to you," she puts the ball in his court as she follows him to the elevator. He asks her how her morning went, and she tells him things she has done so far. Once inside the elevator, he asks her about her dad.

She tells him about the firm her dad works for. A small whistle escapes his lips, "Wow that's an impressive firm. I'd like to work there one day. How come you aren't doing your internship there?"

Kinsey shrugs, "He offered but I didn't want to be the boss's daughter. I want to make it on my own."

"Wait!" Sam stops her, "He's the boss? Holy shit your dad is Pierce Marshall? The CFO?"

"The one and the same. Please don't tell anyone though. Like I said I want to make it on my own merits."

"Say no more," Sam assures her.

"Thanks. What about you? What do your parents do?"

"My dad is an electrician, and my mom is a teacher."

"What does she teach?"

"Second grade."

"Awe, that's sweet. Any brothers or sisters?"

"Two brothers." The elevator doors open, and they step out into the lobby. Sam heads toward the door and she realizes they would have gotten out on the second floor if they were going to the cafeteria. He holds the door open for her. They join the hustle and bustle of the street as he leads the way down the sidewalk. Around the corner, he opens the door to a deli, a tiny bell overhead announcing their arrival.

Standing in line they read the menu board before ordering. "Older or younger?" Kinsey asks.

"What? Oh, my brothers?" Sam picks up where they had left off in their conversation. "One older one younger."

"Middle child, how do you cope?"

"Fairly well. What about you any siblings?"

"Nope, just spoiled me. My mom died when I was little. It's just been me and my dad for a long time."

"I'm sorry to hear about your mom. Did your dad ever remarry?"

Kinsey gives him a sad smile, "Thanks. Nope, he said my mom was the love of his life and he didn't want anyone else." Their order is called, and it saves them from having to go down the sad road anymore.

They carry their food to an open table near the window. Sam pulls out a piece of paper and smooths it out on the table. "I ran some numbers this morning and this is what I came up with."

Kinsey who is unwrapping her sandwich stops to reach for the paper. Scanning his figures, she says, "This is good. Really good." She looks up at him he is nodding his head with a smile on his face.

"Thanks, any input you have I'd love to hear," he offers.

"Okay well, I was thinking along the lines of a presentation." She digs a pen out of her purse and turns over his paper. Quickly drawing some graphs and pie charts she sections the page up into smaller grids labeling them and showing her proposal for a power-point presentation.

Sam seems impressed, "How do you feel about public speaking?"

"I thrive on it. It's like my drug of choice."

He laughs, "That's perfect. You can do the presentation and if you need help on the power-point let me know we can work on it together?"

"That would be great." They eat their sandwiches working out the details of their proposal. She asks questions and offers suggestions. By the end of lunch, they have a good head start on their project.

They walk back to work, "I'm surprised I haven't had you in any of my classes," Sam observes as they enter the high-rise.

"I know. What are the chances? Do you recognize anyone from our work-study?"

"Yeah, a couple of people, no one I like though."

Kinsey laughs good-naturedly at the way he said it, "Oh really? What about me?" They enter the elevators as he assesses her. She had guessed it would be a quick well of course but now she is worried.

"I think you'll do," he finally allows.

"Well, la-dee-da. I get your approval. I should be so lucky."

"You should," he tells her, a twinkle in his eye. She grins at him. The door opens and he steps aside for her to exit first.

"Why thank you very much, kind sir."

All week they work together strategizing and planning for their Friday meeting. On Wednesday Kinsey rushes to Sam's desk. She hops up on the corner, "I have amazing news." He raises an eyebrow at her butt planted firmly on his desk, but she ignores him, "I just spoke to Janice, Roger's secretary. She gave me the 411 on our clients. She also told me that I can put in a request for petty cash and order food and drinks for the meeting on Friday I just need to fill out these forms and have them on Roger's desk by the end of the day." She holds up the paper waving it in his face.

He takes it from her and looks it over, "And she just told you this information?"

"Not exactly. I just started a conversation with her and complimented her outfit then bit by bit interrogated the info out of her."

"I like it. Good work Marshall."

Kinsey hops off his desk just as quickly as she had appeared and snatches the paper from his hand. "Thanks."

"What are you going to order?"

"Well, they are from Chicago, and they can't get enough of our New York bagels."

"I know just the place," he writes down the name of a local company, "You should use them."

"Great, thanks."

Friday morning rolls around and Kinsey dresses to impress. She is wearing all black, her hair in a sophisticated updo to look older and more in charge. She notices the looks in the office and knows she knocked it out of the park. Kinsey wears make-up instead of her usual lip gloss only.

Sam also looks good in his suit and tie. Roger waits with them at the elevator. When the clients arrive, he introduces them, and everyone shakes hands. Roger allows Kinsey and Sam to take the lead down the hallway to the conference room.

Roger has already seen their presentation, he made them do a dry run last night. He also gave a few suggestions on what he would do differently but otherwise, he seems happy with the result. There are four men and two women in the group. Roger sits in the back of the room closest to the decision-maker and Sam sits up front facing her. Kinsey is happy to see the clients help themselves to the bagel and cream cheese spread in the middle of the table.

Janice also joins them and after Kinsey's introduction Janice turns off the lights for her power-point presentation. Sam looks laid back as he watches her move about the room her hands gesturing. Kinsey is animated and personable warming up even more when she sees approving head nods.

Afterward, Janice jumps up to turn on the lights for the Q&A session. Sam jumps up to clarify any points they want to know more about. Kinsey watches him and knows instantly that his line about public speaking not being his forte is a load of crap. She also realizes that he let her have the spotlight.

In the long run, the clients are pleased, Roger is satisfied, and Sam and Kinsey are ecstatic. Roger and Janice leave the conference room to walk the clients out. Kinsey squeals and Sam wraps her up in a huge bear hug lifting her off the floor.

"We did it!" Sam says depositing her feet back on solid ground.

"Holy shit, we did it," Kinsey's hands press to the side of her face.

"I never had any doubt," he says confidently.

"Yeah, okay." They walk down to the staff room and a few co-workers are mingling and grabbing snacks.

"How did it go?" Fiona wants to know.

"Amazing," Kinsey said, "Sam was the brains of the operation though. I barely understand this stuff," she jokes.

"That's not true," Sam's voice is low and serious. Others are talking around them, so she isn't sure anyone else heard his statement, but she does and it makes her heart soar at his defense of her brainpower.

Kinsey and Sam exchange numbers right before going home for the day. On Saturday, Kinsey decides she is going to call Sam. It takes a good twenty minutes before she works up the nerve.

"Hello?" a female answers the phone. Kinsey pulls the phone away from her ear to look at it like it can answer the question of who is on the line. "Hello?" comes again.

Pulling the phone back to her ear she responds, "Sorry. I think I might have the wrong number. I'm looking for Sam."

"This is his phone. Can I take a message?"

"Sure, can you tell him Kinsey called? I have a work question."

"I will let him know."

"Thank you," she says to the dial tone in her ear. The woman had already hung up. Sam never returns her call.

Chapter Nine

♥

On Monday they walk in together. "Hey, I called you Saturday." They get into the elevator by themselves.

"Oh, did you leave me a message?"

"Yeah, I talked to your mom?" she asked hopefully, she's had a knot in the pit of her stomach since the phone call.

"That wasn't my mom."

"Roommate?" she asks hopefully.

"My girlfriend."

"Oh, I didn't realize you were dating anyone. Have you been together long?" Please, say no.

"About a year." No! Her brain screams. What is even happening? She studies her fingers and the way they entwine. "Kinsey?" She meets his gaze he is standing close. Closer than someone with a long-time girlfriend should be.

"Why didn't you tell me?" Suddenly, his shoes seem interesting because he is giving them the same consideration, she had been giving her hands moments before. His shrug is almost imperceptible. They had been flirting all week and she had no idea he was with someone. She had been positive that he was going to ask her to date him.

Tension is building in her chest, and she feels nauseous, thank God she had skipped breakfast this morning. When the elevator doors open Fiona startles them apart, "There you two are! Roger has called a meeting.

Let's go." She grabs Kinsey by the wrist and pulls her from the elevator and down the hall. Looking back toward Sam he follows at a much slower pace his eyes not leaving the ground. He has his serious thinking cap on.

Fiona pulls her into the meeting, and they take a seat at the long conference table. Sam comes in and takes an open seat opposite of her and a little further down rather than his usual spot next to her. "What the hell is going on with you two?" Fiona whispers in her ear.

"Good morning!" Roger silences everyone in the room. All eyes focus on Roger except Kinsey who steals a glance at Sam. Sam's eyes meet hers. The room goes dark as the power-point presentation begins, but they don't break eye contact.

Fiona's sharp elbow jabs into her ribs causing their spell to break. "Ow!" Kinsey whispers, rubbing her side.

"Pay attention," Fiona whispers back. Kinsey swivels in her chair to face the presentation but she isn't absorbing any of it. She hears the soft click of the back conference room door and instantly knows Sam has left the meeting. She glances at her dainty wristwatch and counts two and a half long minutes before quietly leaving out the same door.

It's quiet in the halls. She starts heading towards the restrooms, not sure where she is going or why. Outside Roger's office at the end of the hallway, a hand reaches out and grabs her upper arm pulling her inside the darkened room.

Gasping, her heart racing, she clutches her chest. Spinning around she sees Sam close the door behind them. Her breathing is labored, and she isn't quite sure why. Her fists clench down at her sides as she watches him lean against the door.

"I should have told you," he says quietly. She can tell this is hard for him, but she doesn't think he realizes how difficult it is for her.

"I thought you liked me," she can't stand the dejection in her voice.

Sam pushes himself from the door walking towards her. She takes a step backward but he continues. "I do like you." He stops not touching her. Kinsey tilts her head back so she isn't staring at his chest to look at him. "I do like you," he repeats.

"You have a girlfriend."

"I do."

Kinsey takes another step back and shrugs her shoulders dramatically, "Okay then discussion over."

"I'm sorry if I hurt you." The lump in her throat is getting larger and her chest is tighter. It feels as if all the air is being sucked from the room. "I need to go," she tries to push past him but his hand clamps around her upper arms bringing her around to face him. Her hands are on his chest which is warm and solid. Kinsey can feel his heart racing under her palm. "There is no excuse for my behavior. I like you and I love getting to know you and working with you. You're beautiful."

Why is he telling her this? It's everything she wants to hear from him, but he has a girlfriend! He should not be telling her any of these things and he sure as hell shouldn't be touching her. He shouldn't be looking at her like he wants to devour her. It isn't fair.

"Let's be friends," she says far more cheerfully than she feels. Instantly, he stiffens beneath her. Sam drops her arms, and she clasps her hands together not trusting herself not to touch him.

A smile emerges for the first time today after their conversation in the elevator. Kinsey loves that smile. Internally she is kicking herself. "Friends. I can do friends."

"Great. Glad that's settled. We need to get back to the meeting. You go first."

"Are you sure you are okay?"

"Totally."

Sam lets out a nervous laugh and swipes his hand over his forehead, "Phew! See you in there, Champ." He lightly and slowly swings his fist in a friendly fake punch to the arm.

"Don't call me Champ."

"Got it. Trying something out there. Didn't work though, moving on."

A sincere smile touches her lips, "See you in there."

"Right, better get back before anyone notices."

Sam heads to the door and slips out leaving her alone in the dark. This is not how she had seen her day going. Of course, he is off the market. Why hadn't she considered that fact? He is adorable, funny, and fun to be around, he makes her feel special, and his nose crinkles when he gives her a lopsided grin. Sam doesn't look at anyone else in the office like he does with her, she is sure of it.

She leaves the office but doesn't head back to the meeting. Instead, she heads toward the bathroom. Inside she finds Fiona waiting for her, her finely shaped eyebrow highly raised, her arms folded across her chest. "You need to start talking."

Kinsey debates how much she wants to tell her work friend. They are in competition after all, and Sam is her friend. "We had a little fight, but we've made up."

Fiona smiles, "Thank God. Are you okay? Do I need to poison his coffee or anything?"

Kinsey laughs, "God, no. Don't do that. We're fine."

"Okay, good. You better get back in there before people start to notice."

"Who is going to notice?"

"Probably Roger."

Kinsey groans. "You're right." Turning she makes her way back to the conference room. Sam has stolen Fiona's vacant chair and is waiting for her. Sitting next to him he hands her a piece of gum. Smiling she takes it from him, her fingers grazing his, it means nothing, they are just friends. Then why is her entire body tingling? Removing the wrapper, she pops the cinnamon gum in her mouth and begins to chew, still not paying attention to the presentation.

Chapter Ten

♥

The following day Kinsey is at her desk when Sam comes in. He places a brown paper bag on her desk, and it lands with a thud. "What's this?" she asks.

He places his work bag down and takes a seat swiveling his chair so he can face her desk. "Why don't you open it and see? It's a peace offering."

Smiling she opens the top of the bag and pulls out a porcelain mug. It's a swirl of pink, blue and purple. Turning it over in her hand she finds a saying etched in gold on the front. "You're Tea-riffic." It has a picture of a teabag with a smiling face. On the end of the teabag string is a tiny heart and she wonders if he had noticed.

Kinsey laughs at the pun, "Awe, thank you. I love it."

Sam grins, "You're welcome. There are some teas in there for you too."

Kinsey pulls the bag towards her and pulls out a tin full of different flavored teas. She holds them to her chest in excitement before opening them up to see which one she wants to try first. "Oh, I'm going to try the peach one. Do you want to come to the break room with me?"

"Sure," he stands, and they walk together down the hall. She fills her mug from the cooler and Sam fills one of the disposable cups with the coffee from the coffee pot. She pivots around Sam placing her mug in the microwave. His hands rest on her back as he reaches around her for a lid and stir stick.

Removing the mug from the microwave Kinsey steeps her tea they are standing shoulder to shoulder neither moving away from the other. Reaching for the sugar his hand grazes hers as they both make a move for it at the same time. They fix their drinks in comfortable silence.

The next couple of weeks is tiny moments of touching at work. They don't move away from each other when one of them gets too close or hands casually brush one another. Sam tells her he doesn't like certain people at work.

Laughing Kinsey tells him, "You don't like anyone."

"I like you. That's all that counts," he says with a wink, making her wish his girlfriend would disappear for the millionth time.

Chapter Eleven

♥

    Kinsey's dad's sister dies suddenly, and she is forced to miss a week of work as they travel to upstate New York to make arrangements and attend the wake and funeral.

    When she comes back to the office, she is in the elevator to go up when Sam walks in. He stops when he sees her. They are on the elevator alone. The door slowly closes behind him and she breathes out a sigh of relief. Sam opens his arms to her. She walks into his embrace as if she has done it a thousand times. Her arms wrap around his waist and his arms go around her shoulders. The intoxicating smell of his cologne has her nostrils flaring at the scent. Kinsey presses her ear against his chest, his chin resting on top of her head. "How are you holding up?" Sam asks softly.

    At the moment she is doing pretty fantastic. She is having a hard time concentrating on what he is trying to ask her. Shrugging her shoulders she says, "I'm holding up."

    "I missed you," he confesses.

    She smiles and squeezes him tight, and he squeezes her right back. The door dings and they pull apart. "Did I miss anything?" She asks as they walk to their desks.

    Sam raises an eyebrow at her, "I don't know, did you?" The meaning makes her smile.

    "I missed you too," she allows and is rewarded with one of his nose-scrunching smiles.

"Let me take you out to lunch," Sam says to her as Kinsey takes a seat at her desk.

Smiling she puts her purse down, "Sure, that would be great. Where do you want to go?"

"I was thinking of the pub down the street. I know you like their burgers."

Her grin gets bigger. She is now sitting her shoulders relaxed as she responds, "Oh my God thank you. I need that so much."

"Of course." He twirls around to face his computer. They work all morning and when the clock hits one they both stand to leave. They walk down to the pub and get a booth in the back. They look at the menu but already know what the other wants. Sam puts in their order as she goes to the bathroom.

Their burgers come out and she gives him her tomato and onion on his bun, and he puts his pickle spear on her plate. She uses her butter knife to slather a healthy amount of mayo on her toasted bun. Sam asks her about the funeral and she tells him about her favorite aunt.

When they are done eating, they are sipping from their free refills she gets the nerve to bring up his flirting. "You flirt too," he says casually unaffected by her comment.

She picks up the pickle and puts it in her mouth sucking on most of it before slowly pulling the length of it out, her eyes locking on his. His lips press together as his eyes close, and he throws his head back.

She giggles, "Yeah but I'm single. Did that turn you on?" she asks surprising herself with being so forward. His eyes snap open.

Her eyes widen as he gets out of the booth and joins her on her side of the table. She scoots over, closer to the wall making room for him. His arm slings around the back of the booth his body angling towards her his elbow on the table. "What am I going to do with you?" he asks.

Kinsey's eyebrow raises. "Whatever do you mean?" Her hand clutches her chest, "What do you want to do to me?"

Sam's voice is low as he leans toward her, "I want to eat you out," his eyes are watching her lips as they part open in surprise. His eyes darken.

Kinsey's breath hitches in her throat and her heart starts to race. She had not been expecting an answer like that. He is observing her wanting to know if what he said had gone too far. "What else?" she presses. His lips brush against her ear as he whispers sending goosebumps across her flesh, "I want to make you cum without touching you."

Her hands grip the table, "You think you can do that?"

"I'd like to try."

Her eyes widen, he is serious. She had been playing around, "Okay," she says softly, "Do your worst."

"Oh no, I'm going to do my best," he promises a gleam in his eyes. "I'm going to eat you out until you are begging me to stop."

"Oh yeah? What are we talking about? Like five-ten minutes?"

"What a sheltered life you have lived," he tells her. He isn't wrong, she has been with two guys, one in high school and one in her sophomore year of college. She didn't have time to date and when she did it wasn't anything spectacular. "Forty-five minutes." Kinsey catches the tail end of his conversation.

"Excuse me what?"

"I plan on sucking you, licking you, snacking on you for about forty-five minutes to an hour."

She laughs, "No sir, that isn't possible."

"Oh, it's extremely possible."

She swallows hard as she stares at him suddenly feeling claustrophobic. Turning in the booth she faces him her knee bending her elbow resting on the table her hand next to his. They stare at their hands so close they can feel the heat generated by each other. Her fingers tiptoe across his hand as she speaks, "You're telling me that you would set up camp in between my thighs and do nothing else."

"Not entirely true. I would use my hands on you while my eyes memorize your body. My fingers would be deep inside you working you over while I listen to the sounds of your moans and gasps of gratification. I would be getting rock-hard thinking of all the ways I want to give you pleasure."

"Do you like your neck kissed?" Kinsey asks.

His eyes are half closed, "Love it. You?"

She nods her head, "Same. I can't get enough of it." Her hand continues to play with his.

"Good to know. I would kiss your lips next. I want you to taste yourself on me." Kinsey is highly aroused by this conversation. "Then I would move to your neck. Do you like it soft and gentle or rough and hard?"

"Both," she whispers.

"I can do that. I'm at your entrance. Do you want me inside you?" Kinsey's eyes are now half-closed with passion as she nods her teeth working over her lower lip, "Good girl," he coos. "Will you wrap your legs around my hips?"

"I'll wrap them around your neck if you want me to," she breathes.

"Fuck yeah," Sam groans and she smiles at him. "Do you like your nipples pinched?"

"I-" she hesitates.

"It's okay you can tell me," He encourages.

"I don't know."

"Well, I guess we are going to have to try and see. Would you like that?" He asks and she nods her head enthusiastically.

"Do you like your balls sucked?" she asks out of the blue.

Sam shifts in his seat, his eyes dipping to her lips, before clearing his throat and answering the question, "I do." Kinsey beams at him and he rewards her with a smile.

"Can I get you anything else?" The waitress appears at their table the check in her hand.

Sam clears his throat as Kinsey gasps and jumps at the same time. "No, we are good thanks."

"I'll take this whenever you are ready," she clears their dishes and leaves the check folded and upside down at the end of the table.

After she walks away, they burst out laughing and Kinsey rests her forehead on his shoulder. "I guess we better get back to work." They pay the bill, and the sexy talk is over.

As they walk out of the restaurant, he hugs her from behind and she can feel his erection pressed up against her. Her hands come up to hold his arms wrapped tightly around her neck relishing the moment before it is gone. Releasing her he falls into step next to her.

She can't sleep that night, tossing and turning. Kinsey replays Sam's words over and over in her head. Only after she decides she will talk to him before the holiday break does she fall into a fitful sleep. They don't know if they will be asked back. They are down to fourteen people.

Chapter Twelve

♥

In November Kinsey opens the fridge at work and sees a cake with the words in cursive spelling out, "Happy Birthday Sam" Without taking anything out she slams the door and turns to face Sam.

"Traitor," her eyes narrow on him.

Sam is casually leaning on the kitchen island eating an apple. He frowns, "What did I do?"

"You didn't tell me it's your birthday!"

"Oh, that." He shrugs casually, "It's just another day."

She walks over to him leaning on the counter. "I wish I would have known. I would have gotten you something. I'll have to owe you," she tells him.

Sam wiggles his eyebrows at her, "I like the sound of that. Hey, when's your birthday?"

She folds her arms across her chest. "I don't think I should tell you."

"It's December 14th," Fiona says helpfully as she walks by.

"Fiona!" Kinsey admonishes. Winking at Kinsey over her shoulder Fiona just smiles and keeps walking. Kinsey pulls out her lip gloss applying it to her lips. The apple is forgotten. Sam watches her. Giggling she tells him. "It tastes better than it smells."

"How would I know?"

She leans millimeters away from his lips and then pulls away. His nostrils flare, "Well it smells pretty damn good."

"Too bad you won't ever get to taste it."

"Says who?"

"Me."

Sam's hand gestures to her and she leans in again. He is just a breath away from her, his eyes dip to her lips when she feels him remove the lip gloss from her fist. Pulling away he untwists the cap and applies the lip gloss, his lips becoming shiny. Kinsey bursts out laughing, "You look ridiculous."

His tongue darts out, and one eyebrow shoots up, "It does taste good."

"See I told you." Kinsey pulls the lip gloss out of his hand and puts it in her pocket.

The following week Sam and Kinsey are sitting in the back stairwell. They hang out in here sometimes to get away. No one is ever in there. "Top five foods. Go." Kinsey holds up her hands.

Sam ponders her question, "Tacos."

"Hands down," she nods in approval and puts a finger down.

"Steak."

"Eh. I could take it or leave it," she puts another finger down.

"No one has ever cooked you the perfect steak then."

"Are you offering?"

"I could cook you the best steak of your life. Anything pasta," he continues.

"Now we are talking."

"Chinese and-"

"Wait!" Kinsey holds her hand out. You have to elaborate on what specifically you like for Chinese."

"What don't I like? Crab Rangoon, beef teriyaki, chicken chow Mein-"

"With the crunchy noodles?"

"Is there any other way to eat it?" he asks

"Okay I'm sorry, please continue," she waves her hand at him.

"Where was I? Oh, I love pork fried rice and lo Mein."

"Love lo Mein."

"I like beef and broccoli and General Tso chicken."

"This conversation is turning me on," Kinsey admits.

Sam barks out a laugh, "You're easy."

"Yeah, I am," she teases batting her eyelashes at him and he grins at her. He pulls a piece of gum out of his pocket, unwraps it, and pops it into his mouth. "Would you like a piece?" he holds the chewed piece in between his teeth and another one in his hand. Not trusting herself to remove the piece from his mouth she takes the one from his hand.

"Chicken. Do you want to go to lunch?"

"Always," she smiles at him, and he winks at her. "Can we do Chinese?"

"Obviously," they stand.

"You never finished your list," she says as he holds the door open for her.

"My mom's homemade mac and cheese."

"Wouldn't that be the same as anything pasta?"

He is already shaking his head, "No this is in a class all of its own."

"What makes it so good?"

"She makes it with love," he says with a laugh, "at least that's what she has always told us. That and the cracker topping is to die for."

"I would love some of your mom's mac and cheese. Can you bring me in some next time she makes it?"

"First of all, there are never any leftovers, and second nuking it the next day is never the same. It needs to be fresh out of the oven." Kinsey pouts at this information.

"I'll see what I can do," he shifts his body, so he bumps her hip while walking down the hall. She smiles up at him.

An hour, later, when they drive back to the office, he rolls down the window, and turns off the car but leaves the radio on. "I like you." She tells him.

He shows no surprise, "I like you too."

"I think you are cute."

Sam laughs at her confession, "I think you are gorgeous."

"Really, what do you think is my best feature?"

"I can't stop admiring your lips." She puts on lip gloss, and he says, "You're killing me, Smalls."

"These lips?" Kinsey looks at him.

He is looking relaxed in his seat but as far away from her as possible, "Yes, those lips. I also love your voice."

"My voice?"

"Yes, it is really sexy."

Kinsey puts her hand on his thigh. He shifts in his seat his elbow resting on the console his right side touching her from her shoulder to elbow. His jawline is within kissing distance. Sam is staring at nothing out of his car window.

Taking a chance, she kisses his jawline. He doesn't flinch. Her lips glide down his neck as he had once told her he liked. Her tongue flicks over his earlobe. Sam moves away from her and she falls back into her seat removing her hand from his thigh. Well, she tried.

Staring out the windshield like Sam, she takes in her surroundings. It is a beautiful fall day. Sam has parked them on the rooftop so she can see the crisp blue sky, hardly a cloud in sight. The sun is bouncing off the hood of his car, cool air swirling inside the car through the open window. In front of them is a light grey cement barrier.

Kinsey is taken out of her trance when he takes her hand in his. His fingers interlocked with hers. Both are engrossed in the way her fingers curl over and through his. His thumb rubs over her knuckles. Lifting her hand to his lips he kisses her fingers.

Turning in her seat she lifts her free hand to cup his jaw and turns him to face her. There is so much depth and emotion when he looks at her. Her thumb brushes over his lower lip. "I want to kiss you."

"I know," his voice is rough. She is disappointed he doesn't respond with I want to kiss you too. His eyes dip to her chest. She is wearing a red button-up blouse today and her cleavage is visible. "Your breasts are beautiful."

Kinsey assesses her chest, "Thanks."

The next thing she knows his hand is down her shirt giving her a slight squeeze. His lips are on hers in a crushing kiss. His tongue is tangling with hers. Their mouths are stretched to max capacity trying to get as close as possible. He takes her hand and places it on his arousal through his trousers. Then just as quickly as it had started, they are apart. Hands and lips returned to the proper person.

Well then. She is trying to regain her composure but it's difficult. After a minute her heart rate begins to slow, and the palm of her hands begin to dry as they sit in silence. "Are you happy?" Kinsey wants to know.

"I'm happy when I'm with you."

"What about when you aren't with me?"

"Sometimes," he allows. What does that mean? She wants to scream. She wants another kiss and she isn't sure she is going to get one.

They go on Thanksgiving break. She calls him avoiding the subject. He asks her why. She says she would rather talk to him in person. He wants to know if she hates him.

"I don't hate you."

He sighs in relief, "It was hard to kick your ass out of my car."

She laughed, "I had a hard time leaving your car."

"I noticed," he teases then sobers, "I've never done that before, with anyone. I swear."

"I feel bad for your girlfriend then. You're a pretty good kisser. How have you kept her this long without kissing her?"

"You know what I mean."

"I do," Kinsey murmurs and they fall into thoughtful silence.

After a beat, he asks her, "So what are your plans for Thanksgiving?" She tells him even though they have already gone over this, and she asks him the same even though she knows he is going to his parent's house with her.

Chapter Thirteen

♥

In the parking garage, Sam and Kinsey are walking toward his car. He holds his remote out and the lights flash as he unlocks it. "Are either of your brothers single?" She asks over the hood of his car before sliding into the passenger seat.

"You are not dating either one of my brothers," Sam said as he clips his seat buckle.

"How come?" Kinsey follows suit as she buckles.

"You know why." His look is intense towards her their shoulders touching both of their elbows resting on his console.

"No, I don't. Are they bums?" She holds his gaze.

"One has a lazy eye and the other has a gimpy leg."

Kinsey bursts out laughing. "You are so full of shit. What's the real reason?"

His right-hand rests on her thigh. They both look down at it his thumb rubs against her skin before their gaze meets again. "I can't bear to see you with someone else." He kisses her as his hand slips between her legs. She doesn't want to ruin the moment, so she doesn't mention the elephant in the room. Even though she doesn't have to see Sam with another woman she knows he isn't hers and he goes home to someone else.

She spreads her legs for him, and he slips his finger inside her. Her hand reaches across the console rubbing his erection through his trousers. "Kinsey," he whispers in her ear before nibbling on her lobe.

"Hmm…I wonder if your brothers are as good at this as you are." He growls and bites her neck. She giggles and then gasps at the sensation.

"You will never find out," he vows before capturing her lips again.

He drops her off at the subway station. She walks down the stairs and heads toward the train. The doors are open and she is stepping on when she is pulled back. With her heart in her throat, she wonders if she is being mugged.

Swiveling around to face her aggressor she is surprised to see him. "Sam! What are you-" he wraps her up in his arms and kisses her. Right there on the platform for all to see. People walking all around them. It's the first kiss they've shared where it's a full kiss, unhurried, neither pulling away and in public.

"I just needed to give you a proper goodbye."

"I'm all for it." The doors of the subway have long since closed and left the station by the time they break apart. "What brought that on?"

He shrugs, "I don't know. I just didn't feel like letting you go yet, but um I'm double parked so I do have to go." Sam doesn't let go of her.

"You made me miss my train."

"How about a ride home?"

"I'd love that."

They separate realizing that in public anyone that knows either one of them could spot them causing a problem. They walk side by side with a respectable distance between them, back up the subway stairs. He opens the car door for her, and she crawls back inside the seat she vacated minutes earlier.

Kinsey gives him directions and it takes a while to get home with the evening traffic. They talk as he drives neither one seeming to mind the delay, in fact relishing in each stoplight. When he finally pulls up to her building he parks, and they continue their conversation.

"Do you want to come upstairs?" Kinsey asks.

A knock on her window startles them both. Turning, Kinsey laughs with relief at her dad's face peering in at them. "It's my dad," she tells Sam before rolling the window down.

"Hey, dad. This is my friend from work, Sam Anderson," Kinsey introduces them.

"Nice to meet you, sir. I'm a big fan of your work," Sam reaches across Kinsey and Pierce reaches into the confines of the vehicle to shake his hand.

"Nice to meet you too, Sam. Would you like to come in for dinner?" Pierce releases his grip.

"I appreciate that sir, but I need to get going. Thank you though."

"I'll be up shortly," Kinsey tells her dad.

"Okay, sweetheart. Take care Sam," Pierce straightens giving Sam a wave.

"You too, Mr. Marshall," Sam returns the wave.

"Pierce, please."

Sam smiles as her dad retreats into the building. Kinsey is smiling when she turns to look at Sam. He appears star-struck, "Your dad just told me to call him by his first name. Pierce Marshall just shook my hand. I want to be him when I grow up."

Kinsey laughs, "He is a person, you know?"

"I know. It's just wow."

Kinsey's grin gets wider, "Okay, I'll see you tomorrow."

"Yeah, I'll see you tomorrow."

"Thanks for the ride."

"Of course, it's the least I could do after making you miss the subway."

"Worth it," her eyes lock on his, her voice low. His eyes dip to her lips and she licks them.

His hand cups her face drawing her closer, he presses his lips to hers ever so gently, "So worth it," he whispers before deepening the kiss his tongue sweeping inside her mouth. Her hand rests on his wrist. They pull away slowly and she takes her time stepping out of the car. Sam doesn't rush her just watches her movements from his side of the vehicle.

She sighs heavily as she watches him drive away. Grinning she turns and walks confidently into her building. Stopping abruptly just inside the door she finds her dad waiting for her. He is pretending to go through their mail as he stands by the elevators. His eyebrow arches but he says nothing.

Inside the elevator, he finally says, "Sam seems like a nice guy."

Kinsey grins, "Yeah, he is."

"Are you two dating?"

"No, we are just friends." Her dad snorts but doesn't say anything else and she doesn't offer to elaborate.

Chapter Fourteen

♥

The following week Kinsey and Sam are leaving for the day heading towards the elevator when they hear Roger ask for volunteers to stay late. Wide-eyed they reach for the button to go down trying to vacate the premises before they get roped in.

As they step onto the elevator they hear, "Hey!" Sam pushes her up against the elevator wall tucking her in near the buttons hiding from Roger's view. Quickly pushing the button for the upper-level parking garage. The door closes moments before Roger gets there. Kinsey's heart is thudding in her chest all too aware of Sam's body pressed against hers his hands on her waist. She is watching as the pulse quickens in his throat. He is still preoccupied with the near-miss to realize the effect he is having on her.

Grinning down at her he says, "That was a close call-" His words freeze in his throat as he sees the desire in her eyes. The door opens far too soon. The spell is broken as he moves away from her, and they walk out into the parking garage. The elevator next to them is fast approaching.

"You don't think Roger is chasing us down here, do you?" Kinsey asks.

"Let's not find out," Sam starts running. Laughing Kinsey follows his lead. As they round the corner, she sees Roger step out. Squealing, he turns their way and shouts.

"Quick get in," Sam and she are laughing as he unlocks the car, and they hop in the backseat. As Roger rushes by the car, she gasps, and they duck down behind the seats sliding down on the cushions. Her legs are on his side of the car she is fully laying on her back her hair in her face from her haste. Her neck is awkwardly angled in the corner of the door.

Sam on the other hand is bent sideways and his head is pressed to her hip bone his arm slung casually across her belly. She moves her hair out of her face and watches as he shifts, not away from her. He presses his lips to her belly, his hand running down her back. She bites her lip and peers up at him through her eyelashes knowing that turns him on. Kinsey sees it in his eyes. They didn't have to talk a lot these days their gaze communicating everything they need to tell each other.

He shoves her skirt up past her hips and his teeth latch on her panties. Slowly, his eyes locking with hers he easily removes them. He spreads her thighs and pulls her womanhood towards his face. Her neck feels better, in this new position, as she lay more comfortably on the seat cushion. Her thighs cradle his face, and she can feel his hot breath on her. Kinsey's knees bend over his shoulders. Her whole body is quivering in anticipation.

His tongue is greedy when it tastes her. Kinsey's hips rock in response to his demanding administrations. She whimpers and cries out as his methods of pleasure change. Her fingers twist in his curls tight against his scalp. Her other hand reaches behind her to clutch the arm of the door. Sam is both gentle and playful and rough and domineering she isn't sure what she likes better but the combination of the two is explosive.

When she feels like she is ready to cum she uses her right heel on his shoulder and pushes him away. He is now in a sitting position facing her. He wipes his face, "I'm sorry. I know I shouldn't. I just got carried away." She sits up on her knees facing him when she notices the large bulge in his pants. He is affected by her.

Her hands reach out and touch him. She secretly revels in the power she has over him. "Don't," he croaks.

She leans forward, his lips inches from his. "Don't what?" she whispers as she continues to stroke him through his pants.

"God, Kinsey. You're going to be the death of me."

"Good, at least you'll die a happy man," she promises as she unbuckles his pants. He growls as he reaches for her. His lips are crushing this time as he bites her, but she doesn't care it just turns her on more.

She lowers his pants and underwear down to his knees and straddles him. This is the moment they had been building for all these months. He is huge and it takes a moment to adjust to his size. They share an astonished look, their breathing ragged. "Holy Christ," he says, and she laughs reveling in his desire as much as her own.

She begins rocking her hips back and forth and he clings to her his hands digging into her shoulder and hip slamming into her. The feeling she is having is so overwhelming she cries out, "I love you."

He stops and looks at her, "What?"

"Nothing."

"You said something."

"I said you had a nice cock. Geez, desperate for compliments much? You're huge! I wasn't expecting that from your skinny ass." He frowns at her. She isn't sure if he had heard her and wants to confirm or if he hadn't heard at all.

A rap against the window startles them, causing both to flinch and look at their disruption. The security guard is shuffling on his feet his hand scratching the back of his head. "You two can't do that on company grounds."

Embarrassed Kinsey puts her hands up, "Sorry Hank! We were just leaving."

"Okay then, Miss Marshall," he backs away from the car but waits at the hood while they readjust. She scrambles off Sam's lap and he hastily yanks his pants up not bothering to re-tuck his shirt. Kinsey promptly shoves the discarded panties she finds around the stick shift in the front of the car, into her purse, not bothering to put them back on.

She gets out leaving Sam in the car without as much as a backward glance. Kinsey walks briskly towards the elevator so she can catch the subway home. Sam had been giving her a ride down to the station, but she needs time to clear her head. What is she doing? She is madly in love with a man that can't or won't love her back. She knows it's wrong of her to want him. Why is he in her life? To torture her? Because it is working.

Chapter Fifteen

♥

The next day Kinsey finds Sam already at his desk. "Good morning," she keeps the emotion from her tone.

"Hey," he says over his shoulder not meeting her gaze. What the hell?

Kinsey takes off her coat and slings it over the back of her chair and puts her purse away in her desk drawer. Sitting down she turns on her computer. He doesn't turn around the entire day. Instead, he asks Becky for help on their project. Becky is all too happy to oblige. She is even flirting with him! Again, what the hell?

At lunchtime, Kinsey asks if he is going down to the cafeteria. "No, I brought my lunch today. I think I'm going to just eat at my desk. I want to finish up a couple of reports Roger asked for."

"I'll go down to lunch with you," Becky offers.

Looking again at the back of Sam's head Kinsey says, "Okay, I'm starving. Let's go."

"Are you sure you don't want to join us?" Becky offers sweetly her hand running across his desk her hip leaning against it. Um, excuse me but, did this dumb bitch think he wanted her company over Kinsey's?

"I'm good, thanks though," Sam says, his focus returning to his reports.

Kinsey feels some satisfaction that he turns her down too. Kinsey wants to growl and throw her stapler at his face-no-nut sack. Instead, she grabs her purse and leaves for lunch.

The final straw comes at the end of the day when Becky is saying goodnight. Sam quickly puts his paperwork aside, turns off his computer, grabs his bag, and says, "Wait up. I'll walk out with you." Without looking at Kinsey he walks past her desk.

"See you in the morning!" Becky's confidence is so heightened at this point it is sickening. Oh, hell to the no.

At the last second Sam turns, "See you tomorrow, Marshall."

"Bye, guys," she combos up her bye to both of them. Fiona and Gabe both shoot Kinsey a look to say what the hell is up with that? She shrugs her shoulders and returns to her computer. Kinsey ends up staying late until Roger kicks her out. She hadn't been working she had been devising a plan.

The following morning, she takes her time to curl her hair down her back and wears her shortest, tightest, form-fitting dress and highest heel. She picks out dangly earrings and a delicate necklace that slips down to nestle in between her breasts. Kinsey applies her make-up carefully wearing his favorite lip gloss and a spritz of perfume. She will not be ignored.

They arrive in the elevator at the same time. Someone joins them in the compartment, and he keeps his distance. When the elevator door opens, he grasps her arm and leads her away from their desks and down the opposite hallway. "What do you think you are doing?" he growls.

"What do you mean?" she asks coyly but she knows she is affecting him. She is practically running trying to keep up with his long angry strides, the sounds of her heels clicking resonating down the hallway.

"How am I supposed to get any work done with you dressed like that?"

She looks down at herself as if just realizing what she is wearing. "This old thing? Do you like it?"

"You know I fucking do. Christ, are you wearing any panties?"

"Only one way to find out…"

"Kinsey," he warns. He opens the door to the stairwell and pushes her out into the quiet landing. No one ever uses the stairs. He forces her back up against the wall his body covering her in an instant. Sam's lips find her eager to show him she had missed him. His hands roam her body and hike one of her legs up on his hip. His fingers find what he is looking for. She is wet and not wearing any panties. She clutches his shoulder and around his back as his fingers sink into her. He pulls away watching her passion build.

It is unnerving how he can hold her gaze as his thumb begins slow circles around her nub. She throws back her head and rocks her hips forward. "Look at me," he demands in a rough whisper. Kinsey does, biting her lip her eyes dipping down to look at his lips.

"No," he tells her.

"But I want to kiss you," she whines out of need.

"You've been a bad girl and I need to teach you a lesson."

"You know you want to."

A smile touch his lips, "That's not the point."

She gasps as he works her harder, "You are only torturing yourself."

"I deserve to be punished too." Sam's eyes are sorrowful.

"Sam," her hand cups his face she wants to take away his pain but knows she is part of the cause. He kisses her then. His lips are gentle, lingering. His fingers are attempting something new and it causes her to break away from the kiss with a gasp. His lips continue down her neck and in between her breastbone. Both hands cradle his head as he works his way back up a trail of kisses leading to the other side of her neck.

Then as abruptly as he had started, he stops taking several steps back. He shoves his hands into his pockets, more than likely stopping himself from touching her again. This simple action makes her smile. He looks at the floor not meeting her gaze. "Now, we are even."

"What do you mean?" Kinsey asks trying to compose herself.

"I think that is only fair that if I have to look at you in that dress all day, you get to think about not cumming in the stairwell."

Dawning reaches her, and she gasps, he is punishing her. "You bastard," she says without much malice.

"After you," he holds the door open for her. Sam slaps her hard on the ass as she walks by.

"Be careful, two can play this game," she warns in the hallway. As they meander back to their desks, she glances at him, a sparkle in her eye, "Um Sam? This isn't our floor."

Sam looks around then belts out a laugh, "Well shit. That is one hell of a dress." She joins him in his merriment. They had both been so distracted by each other that neither one of them realized they had gotten off on the wrong floor. They go back to the elevators and rise to the correct floor.

She does think about the stairwell all day. That and what they had started in his car. This is torture. Kinsey needs a release she worries he won't be able to commit to. She is being selfish. She wants him all to herself and he isn't budging. Yes, he has kissed her, yes, he flirts with her constantly, yes, he touches her in places a friend shouldn't, and yes he has even had his dick inside her. Did it count if neither person came? If they didn't have time to finish? She doesn't feel like it should count. She wants a do-over.

Chapter Sixteen

♥

The following week, Sam and Kinsey are snuggled together in a napping pod. If anyone were to walk by, they would see two pairs of legs sticking out of the ends but not necessarily know what is happening under the dark dome closing them in. They are done work for the day and are trying to enjoy a few moments alone before they have to go home.

Sam tucks Kinsey's hair behind her ear, "I like who I am when I'm with you." he tells her. His breath is warm on her face. His words wash over her.

Her heart seizes in her chest. "I don't like who I am when I'm with you," she confesses.

Sam's head jerks back at this response. His hand has migrated to her neck his thumb caressing her jaw. His eyebrows furrow as he studies her face, "Why? I think you're terrific."

She smiles but it is not her normal dazzling smile. She goes on to explain, "I'm selfish when I'm with you. I know I can't have you and that doesn't stop me from wanting you." Her hand rests on his chest and she can feel his heart beating wildly inside. "It doesn't stop me from pursuing you."

Sam nuzzles her neck, "I'm sorry," he breathes. "I want to tell you to stop. I want to stop, but I can't. I know that makes me a terrible person. I'm selfish when I'm with you too. You just make me feel alive and whole when I'm with you."

Kinsey sighs rolling away from him. "Can we just stay in here forever?"

His arms wrap around her waist pulling her back up against his chest, "I wish." He doesn't speak and neither does she, enjoying the sensation of being in his arms. She closes her eyes as her breathing starts to match his and before they know it, they are both sleeping.

Waking up, she doesn't know where she is at first. It's dark and quiet. The office has packed up for the night. Her eyes adjust to the dimness recognizing that there are sparse emergency lights on.

Rolling over she faces Sam he is still sleeping. He looks so young and worry-free. Her fingers run over the features of his face trying to memorize every inch of him. The pad of her thumb runs across his lower lip there is a single freckle. His eyes are still closed but a smile starts to form on his lips.

"Are you about done?"

"Not even close," she says a second before leaning in, her lips pressing against his. Instantly he deepens the kiss, his hands cupping her ass bringing her closer. His tongue swirls with hers. They kiss for hours barely coming up for air. When they do, they speak in hushed tones about what they like in bed turning each other on. They don't go any further than kissing and some heavy petting.

Eventually, when it is too late for either to explain why they are coming home so late they crawl out of the napping pod. Kinsey feels satisfied and disappointed at the same time. She loves spending time with him, in any capacity but it's days like this when she craves a future with him so badly, she could cry. Especially knowing it will never happen as much as she wishes for it to come true.

Chapter Seventeen

♥

Kinsey and Sam get their letters of intent to continue with the company before Christmas break. Kinsey secretly rejoices at the fact that Becky doesn't get one. Sam, Gabe, Fiona, Tyler, Justin, Sierra, and Marcus are all asked to stay on for the spring semester. Justin suggests they all go out to celebrate.

They go to a karaoke bar. Lining up at the bar they order shots of Tequila. "Who is singing first?" Fiona wants to know as they slam their shot glasses down on the wooden bar. The bartender hands them a laminated book with a list of songs. As people pick their songs, they make their way up to the front to put their names on the list.

Sam suggests a duet and Kinsey quickly agrees. When it is finally their turn, they are a couple of drinks deep and they have been laughing hysterically at everyone that has gone before them except Justin who did surprisingly well.

Making their way up to the stage Kinsey wonders if this is a good idea. They are each given a microphone. Sam's part starts first, his voice sends chills down her spine. Kinsey looks away because she is afraid, she won't know when it's her turn to start singing.

Kinsey opens her mouth, and she is surprised by her angelic voice mixing with his deeper tone. She hears the crowd hooting and hollering. Smiling, she gets into the song turning towards Sam. The look he has in his eyes has her heart thudding.

It's just them and the music, everyone else fades into the background. "Get a room!" Kinsey hears Gabe shouts when they finish the song still staring at each other. It snaps Sam out of the trance first. Grinning he takes her hand, and they take a bow to the standing ovation. Tugging her hand, he pulls her off the stage and down the back hallway.

"You were so good," he tells her.

"So were you! I didn't know you could sing. You are always humming to songs."

He grins like he is proud he was able to keep this secret from her. "We were good together."

"Guys!" Fiona interrupts, "We have another round of shots ready to go. Come on!" She waves them back to the bar. Their co-workers cheer when Fiona returns with them. Hours later the crowd is standing on the street corner flagging down taxis to take them home or heading to the subway.

Sam and Kinsey are huddled shoulder to shoulder in the chilly night air. Shivering, Kinsey runs her hands up and down her arms to keep warm. Sam slips out of his long coat and slips it over her shoulders even though he is now pretending to not shiver in the cold. Kinsey looks up at him smiling her thanks when her expression freezes seeing the way he is looking at her. She isn't sure how his eyes can search her soul so completely.

"Bye guys!" Fiona wraps them both in a hug then she and Gabe jump in the same cab leaving Kinsey and Sam standing alone on the curb.

Sam tugs Kinsey into the dark alley. He leans his back on the brick wall pulling her up against his chest. Reaching for him his coat cascades down her back and onto the ground unnoticed. His head dips, his lips capturing hers. She moans into his mouth, and he growls his hands cupping her ass and grinding her to him. Lifting her, he turns her, so she is up against the wall the warmth of his body cradling her.

His lips trail down her neck and she plays with his hair and down his back clutching him to her. "Do you love her?" Kinsey realizes this is not the best time to ask this question, but they aren't going to see each other for a month.

Kinsey may as well have poured ice-cold water over him. It would have produced the same effect as her words. Sam stiffens and releases her, so her legs are no longer wrapped around his hips but firmly planted on the ground. He can't look at her when he responds in a low whisper, "Yes."

Tears burned her eyes, "Will you ever leave her?" She desperately wants to add, for me? His fist slams against the bricks behind her head making her jump.

Kinsey waits patiently for his response her throat constricting with all the pent-up tears she feels coming. He pushes away from the wall, away from her. It's a physical pain she feels at the separation, and she can see it in his tight jaw he feels it too.

This time he does look at her as he responds. "I can't." Not no. Not I don't want to. Not never, but I can't. What the fuck does that mean?

"Why?" Kinsey demands instead.

"It's complicated."

"This is complicated!" Kinsey half shouts, waving her arm between herself and him.

"I know!" Sam takes a steadying breath, running his fingers through his hair. "Kinsey, I never meant for this to happen, and I'm kicking myself that I let it get this far. And I'm fucking pissed with myself that I'm hurting you. It's the last thing in the world I want to do to you. You deserve so much better."

"I don't want better!" she cries.

He lets out a small laugh and comes back to her crushing her against him. He wipes away her tears and she sees the damage on the side of his hand from hitting the wall. It is bloody and scraped. She kisses his hand gently.

"I can't do this anymore." Tears are still streaming down her face, and she is mad that he is witnessing her weakness.

"I understand," Sam's voice is rough with emotion. How can he let her go this easily? Kinsey shoves him away from her hard and he lets her.

"Fuck you, Sam," she doesn't even say it with malice, just defeat. The other woman has won. Kinsey is actively fighting for Sam and this woman is oblivious at home doing nothing and winning. Sam doesn't respond just stands there and watches her leave.

Chapter Eighteen

♥

When Kinsey gets home, she slams the door behind her and instantly regrets it. Hanging her purse carefully she slips out of her shoes and runs barefoot on the marble floor to her room. Her bedroom has a plush cream-colored carpet. Kinsey had remodeled it from the princess bedroom her dad had created for her to a more sophisticated décor her sophomore year of high school. Flinging herself onto her bed, clothes and all, she sobs into her pillow.

At first, she doesn't hear the soft knock on her door but the second one is louder. Sniffling she rubs her hand across her nose and mouth, "Come in," she calls.

Her dad cautiously opens her bedroom door. "You okay, sweetheart?"

"Of course, sorry I slammed the door I didn't mean to."

"I don't care about the door. Do you want to tell me what's bothering you?"

"Nothing," she attempts and fails to sound chipper.

He is silent for a second then offers, "Do you want a hug?" Kinsey jumps off the bed and flings herself into her dad's arms. Her crying starts all over at her dad's kindness and knowing what she needs. Kinsey can't tell him about Sam, she knows he wouldn't approve of her going after someone in a relationship. Pierce doesn't press his daughter anymore just kisses her goodnight after most of her tears have dried.

Kinsey doesn't wake up until noon the following day. She never sleeps in this late and she is shocked her dad hadn't bothered to wake her. She stays in her PJs all day eating every ounce of junk food she can find in the cupboards. Sitting on the couch wrapped in a blanket, she watches mindless TV. Sam doesn't call her, and she doesn't call him.

She doesn't shower and she cries herself to sleep for three days. On the third night, it is midnight, and she is polishing off a bottle of wine by herself in her room. This needs to stop, this isn't her. Putting down her empty wineglass she stands and walks to her attached bathroom.

Turning on the shower she closes the door and allows the room to fill with warm steam. Stripping down out of the same PJs she has been in since coming home the night she had left Sam in the alley. Should she go to a bar? Maybe pick up a stranger for a fling? She has an abundance of pent-up sexual frustration, but that just isn't her style.

Kinsey needs a boyfriend someone to take her mind off Sam. Someone to do things with, someone to love her. She is freaking amazing, and Sam is stupid not to realize that. Okay, how is she planning on meeting someone? Online dating seemed to work for some.

Turning off the shower she dries herself off and slips into a robe. Turning on her computer in her bedroom she waits for her modem to wake up. Dressing in fresh panties and PJs she sits down and signs up for online dating. The quiz, to begin with, takes her over an hour. Then she begins to work on her profile.

Kinsey scrolls through her pictures on her computer trying to find one of just her or one she can crop. Eventually, she settles on one from her friend's wedding last year. Once she finally finishes, she crawls into bed and does not cry herself to sleep. She is excited about the future.

Chapter Nineteen

♥

The following morning, she wakes up, dresses, does her hair and make-up, and is early enough to catch her dad before he heads to work. The smile that crosses his features makes her feel guilty when she realizes she made him worry about her behavior this weekend.

"Hey, Dad. I'm going to get a coffee do you want anything?" She kisses him on the cheek and his hand squeezes her upper arm.

"No thank you. I'm headed to the office shortly. What do you plan to do today?"

"I'm going to lunch with one of my friends."

"That's nice. Have fun. Will I see you for dinner?"

"I'll be here. Do you want Mexican tonight?"

"That sounds delicious, I'll be home by six."

Kinsey waves goodbye before leaving their apartment to head down the street for a coffee. When she returns to the quietness, she boots up her computer again and waits to see if there are any results from last night's experiment.

She has three matches! Kinsey claps her hands in excitement. Clicking on the first one she scans the photo before reading his profile. His name is Jon. He is thirty-two, clean-shaven, and works on Wall Street. She had heard some rumors about guys that work there, and her dad had told her to steer clear. That and the age difference is ten years, not that it was a deal-breaker, but she moves on to her next match.

Bryce is a twenty-eight-year-old firefighter. She loves a man in uniform and his profile pic doesn't disappoint. Clicking through his photos she melts when she sees him posed next to his dog. The next picture has her frowning, he is running a marathon a number taped to the front of his tank top smiling and waving to the camera, he is sweaty with the excursion. Kinsey is not a runner she had tried once but it hurt her knees and she couldn't get her boobs to stop bouncing even with two sports bras and that hurt too. Did runners date non-runners, wasn't there a rule? She chews on her fingernail as she contemplated this.

She moves on to read his profile, he is witty and some of his comments have her laughing out loud. Bryce comes from a big Irish Catholic family, with two brothers, three sisters, and tons of nieces and nephews whom he seems to adore.

She decides to respond and sends him a message through the dating website. "Hi Bryce, I love that you have such a large family. My mom passed away when I was young, so it's always been just me and my dad. I'm a little jealous I've always wanted a brother or a sister. Cute puppy, boy or girl? I hear firefighters are good cooks, is this true?"

Kinsey clicks on the next profile his name is Travis, a twenty-six-year-old bartender. His profile picture is of him at the gym flexing his muscles. All his photos are of just him and his chiseled jawline. He has a body that just won't quit. Kinsey starts rejecting herself on his behalf before he can. He seems self-absorbed and probably wouldn't appreciate Kinsey's lack of exercise.

She is going to close his profile when she sees he has sent along with a message to her. "Kinsey, you have a beautiful name just like your eyes. I would love to meet you in person for a coffee or a drink?"

Wow, okay well, maybe she shouldn't count this one out. She responds to his message, "Hi Travis, thank you for the compliment. I would love to grab a drink with you sometime. I'm on winter break from college so I'm free for the next three weeks."

She reads her message over and it seems too eager and desperate. She erases the last sentence and sends the message. She picks up her phone and shoots Fiona a text, "Hey do you want to grab lunch today?"

"I'd love to. Name the time and place and I'll be there." Kinsey shoots her an address, and they agree on one o'clock.

Fiona is standing on the sidewalk in front of the restaurant wrapped in a beige pea coat and tall deep brown leather boots her blonde hair whipping in her face as the bitter wind picks up. Fiona brightens, a smile appearing, as Kinsey rounds the corner. Responding in kind, Kinsey matches her with a huge grin, it's good to see her. The women hug and then rush to get inside out of the harsh weather.

They are escorted to a booth and the women shed their outer garments before sliding into the hard leather seats. They are looking over the menu when Fiona asks, "So how was your weekend?"

"Shitty, how about yours?" Kinsey replies putting down her menu.

Fiona frowns her lips pursing, "Why what happened?" her voice concerned.

Kinsey assesses her friend she wants to tell everything, but she is also loyal to Sam and wants to protect his secret-their secret. "Sam and I fought after you got into the cab to go home."

Fiona's face registrars shock, "Is this like the fight you had when we first started? Will it be over in a couple of minutes? Or the other fight that lasted a day? You seem so right for each other."

Her comment both stabs at the very core of her and in the same breath exhilarates her yes, they are perfect for each other! Fiona is referring to the time she first discovered he was in a relationship and the day after they got caught having sex in his car and he was feeling guilty. Instead, she answers her questions and ignores the statement. "Our first fight was over a misunderstanding, the second fight I'm no longer willing to do what fixed that, this one is much bigger. I can't get into the details with you, but I've decided to move on. For my sanity, I need to. Last night I joined a dating website."

"Tell me everything!" Fiona exclaims. The waiter comes over and they order their drinks.

"Well, I had three matches this morning."

"Look at you go!" Fiona encourages. Kinsey tells her about all three men. Fiona suggests that she shouldn't rule out the Wall Street guy. "Listen a girl has to eat. Go out on one date with him. He could be the one you just never know."

"Okay," Kinsey decides to message him when she gets home.

"I slept with Gabe Friday night," Fiona adds casually to the conversation.

Kinsey instantly starts choking on her food. "What?" she asks after drinking her water and pounding on her chest.

Fiona smiles, "He just slipped into my cab. I thought maybe he lives close to me but nope. He told me I was beautiful, and he has wanted to kiss me since the first day."

"How did you respond to that?"

"I kissed him."

Kinsey laughs, "Well okay then. So, are you guys dating now?"

She giggles, "He is still at my place. Gabe hasn't left. We've gone to dinner, the movies, ordered in, sex in between." Kinsey is happy for them. It should have been her and Sam as the office couple, but it isn't. The women finish their lunches and hug goodbye at the door.

Kinsey rushes home to see if Travis or Bryce has responded and to send Jon a message. Travis has responded but Bryce has not. She is a little disappointed she likes him most out of her options right now. Travis' message, "Kinsey, I'm working tonight and the next couple of nights, but I do have Thursday night off if you would like to get a drink then say around 8?"

Kinsey responds that that sounds lovely and suggests a place she knows nearby. He responds, "It's a date. See you then, Beautiful."

This guy is extremely complimentary, and she loves it. She sends Jon a message and then notices a red bubble in the top toolbar with a white four in the middle. Clicking on it she realizes she has four more matches!

Oh my. Now what? She looks through the profiles. Murphy is heavyset, his face split in a wide, contagious grin. She instantly likes him but isn't attracted to him.

Will is a real estate developer. His beautiful golden brown skin and chestnut brown eyes are mesmerizing her through the computer screen, attraction to him is instant. She reads his profile and shoots him a short flirty message and moves on.

Patrick is twenty-one and a bike messenger by day and an exotic dancer by night. She quickly checks out her next prospect. Shaun is an Asian photographer. He has one black-and-white profile picture he is bald and attractive. The rest of his photos include his work displaying buildings all in the same black and white photography. Kinsey sends him a message.

Sitting back in her chair she begins to panic a little. Maybe she should have only picked one guy to start with and see how that goes now she is in communication with multiple men, and she isn't sure if she can manage it. If she had been looking for a distraction from Sam, this is it.

Roger has given them a project over the winter break. Originally, she had been excited thinking she and Sam could see each other over the break but Roger specifically stated he wants these done individually. She needs to email him a proposal by Friday.

She researches the company and goes over the data given. Three hours later she orders Mexican food for her and her dad. Kinsey walks down to the local Bodega and picks up a bottle of margarita mix and salt. Walking two more blocks she picks up the food.

That night after dinner she gets a message from Bryce and her heart speeds up. "Hey Kinsey, I was on shift today and there were several calls I had to go out on. I'm back at the station now. I'm working a 24-hour shift. Yes, most firefighters are good cooks. I however happen to be exceptional, not to brag or anything. I would like to cook for you sometime so you can judge for yourself.

I'm sorry to hear about your mom that must have been tough, I couldn't even imagine. As for siblings you can borrow any of mine, seriously take your pick. As for my dog, her name is Riley. I rescued her after a house fire she was the only survivor. Sorry, that took a sad turn. Do you have any pets?

What do you like to eat? I can start planning the meal I'll make for us. I have tomorrow night off and the night after if you are free for dinner. I'll take you out to a restaurant before inviting you into my apartment. I'm sure your dad wouldn't approve of you meeting a stranger for the first time in his tiny basement apartment."

Clapping her hands together in excitement, her face in a grin she responds. "I appreciate your concern for my dad's feelings, and I assure you the restaurant is a good first move. I have plans for Thursday night, but I can go to dinner on Wednesday. You name the time and the place.

I love that Riley is a rescue. I can't wait to meet her. What type of breed is she? I have no pets. I asked my dad for a pony when I was eight. The best he could do was let me start riding lessons and I got into competitions. I did that for years but not since college. Did you play sports or do any clubs? I see you are a runner. I must confess that is not something I enjoy. Only if a bear is chasing me and in the city the possibilities are slim.

As far as food goes, I like most things oh except seafood. I'm not sure why if it's a combo of the sight and smell but I just can't bring myself to do it. Most people find that weird."

Kinsey checks her messages a couple of hours later before going to bed and she sees that Jon, the Wall Street guy has responded. "Hello, Kinsey. You have a unique name is that a nickname? I'm working all week but free this Saturday. Can I interest you in a date? There is a comedy show this Saturday night, it's dinner and a show."

That sounds fun. Kinsey accepts his date and then crawls into bed. She doesn't cry but instead lays awake staring at the ceiling thinking about Sam. Kinsey tosses and turns for hours before falling into a fitful sleep.

Kinsey arrives at her date with Bryce right on time. He is standing just inside the restaurant next to the hostess counter. He is a little shorter than she would have pictured him to be in person but still taller than her.

He smiles when he sees her and comes over to give her a hug which she accepts.

"Nice to meet you in person," he tells her warmly.

"Same," she murmurs. The hostess takes them to a table and Bryce helps her out of her coat. They slide into chairs opposite each other. Bryce engages her in small chit-chat about the weather and the area of town while they browse the menu and order drinks.

Their conversation is light, and he is easy to talk to. He asks her about school, and she tells him about her internship leaving out the boy she wants to spend the rest of her life with but can't. He tells her stories of the fire station some of them scary rescues and other funny stories of his co-workers.

The night seems to fly by. She reaches for her purse to pay but he insists he has it covered. At the end of the date, they are standing face-to-face outside the restaurant each holding their to-go containers. When they go to say goodbye, he hugs her and she is disappointed she didn't get a kiss. Feeling a little rejected she smiles and waves hurrying off to her subway stop in the opposite direction he is going. When she gets home her dad is waiting up. She puts her leftover Styrofoam container in the fridge and joins her dad on the couch. He is watching an old movie rerun on TV. The room is dark except for the blue glow coming from the screen.

"How was your date?" he asks.

"It was fine. He is super nice."

"But…" her dad wants to know.

She smiles at how well he knows her. She shrugs, "We'll see, not sure if there will be a second date."

"Well, you win some you lose some," her dad offers in way of advice.

"Yeah, I guess so." They sit in silence watching TV until she hears her dad's soft snoring. Smiling she turns on a lamp before turning off the TV with the remote. "Come on dad time for bed."

Her dad gets up and hugs her before shuffling down the hall. When she reaches her room, she decides to turn on her computer before going to bed. There is a message from Bryce. "Kinsey, I had a nice time with you tonight. Please forgive me for not kissing you. I should have and I've been kicking myself all the way home that I didn't. Please give me another chance. I've talked it over with Riley and she wants to meet you."

Kinsey smiles as she replies, "Bryce, you don't fight fair bringing your dog into this. You're lucky she is on your side. I suppose I have no choice but to forgive you. I'm going out of town next week for the holidays. What does your schedule look like after the new year maybe we can take her to the park together?"

Bryce responds almost immediately, "Phew, saved by the dog, she says thank you and so do I. I'm off Wednesday and Thursday of that week. I have errands to run on Wednesday, but I would love to go to the park and then out to lunch on Thursday?" She replies that she would love to, and they work out the details.

As she is about to log off, she sees that Will the real estate developer has sent her a message, "Hi Kinsey, I'm sorry I didn't respond right away I was away on business and just got back. I'm free this weekend if you would like to get a bite to eat. I know this great Italian place if you are interested?"

Kinsey tells him she has plans for Saturday, but Friday night or Sunday would work for her. They agree on Sunday night.

Thursday, she meets Travis for drinks. He is a little too touchy-feely for her liking. He orders her drink for her telling her as a bartender he can usually tell what someone is going to order but he knows what they really should have. She thinks this is a little cocky, but she has to admit she does like the drink he gets for her.

At the end of the night Travis kisses her, well really goes all in for a full-on make-out session. There is slobber and he is way too aggressive she is not into it at all. She breaks away from the kiss and tells him to have a good night. "You aren't coming home with me?" he asks.

"Um no."

"What a waste," he mumbles before walking off. Kinsey's eyebrow shoots sky-high. The nerve of this guy. She calls Fiona on her way home to tell her about him.

"What a loser," she says but she is laughing. "How was your date with Bryan last night?"

"Bryce? Good. He is the complete opposite of Travis."

"Yeah, we hate Travis, moving on. Who is next?"

"I'm going to a comedy show Saturday night with your pick, Jon the wall street guy. I also have a date with Will the real estate developer on Sunday."

She squeals on the other end of the line. "I can't wait to hear all the details."

"I'm also seeing Bryce again when I get back into town after the holidays. We are taking his dog to the park and having lunch."

"Ahh, that sounds adorable. Yes, keep me posted on all of this," Fiona says. Kinsey agrees she will, and they hang up.

The comedy show with Jon is so much fun. They don't get to talk much because they are eating while watching the show. She learns he is Italian. He has broad shoulders and is bigger in person than what his profile shows but still attractive.

The lights come on at the end of the final act and people are standing to leave. He reaches over his hand cupping her face his thumb on her chin. He draws her closer for a kiss. It's a nice kiss and she feels a little tingle. She can't wait to tell Fiona.

When they break apart, he asks if he can see her again. He explains that he is divorced and gets his son every other weekend. Next weekend he is busy so it will have to be the following weekend. Jon explains he doesn't want to introduce anyone to him unless things are getting serious. Kinsey understands and they agree on a Saturday date in two weeks.

Will the real estate developer is yummy for lack of a better word. He is dressed to impress and takes her to a fancy restaurant. He offers to pick her up outside of her apartment and has a luxury sports car that is just as sleek as he is. He jumps out and comes around to open the door for her.

"Thank you," she murmurs as she slides inside. He uses valet parking and his hand rests on the small of her back as he guides her through the restaurant that he frequents because everyone seems to know him smiling and saying hi. Will is gracious and did she mention beautiful? They have a lovely dinner, but he seems preoccupied with his phone. He keeps apologizing as he tends to business.

Will drives her home, parks, and not only walks her to the building but rides up in the elevator with her. "I had fun tonight," he tells her. Smiling Kinsey tells him the same. She can see it in his eyes he is going to kiss her, and she feels like swooning before his lips even reach her. Her arms wrap around him, and he envelops her in his embrace.

The door to her apartment opens and her dad is standing there. They jump apart like teenagers getting caught. Will offers his hand out to her dad, "Sir, so nice to meet you I'm Will Coleman."

"Pierce, nice to meet you. Would you like to come in for a drink?"

"Thank you, sir, for the invitation but I really must get going I have work in the morning."

"Raincheck. Where do you work?"

"I own Coleman Properties."

"That's impressive, good for you. Well, I'll let you two finish saying goodnight. It was nice to meet you, Will."

"Thank you, you too sir."

Her dad shuts the door, and she is ready to die of embarrassment when he says, "I like your dad."

"I think he likes you too."

He takes her in his arms again, "Does he now? What about his gorgeous daughter? Does she like me?" Kinsey bites her lower lip trying to hide her smile, but it isn't possible as she nods her head in affirmation. "Can I see you again?"

"I'd like that," is all she manages to get out before he is kissing her again. Oh my. That night as she falls into bed, she doesn't think about Sam but about Will's kisses.

Chapter Twenty

♥

The following morning, she and her dad are in his car driving upstate where there is little to no reception. She won't be able to talk to anyone until she gets back. It gives her a chance to think which, is turmoil in itself.

Kinsey does her best to enjoy her aunts, uncles, and cousins but her head is still in Manhattan trying to figure out her life. These are the moments especially when she misses her mom. Would she know the right things to tell her? Had she ever experienced any of this? She desperately wants to talk to her.

Thursday when she returns there is a huge snowstorm, and the city is under a state of emergency. "Do not go out if you don't have to. Visibility is poor and the snowplows are just trying to clear this mess. Snowfall is coming down at a rate of an inch an hour. Stay tuned…"

"Ugh," Kinsey shuts off the TV. Going to her room she sits down at her desk. Next to her computer is a giant bouquet of flowers from Will. He had sent them the morning she had returned after their date. "I can't wait to see you again. Will." The card read. She had sent him an email immediately thanking him for the flowers gushing over how beautiful they are.

As she suspects Bryce is canceling their date. "I guess we will just have to take a rain check. I'm bummed I was looking forward to you meeting her. Riley is depressed she won't eat. She tossed and turned all night worried about if you would like her or not."

Kinsey laughs, "Oh no, poor Riley. Tell her not to worry, I was smitten when I first laid eyes on her. When is your next day off? I need that kiss you've promised me."

Kinsey works on her project, and cleans the apartment, before making herself lunch. She hears a knock on the door. Frowning she shuts off the stove and wipes her hands on the dishtowel. Walking to the door she looks through the peephole. Surprised, she steps back, an anxious Bryce is standing in the hallway. They had discussed on their date where the other lives in the city. She was on the Upper East Side with her dad, and he was farther north in Harlem in a tiny basement flat by himself.

He knocks again startling her. Oh yes, she needs to open the door. Looking in the mirror over the entryway table she smooths her hair down. Thank God she had dressed this morning and not bummed around all day in her PJs. Twisting the handle, she pulls the door in towards her. Bryce's hand is raised again to knock.

Bryce looks worried and Kinsey instantly takes pity on him. Smiling she says, "Well this is a nice surprise."

Relief instantly washes over his face his hand in the air moving to rub the back of his neck, "Good."

"Would you like to come in?" Kinsey steps aside. He moves forward and she shuts the door. "What do I owe the pleasure?" she asks.

Instead of answering her in words, he takes a step forward pulling her to him. His lips land on hers that are parting in surprise. Closing her eyes, she gives in to the kiss. Oh my, her brain is trying to process. If Bryce had kissed her that first night like this, she would have canceled all her other dates.

Bryce's head lifts but he keeps her wrapped in his arms. "You said you needed a kiss, and I didn't want to disappoint a second time."

She smiles up at him "I'm glad you came through on your promise. I'm thinking I should collect interest though. I mean I think it's only fair since you made me wait so long."

Grinning his lips lower to hers. She invites him to stay for lunch and watch TV. He joins her and they hang out on the couch all afternoon. Snow is falling fast and fierce outside. Bryce lights a fire in the fireplace for her. They talk and flirt and make out until her dad comes home.

She introduces them and Bryce heads home after hearing it has only gotten worse out there. He tells her he needs to take Riley out anyway. They make plans for Saturday night, the same night she has plans with Jon. She is going to cancel with him and suspend her dating account for right now. Kinsey however is not breaking her date with Will on Sunday night. She hasn't officially made up her mind yet.

For the next couple of weeks, she dates both men and it becomes clear that Will is too busy to date. He is charming but distracted by running his own business and cancels on her twice. Bryce however is funny and kind and just the distraction she needs from the man she cannot have.

Chapter Twenty-One

♥

Kinsey braces herself for seeing Sam again. She couldn't sleep last night, tossing and turning. She is with Bryce now, she has moved on, yet somehow, she hasn't moved on at all. Walking into the office Sam is already at his desk working.

It's like he feels her presence when she enters the room. He turns in his chair his eyes lighting up when he sees her, she can't help but smile back at him. They are both early no one else is in yet, and their entire floor is quiet. He looks relaxed and well-rested. He swivels in his chair his legs spread wide a pen dangling in one hand.

"Hey," she says.

"Hey, yourself," he sounds happy to see her and her heart swells.

Kinsey approaches, but he doesn't stand to greet her. She puts her purse on her chair and comes into the space between his desk and hers. She takes a seat on her desk facing him her legs crossed. "How was your vacation?" she asks.

"It was good. How was yours?"

"It was good," she allows.

"I missed you," he tells her. She uncrosses her legs and leans forward.

"That's not fair, Sam," she says softly.

He leans forward in his chair his face sobering, "I know. I'm sorry." He seems contrite.

"How did you do on your project Roger gave us?" Kinsey changes the subject.

He grins seeing what she is doing and goes along with it, "Good. How about you?"

"I think I did well. I would have liked your take on it before I handed in my final draft."

"You should have called me," Sam tells her.

Kinsey cocks her head to the side searching him quizzically. He means it. Shrugging her shoulders, "I won't always have you around to help me."

"Says who?" he wants to know.

"Come on Sam, be realistic. We won't see each other after this internship, you know that, right?" She is pissed because she has only spent five minutes with him and it's like they never separated. It doesn't matter that Bryce is a good guy. It doesn't matter that Bryce only has one girlfriend and it's her. It doesn't matter that Bryce likes her a lot. When she is with Sam that is the only person, she wants to be with.

Sam shrugs non-committal, "You never know." But they both know if nothing comes from this experience they would move on and go their separate ways it was the only way to keep their sanity.

Kinsey hops off the desk coming in close contact with Sam. His hand reaches out and touches her outer thigh. They both look at his hand.

"Hey, guys!" Fiona's voice fills the room. Sam's hand quickly shrinks away from her and she walks around to greet her friend. They hug and Fiona settles into her chair behind Kinsey. "Hi Sam!" she waves enthusiastically to him. He smiles and greets her. "It was so much fun last night," Fiona whispers to Kinsey but Sam overhears.

"Oh yeah, what was last night?" Sam asks.

Fiona looks guilty but Kinsey knows she did it on purpose and she is not ready for the cat to be out of the bag. "Oh, we had a double date. Bryce is such a nice guy."

Sam is quiet for a minute and Kinsey forces herself to stay facing Fiona who gives her a wink. Her heart is racing. Will Sam demand she break up with him? That he will call his girlfriend right now and end things. Is he jealous? She freaking hopes so. It has been a bitter pill she has had to endure the past several months. She doesn't want to revenge date she wants Sam to want her. Why is this so complicated?

"That's nice," is all Sam can muster up to say before turning around.

Later that morning, Sam catches Kinsey by herself in the breakroom. He is behind her, "So you're dating someone now?"

Turning around with her cup of tea she moves the teabag up and down in her steaming mug of hot water. The same mug he bought her after finding out he was in a relationship. "I had several dates with different guys then settled on one."

"What's he like?"

"Do you really want to know?"

"No."

"It sucks, doesn't it?" She doesn't say it to be mean, well maybe a little. Kinsey wants him to know it hasn't been easy for her and this is only a sliver of how hard it has been on her.

Sam nods before turning around and walking away. Kinsey wants to cry. Bryce is a good kisser, and she likes spending time with him. With Sam, she craves his kisses, she yearns for his touch, and she is desperate to have him look at her the way he does. Sam is such an idiot, and she is stupidly in love with him.

Chapter Twenty-Two

♥

Sam gets into a funk. Both of them are off as their time at the company comes to an end. Kinsey wonders if it is something, she has done to upset him or if he and the misses are fighting again. He had once told her that when he is in that kind of mood, not to talk to him, look at him or touch him. Well, they were halfway there already. She would give him his space and hope he comes back around.

Stu Hersch is retiring, and the entire company is invited with a plus one. "Are you going to bring your girlfriend?" Kinsey asks.

"What?" Sam seems distracted with the invitation in his hand.

"Are you going?" she asks instead.

"Yeah, I think it should be fun. Black tie event on the company's dime. Sure. You?"

"Yes. Do you think I should bring Bryce? I don't know his schedule, but he may be able to request it off with enough notice."

Sam ponders her question. "Sure." Turning around he ends the conversation.

The night of the event she is dressed in a red cocktail gown her hair is pulled off her neck. Bryce looks handsome her arm tucked neatly into his bent elbow. She has only ever seen him in his firefighter uniform which does it for her and casual attire. This is definitely a good look for him.

Inside the Waldorf-Astoria hotel, the ballroom is set up beautifully. Kinsey has been to a few events here and knows that the three-story room has balconies that line the two upper floors. In the decoration of the room, a white banner has been draped across the room closing off the balconies from looking down. Twinkling lights are on the ceiling a blue hue softens the room. A live band is playing, and the hardwood dance floor is empty in front of them. Round tables, covered in fine linen and topped with tall silver centerpieces with an abundant number of flowers have the room smelling of spring. A long table hosts the guest of honor, his wife, and all the higher-ups of the company including Roger.

The interns have a table towards the back but are also stationed close to one of the bars. Walking to the table first she spots Fiona and Gabe talking with Justin and his date. Justin introduces them to his boyfriend Vinny. Shaking his hand Kinsey smiles, "So nice to meet you. Justin, Vinny this is my boyfriend, Bryce." The men shake hands. Bryce already knows Fiona and Gabe from their double dates. The men decide to hit the bar while people are still walking in.

Bryce has his hand on the small of her back, "What can I get you?"

"A white wine if they have it. Thank you."

"Of course. I'll be right back."

Fiona and Kinsey stay at the table they put their purses on the table next to each other holding their spots. "You look amazing," Kinsey tells her friend. Fiona is dressed in a gold sequence gown that leaves one shoulder bare.

"Thank you," she beams doing a little twirl for Kinsey to assess the whole dress. "I love yours too. Red is a good color on you."

"Thanks," Kinsey says. She can feel him before she sees him. Her heart starts to speed up and her palms start to sweat. Looking up, Sam has entered the room his eyes fixed on hers. She looks for his girlfriend but finds him alone. A smile creeps across her face hoping it's the case and she isn't in the restroom. He is walking towards her weaving in and around tables and coworkers.

"Here's your wine," Bryce has returned handing her the glass.

The spell is broken the moment she returns her gaze to Bryce, "Great, thank you."

"You're welcome."

Sam comes to stand directly in front of her. She can feel Fiona shuffle next to her clearly uneasy. "Sam this is my boyfriend, Bryce McGovern. Bryce, this is Sam Anderson, one of my colleagues."

"Nice to meet you," Bryce reaches out taking Sam's hand shaking vigorously.

"Likewise," Sam tells him, and she knows he is lying. Gabe joins them bringing Fiona her drink.

"Sam! Glad you could make it!" Gabe pounds Sam on the back. "Did you bring a plus one?"

"No. We were on our way out the door when she got a call from work. Some marketing crisis she needs to deal with."

"Tough break," Gabe commiserates.

So, she would have been here Kinsey thinks and the thought makes her feel like a knife is buried deep inside her chest. Justin joins them with Vinny and makes the introductions to Sam. Marcus and his date show up and more rounds of handshakes ensue.

"I'm going to get a drink," Sam tells them.

"I'll go with you," Marcus joins him leaving his date with them. They start taking seats at the table. When Sam comes back, he takes the seat right next to Bryce. It's the closest to her he can get. The table fills in and the lights dim as they begin the evening.

"Thank you all for coming. We are here to celebrate...." Kinsey is facing the speaker, but her brain is on the two men behind her. They were having a conversation before they had gotten started. Several speakers get up roasting the retiree. Laughter and clapping happen at all the right times, and she follows along.

Bryce leans forward his lips close to her ear, "You, okay?"

Pretending she is fine; she plasters on her best smile as she turns to face him, but her eyes catch Sam's. "Never better," she tells him breaking contact with Sam and locking eyes with Bryce, "thanks for asking though." He smiles and places a kiss on her cheek. She watches Sam's eyes harden at the gesture and she feels sick with this tug-a-war with her heart.

Afterward, waiters bring out salads and bread. Bryce gets her another drink. At the bar, Sam and Bryce are talking and she sees Bryce laugh at something Sam has said. What did he tell him? Was it something about her?

"Relax," Fiona whispers behind her.

Kinsey swivels in her chair, "Exactly how am I supposed to do that?"

Fiona sighs, "Well I don't know but you can't be so obvious about it. You are glaring daggers at them from across the room."

Kinsey lets out a long slow breath and polishes off the splash of wine she has left. The men return with drinks. Plates are cleared and the dinner arrives. She had ordered Bryce the steak and she has the chicken. Normally she and Sam would share their plate but that was when no one was around. Glancing up at him he nods to his steak, and she shakes her head at him even though she would love a bite of his bacon-wrapped filet mignon. His eyes narrowed as if to call her a liar.

When the dessert plates are removed the dancing begins. Fiona takes Kinsey's hand and leads her out onto the dancefloor. The men all stay at the table drinking and Sam and Bryce are deep in conversation. The dancing is helping Kinsey relax, and she is on her third glass of wine.

After about an hour Kinsey tells Fiona, "I need to go to the bathroom. Do you need to go?"

"No, I'm good!" she shouts over the music.

"Okay, I'll be right back."

"Hurry back!"

Leaving she looks for the restroom. The line is out the door. A woman walking by her tells her, "Go upstairs, there are no lines."

"Oh, good. Thank you."

"No problem."

Taking the stairs, she holds her skirt in her hand, so she doesn't trip. Upstairs it's quieter. She can still hear the music, but it's muted. The bathroom is even quieter. When she finishes, she leaves walking into the hallway.

Sam is directly in front of her leaning up against the wall and waiting for her. Walking towards him he pushes himself off the wall and meets her halfway. Before either can utter a word, they hear laughter in the stairwell. He cocks his head to the side indicating the quiet end of the hallway. She turns and he falls into step beside her walking away from the people coming up to the second floor.

Towards the end of the hall, he opens one of the heavy curtains hiding a balcony. Standing to the side she slips into the enclosed space. Sam joins her dropping the curtain before the boisterous group on the stairs reaches the landing. It takes her a second for her eyes to adjust. The canvas on the side facing the ballroom is lit up allowing a soft glow into the dark space. A slow song is playing downstairs. "May I have this dance?" he asks holding his arms out to her.

She smiles at the gesture. They would never be able to have this dance downstairs. She melts into his arms. Placing her hand on his shoulder the other in his hand, his arm wraps around her waist and they sway to the music dancing in circles. She is studying his face. Is this all he came here to do? Normally she can read his thoughts like an open book, but she is struggling to know what's behind his bright blue eyes. After a few turns, he twirls her in a circle pushing her away from him before tugging her back into his arms.

Laughing she falls into him, this time her fingers lock around his neck, and he encircles her back. They move once again to the music. She lays her face on the lapel of his coat. His hands run up and down her back soothing her nerves.

"I've missed this," Sam tells her.

"What?" she looks up but knows what he is saying she just wants to hear it with her own two ears.

"Touching you." Her body quivers. "Kissing you." Her lips part.

They stand there for a moment. His head dips slowly as if asking her permission. She doesn't tell him no. She pulls him forward their lips are a breath away. Still, he hesitates and it's driving her mad with desire.

Kinsey waits him out. If he wants this kiss, he needs to take it from her, and then he does.

His lips are soft and gentle on hers. Sam inhales, breathing in deep her scent. His hand moves to the back of her head tilting it. His lips roam down her neck and she whimpers. Growling he captures her lips again this time his tongue sweeps inside the confines of her mouth. She welcomes him her fingers gripping the lapel on his tux pulling him closer, but it isn't possible their bodies are nearly one with each other. His kiss is so sweet she wants to weep. He is slow and gentle, and she wants more but he holds her at bay. Taking his time his lips move over hers.

"I can't," he tells her.

"You can't what?" She is confused about what he is trying to tell her.

"I can't watch you with him. It's torture."

"Say the word," she dares him.

"What do you mean?"

"Tell me to break up with him. Tell me you are leaving your girlfriend and we can be together. I'll do it. Right now. I'll march downstairs and tell him it's over."

"I know now what you meant when you said you felt selfish with me. I get it."

"You don't get the half of it. I've had to deal with this way longer than a night."

"You've never had to see me with her."

"Yeah, but I would have if she didn't have a work emergency. I don't think I would have handled the night very well either. What are we going to do?" she presses her forehead to his, her fingers running through his hair.

"Nothing we can do," he tells her mournfully.

"Why? What does she have on you?"

"Nothing."

"Tell me. We can work through this together."

He pulls away from her. "I'm sorry. I should have never come up here or said anything or done anything."

"Like dance with me? Like, kiss me? You're right you shouldn't have."

Sam looks broken at her words, but she knows it's like he is looking in a mirror because she is shattered. "You're right. It won't happen again. I promise," he tells her before leaving her in the alcove of the balcony. The sharp pain she feels at those words leaves her standing in stunned silence for a minute before collapsing into one of the chairs. She wants to scream in frustration, but she knows from experience that will do her no good. He means it. She knows he does. This will be the last time he kisses her, the last time he pursues her, it's crushing. That's not what she wants but what else can she do? To be the other woman forever? No. That will never work, and they both know it.

Standing she makes her way downstairs. Fiona locks eyes with her when she returns, and Kinsey knows that she knows. Bryce is laughing with Gabe and Marcus. She doesn't see Sam and she isn't sure if he has left or not. She walks over to Bryce.

He smiles down at her, "How's the dancing going?" Bryce hasn't even realized she had left the room and just spent the last ten minutes making out with the love of her life, then arguing with him about it.

"I'm not feeling well. Do you think you can drive me home?"

The concern is instant on his face, "Of course." Bryce picks her purse up from the table and they say their goodbyes. Fiona comes running off the dance floor with Justin and Vinny.

"You guys leaving?" she asks her face flushed from the dancing.

"Yeah, I'm not feeling great. I'll see you on Monday though." They give each other a hug and Fiona whispers in her ear.

"Call me."

"I will," even though she doesn't think she will tell her friend about this.

Driving home Kinsey is quiet as she looks out the window. It isn't that late and there is still traffic halting at the lights. Red lights illuminate the inside of the car as the vehicles around them apply their brakes. She turns to Bryce. She needs to break up with him. Not because of the kiss she just shared with another man but because she will never feel about him the way she does with Sam. It physically pains her knowing she is going to disappoint Bryce. He has been hinting at a long-term future with her and she just doesn't feel it. The red glow suddenly disappears as it is replaced by the green light overhead. Bryce accelerates and she looks back out the window on her side.

Parked cars line this side of the road, and she can see pedestrians walking solo and with big groups, couples, and friends, and the occasional hobo laying on cardboard on the sidewalk. She wonders about their conversations. She sees a couple arguing and she wants to know if it is over another person or not putting the toilet seat down for the hundredth time. Kinsey witnesses a couple holding hands and he stops her in her tracks to kiss her. She pictures that being her and Sam one day. A tear rolls down her cheek knowing that won't ever be the case.

Bryce's car comes to a halt, and she realizes she is in front of her building. Swiping away at the tear on her cheek she unbuckles and turns towards him. He is facing her. He knows something is up he just doesn't know what yet. "We need to talk."

He sighs, "I figured as much. What's up?"

"This isn't working," Kinsey can see the confusion in his eyes. "Us. I don't think we should see each other anymore."

His jaw goes slack, "Why? What happened? Was it something I did or said?"

"No," she rushes to tell him placing her hand on his forearm, "It's not you it's me."

"Oh great! Are you seriously giving me that line?" He pulls away from her.

"I know it's awful but it's true. You are amazing, and any girl would be lucky to have you." He is now staring out the windshield. "I just-I'm not ready. I thought I was, and it turns out I'm still getting over someone and it's just not fair to you. I need to sort through some things on my own."

Bryce looks over his shoulder over the top of his arm that he's resting on the top of the steering wheel, "We can work through it together. I'm a patient man."

She smiles a sad smile, "I love that about you and I'm sure you would, but I just can't ask you to. It will only hurt us more if I let this drag out."

"There is nothing I can do to change your mind is there?"

"I'm sorry, no." Kinsey is proud of herself for being firm. Her brain is screaming at her to take this lifeline he is offering her. She knows they will be here in the same situation a month from now or six months from now. Eventually, their relationship is doomed.

"Did something happen tonight?" he asks jerking her back to reality. She doesn't have a good poker face and lying is not in her DNA. Her silence says it all. "Okay then. Have a nice life, Kinsey."

"You too-"

"Get out." He doesn't shout his voice is calm and it scares her. Quickly she vacates the vehicle, and he drives off almost before the door is shut. What she feels is a huge weight lifted and a tremendous amount of sadness.

Chapter Twenty-Three

♥

Kinsey takes a personal day on Monday. Sam doesn't call her but she hadn't expected him to, but she had hoped. Fiona texts her instead, "Are you with Sam?"

"No. I'm home, sick. Why do you ask?"

"He didn't come into work either. I thought you two were together." Fiona tells her.

Kinsey groans. This doesn't look good. "I have no idea where he is or what he is doing or with whom."

"Alright. Sorry, I asked. Are you coming in tomorrow?"

"Yeah. I'll be there. Thanks for checking in."

"Can I ask what happened Friday night? I saw him walk out after you left. You guys were both gone a while. I don't mean to pry but did something happen?"

Kinsey doesn't want to have this conversation with her friend. She wants to hold Sam close in their private world. Kinsey would love to shout from the rooftop that she loves Sam, but he doesn't love her back. Why else would he be putting her in this position? She had stupidly thought he did love her and there was some noble thing holding him back but now she isn't so sure. If he wanted to be with her, wouldn't he just simply be with her?

She flings herself back on her bed. She had half expected Bryce to text her at any point this weekend. Knowing he had to work she wasn't surprised he didn't but knows enough to know he has downtime and could have if he wanted to. It's for the best she concedes.

The next morning Kinsey is first to the office. Anticipation is high as the office begins to fill with coworkers. She almost thinks he isn't going to show up again today when his bag hits his desk. Jumping she chastises herself as he settles into his chair.

Turning around he faces her, "Hey, what did I miss yesterday?"

Sam is back to his old self. Friend zone, Sam. Not her favorite but definitely not her least favorite version of him so she will take it. "Hey yourself," she responds, "I wouldn't know. I wasn't in yesterday."

He frowns, "You weren't? How come?"

Kinsey crosses her arms over her chest, "How come you weren't?"

"I had a family thing."

"Oh."

"So how come you weren't in?" he seems concerned now.

"Same."

He cocks his head to the side trying to read her, his eyes searching hers, and she looks away. "You had a family thing? On the same day, I had a family thing? Okay, Kinsey if you ever want to tell me the real reason. I'm all ears."

Kinsey purses her lips together, "Nope that's it. That's the reason."

"Okie Dokie," he spins around. "Psst, Gabe. What did I miss?"

Kinsey swivels in her chair to face Fiona. She won't meet her gaze. "You, okay?" she asks.

Fiona snorts, "I should ask you. You're the one that's sick." Fiona does air quotes.

"I'm sorry I didn't text you back yesterday. That was rude. It would have taken me too long to get the whole story out and…" Fiona is not paying attention to her. "I broke up with Bryce." There bomb dropped.

Fiona's eyes widen as she looks up at her. "Oh, sweetie, are you okay?" This time she means it. "What happened?" Kinsey can already tell she has Sam's attention. He has turned away from his conversation with Gabe.

"What happened?" Sam is now intervening in the conversation.

Kinsey swivels her chair so she can see both Sam and Fiona. "I broke things off with Bryce."

"When?" Sam's voice is low.

"Friday night when he drove me home from the retirement dinner."

Fiona is watching both Sam and Kinsey as if trying to figure out the puzzle. She has some of the pieces she just isn't sure what goes where. Sam's lips purse together his hands folded in front of him. He looks down at them but doesn't say anything.

"I liked Bryce," Gabe chimes in. Fiona glares at her boyfriend silently urging him to stay out of the conversation. "What? I did," he asks her his hands thrown in the air not understanding the contents of her request. "Ohhhh…" he says quietly backing out as quickly as he can, looking at both Sam and Kinsey.

"I'm sorry to hear that," Fiona offers. "Things tend to work out for the best even if they don't seem like it at the time."

"That's what I'm hoping," Kinsey says.

Roger addresses the group, and she couldn't be happier than to listen to him drone on about an upcoming project for them to work on. Sam seems incredibly happy the rest of the day. Well at least someone is.

100

Chapter Twenty-Four

♥

A couple of weeks later Kinsey and Sam are seated in one of the meeting rooms. They like it here because they can close the door to have privacy. Well, as much privacy as the glass door and window facing the hallway allows but their conversations are confidential with the soundproofing. There is a large window overlooking the city. A table for six is in the middle of the room with upholstered chairs surrounding it. The tables allow for them to spread their work out and sit side by side.

Kinsey watches him work, "Don't even," he says without looking up at her.

"What am I doing?"

"You know what." Grinning, she does know what. He closes his file and looks at her. "Do you want to get out of here?"

Kinsey looks around they just got back from lunch. "And go where?"

"Let's get some fresh air and go for a walk."

"Okay," she packs up her papers and puts them in her bag. They leave down one of the back stairwells and take the elevator from the lower level. They leave their bags in his car and walk to the street. Sam leads them toward the Hudson River. They cross the street to the walkway that follows the water.

"Where do you see yourself in five years?" he asks.

"Married to you of course."

"Naturally," he allows, "And we would have three, maybe four kids?"

"Five," she says firmly.

Sam laughs, "I stand corrected. And we would live?"

"Upper east side, in a brownstone that is close to being torn down but we save it and rebuild it with our own two hands. It's featured in a magazine on the front cover with a spread showing before and after photos."

"I like it. I think we should have two home offices. His and hers."

"You don't want to share your space with me?"

"No, I do not."

Kinsey pouts, "How come?"

He steps closer to her and she stops. They are facing each other, "Because my dear if I had work to do, I would have a hard time concentrating with you sitting in the same room as me."

"You do it now," she reminds him.

"What are we doing now?"

"What do you mean? Oh, you mean the walk?"

"Yes. It is hard to get any work done with you near me."

"I think you do a good job," she tells him.

"Thank you for noticing," they stare at one another before he turns and continues their walk. She falls into step with him, "Our kids should go to the best private schools."

"Can we send them to public school instead? That's what I did, and I think I turned out pretty well," she smiles at him knowing he agrees.

Grinning down at her he confirms, "That you did. We can send the kids anywhere you would like." Her heart sings at the fictional world they are creating. He continues with his narrative, "I want a dog, a rescue from the shelter."

"Big or little?"

"Medium would be good, something that doesn't shed too much. A cute mutt."

"I'd love that. I'm sure the kids would like it too." They continue to talk about the fantasy of being together.

Chapter Twenty-Five

♥

In early May, letters of intent to hire are passed out. She is given one and Sam is not. The look on his face says it all. Kinsey is heartbroken for him. Even worse she isn't going to take the job. How could she stay in this building with all the memories they had made here together?

"If it makes you feel any better, I'm not staying," she whispers to him putting the envelope into her drawer.

He stands up from his desk, "No, actually it doesn't." And he walks away. She isn't sure if she should follow him or not and eventually she does.

She finds him on the roof, she can see her breath as she exits the door to the building. The sun is up and there isn't a cloud in the sky. From all appearances, it looks like a beautiful day but the air is sharp and she finds herself crossing her arms and rubbing her hands up and down on the outside of her arms to warm herself. Kinsey would have grabbed a jacket had she known this is where he would end up.

There is the usual cluster of smokers up here, but she avoids them and walks around to the other side of the building. There is gravel where he is standing and it's difficult to walk in her high heels.

Sam isn't facing her his hands are in his pocket and he is looking out towards the Hudson River lost in thought. She stops ten feet away still. "I'm sorry. I know how much you want this job."

He turns to face her, his face stoic. He opens his arms to her, and she rushes forward burying herself in his warmth. Kinsey's arms wrap themselves around his body inside his suit jacket and presses her face into his chest. His arms encircle her, his hand cupping the back of her head. She fits perfectly into him.

"I'm afraid," Sam confesses.

She turns her head so one ear is up against his chest and the other is exposed to hear him, "Of what?" She asks, her voice a whisper.

"I don't want to make the wrong decision." He pauses and she waits, feeling his heartbeat against her ear, she gets lost in how soothing it feels then her heart lurches into her throat at his next words, "I feel like... you might be the one that got away."

Oh my God, this is it. The moment she has been waiting for. Her heart soars at the proclamation then clenches tight. He still hasn't decided, he is speaking hypothetically. Pushing away from him she is angry, "I'm right here in front of you!" She waits but he won't even look her in the eye. "I will be the one that got away, Sam Anderson if you don't figure out your shit real quick. We are good together but I'm not going to wait around forever."

"I know," he says despondently.

Kinsey wants to cry, to scream and shout and grab him by the shoulders to shake him. She doesn't do any of these things. He is shuffling his feet, unsure of himself which is not what she is used to seeing. Finally, he speaks, "Come on let's go inside. It's freezing out here." She doesn't wait for him she just turns on her heel and stomps back to the warmth of the building. Sam follows slowly behind her.

Later that night, she writes him a letter confessing her love to him. Taking the letter with her to work she contemplates giving it to him all day. It remains in her purse and she never gives him the letter. Kinsey feels it is so obvious that she is madly in love with him and wants to be with him, but she has never voiced her feelings to him. Maybe he thinks she is only in lust with him and that will fade with time.

Sam and Kinsey don't ever mention the rooftop confession. They slip comfortably back into the "just friends" category. They laugh and joke but don't touch anymore, well rarely. Kissing stopped a long time ago.

Sam lands a job and Kinsey grudgingly takes an opening at her dad's firm. On the last day at the office, Fiona and Gabe organize a dinner out. It is a fancy place with linens and low lighting. They all go home to dress up before meeting at the restaurant. They attempt to be sophisticated adults. They drink bottles of wine and have beautifully plated meals. Conversation flows easily as they reminisce and bash Roger behind his back.

At the end of the night, they all throw their cards on the table to split the check, but they are informed the bill is paid. Roger had called in the corporate credit card ahead of time. They are astonished at his generosity and a little abashed they had just been making fun of him. Hugging everyone they all promise to stay connected.

Sam hangs back in the crowd as everyone says their goodbyes. Kinsey stands next to him as they watch everyone else leave. Turning he pulls a business card out of his wallet and hands it to her. She runs her fingers over the raised glossy print with his name and company logo on it. "That's my direct line. You can call me any time."

She looks up at him and her heart squeezes, this is it. "I can't believe we won't see each other again."

"We will."

"Maybe," she allows. "When do you start?"

"Next week."

"Wow, you don't waste any time."

He shrugs, "What about you when do you start?"

"I'm taking the summer off. My dad is sending me to Europe. I'll start in the fall."

"Must be nice."

"Yeah, I guess so." What she wants, is to stay here in his arms. But even if she doesn't go overseas, the option of his embrace is out of the question. She is circling the card between her fingers.

"You are going to set the world on fire, Kinsey." She grins as she finally looks up at him. God, why does he have to look at her like that? It's like when he looks at her, he is parched, and she is the only one that can quench his thirst.

"Thanks, Sam."

"I'll see you at graduation, right?"

She shakes her head, "I leave tomorrow."

His eyebrow arches, she hadn't told him of her plans for this summer. He probably thought she is running away, and he isn't wrong. "I'm going to miss seeing your face every day."

"Same," she replies but she wants to tell him there is one way to fix that. The servers are maneuvering around them as they attempt to clear their vacated table.

"I guess we better get going."

Outside she hails a cab. He opens the door for her. They hug and his lips brush across her temple. "I'm not the only one that's going to set the world on fire, Sam."

"The world better watch out then. Have fun in Europe. Goodbye, Kinsey."

"Goodbye, Sam." She climbs in the cab quickly and he slowly latches the door behind her. Looking out the window she puts her hand upon the glass separating them. Sam places his hand covering hers on the other side.

The cab pulls away from the curb, effectively breaking the moment. Kinsey gets up on her knees to look out of the back window. Sam stands there his hands in his pockets as he watches her leave.

Kinsey has a great summer, thoughts of Sam fade into the background so she isn't thinking of him every waking minute. The second she returns home she finds his card on her nightstand where she had left it the last night she saw him. Going to bed she turns it over in her hand as she stares up at the ceiling. She is starting her career tomorrow.

Chapter Twenty-Six

♥

The following day she settles into work. At lunch, she pulls Sam's card out of her pocketbook. She is still at her desk, looking around, everyone else has disappeared to lunch. Dialing the number, she waits.

"Sam Anderson," he answers his phone with confidence.

"Hey," she says into the phone suddenly unsure she should have called.

"Hey, yourself," she can hear the smile in his voice.

Smiling she responds, "Did you miss me?" She knows she is being flirtatious and not fair.

"You know I did."

"Do I?"

"How could I not? How the hell have you been?"

"Great! Paris was amazing."

"Must be nice. Some of us need to work for a living," he said teasing her.

"God, what's that like?" she gives it back to him.

They talk like they hadn't taken a three-month break. She doesn't bring up his girlfriend and he doesn't either. She would think if anything had changed in that department, he would have told her. Kinsey soon realizes her lunch break is over as people start returning to their chairs. "I have to go," she tells him.

"Talk tomorrow." It was more of a statement than a question.

Smiling she agrees, "Sure." And just like that, they are sucked back into each other's lives. They only talk during business hours and never on the weekend. They also don't meet each other. It feels safer over the phone, they can't touch, make out or cross the line further if they aren't face-to-face. She keeps telling herself they are just friends. No harm, no foul. She can have a male friend and he can have a female friend that isn't his girlfriend, right?

Five months later she meets Grayson. Her phone calls become less frequent. Finally, she makes the call she has been dreading. "Hey."

"Hey, yourself."

"I'm going to San Diego."

"Why?" he drawls out the question. She can tell he is distracted, she can hear him shuffling through paperwork on his desk.

"Grayson bought me a ticket to visit him at his place."

Pause. Now he is paying attention. "Sounds like things are getting serious," his voice is grave.

"I love him," tears are stinging her eyes as she tells him, but she manages to keep her voice upbeat. Her free hand, not holding the receiver, swipes at the tears on her cheeks.

Long pause, "That's great, Kinsey. I'm happy for you."

Are you? She wants to ask but instead says, "Thanks, Sam. Listen I have to go, I have a business lunch today."

"This is it isn't it?" his voice is so quiet she isn't sure he realizes he has said it aloud.

"It has to be, otherwise I'll never be able to move on."

She hears him swear away from the receiver, but he says into the phone, "Take care of yourself, Kinsey."

"You too Sam."

Chapter Twenty-Seven

Kinsey-Present Day

Trish sits back in her chair after Kinsey's condensed version of her and Sam's relationship. "Wow," she breathes. "Whatever happened to him?"

"He married her."

"Still married?"

"As far as I know. I try not to go down memory lane too often with that one."

"If he is still married that probably won't work."

"If he is single, it would be worse."

"How do you figure that?" Trish wants to know.

"Well, if he is still married, he cheated on her once he may do it again as a favor to me. I know that sounds awful, but if he is single, he may get attached, and then I have a real problem on my hands. This way we just go back to our lives afterward."

"It sounds messy either way," Trish sits back in her chair crossing her legs and throwing her hands in the air. "You don't know anyone else that may be able to carry the torch for you so to speak?"

Kinsey is shaking her head vehemently. She has made up her mind that she is going to reach out to Sam and be damned with the consequences. Reaching for her phone she looks him up on social media, still married.

Before she can change her mind, she sends a simple text "Hey," testing the water. It's been over twenty years. A lump in her throat and a huge knot in her stomach form. What if he doesn't remember her? No, that isn't possible. She checks her phone every half a second for the rest of the day. The second her screen goes black, she refreshes it instantly. All day goes by and nothing happens. Kinsey keeps checking her phone, but she isn't even sure if he has seen it.

That night she plugs her phone into her charger and lies down. She kisses Grayson goodnight and rolls over. Minutes later she hears his soft snoring and ping on her phone causing her to jump. Checking, she finds it's her email. With a huge sigh, she replaces the phone on her bedside stand.

"Are you, okay?" Grayson asks half asleep.

"Yeah, I think I'm just going to get a glass of water." She takes the phone off the charger and heads downstairs. She fills a glass with ice and water and is heading back up the stairs when her phone, which she has chosen to leave in the kitchen, goes off. It's eleven at night, there is no way it is him, but she goes back downstairs anyway. Flipping her phone over on the counter her heart leaps up into her chest. "Hey yourself" is on her screen. Kinsey half drops and half throws the phone back on the marble countertop.

Sam has kept her waiting all day she can't possibly respond to him right now. She picks up her phone her palms sweaty as if he can sense she is about to respond. She types, "Do you want to bang me?" Delete. Delete. Delete. "How have you been?" she wants to know but she has seen his social media account. She already knows that he married the woman he refused to leave for her and has two gorgeous daughters. Delete. Delete. Delete. "Can we get together for coffee?" She stares at it. To forward? They haven't seen each other in forever.

Incoming message: "I'd love to catch up. Lunch tomorrow?" Her mouth is dry. She looks at her unsent message. Delete. Delete. Delete.

"Sure. Our old spot?" Send. Oh, God.

"Perfect. Can you do one?"

Shit. Shit. Shit. This is happening. "I'll be there." Fuck. Fuck. Fuck. Feeling queasy she heads to the downstairs bathroom. Kinsey doesn't sleep most of the night, only falling asleep shortly before dawn. The next morning Grayson is already gone to the airport, and she can survey her wardrobe. She tries on an array of outfits before settling on one.

Kinsey barely focuses on work and leaves early to meet Sam for lunch. He is outside waiting for her. He looks even better than she remembers him. How is this possible? He is doing his own assessment of her and she can see the approval in his eyes. They hug. "It's so nice to see you, Kinsey." She glows hearing her name on his lips again.

"You too, Sam. It's been so long."

"It really has. Come on in. I already put our name down for a table." He opens the door for her and they step through. The host walks them to a table in front of the window. He waits for her to take a seat before joining her. She notices his wedding band right around the time he notices hers.

"How long?" he asks.

"Seventeen years. How about you?"

"Same."

"Congratulations."

"Thanks, same to you. Any kids?"

"Yes! Twin boys. They will be fifteen next month. What about you?"

"Two girls, Quinn just graduated high school and Sadie is only a year behind her."

"Wow, time does fly." His timeline isn't adding up with the age of his girls and his wedding, but she doesn't want to delve into his love life.

"It sure does."

"What is Quinn going to school for?"

"She is a business major and has a minor in finance."

"Impressive, sounds like she is following in her dad's footsteps. Does Sadie know what she wants to do yet?"

Sam laughs, "Yes, travel the world and be a free spirit."

Kinsey shares in his merriment, "Oh, boy."

"Oh boy is right we aren't quite sure what to do with her."

Kinsey's heart constricts at Sam's use of the word "we". "She will probably come around," she allows.

Sam shrugs and takes a sip of his water, "I sure hope so. What about your boys? Any idea of what they want to do?"

"Aidan wants to do something with video games or be a professional soccer player. Ethan wants to be a doctor."

"Sounds like we have similar kids, a dreamer, and an overachiever."

"The world needs both."

Sam smiles, "Agreed." The waiter comes over to take their drink orders. After he leaves, they look at the menu. "Burger and fries?" she asks after a minute.

"You know it," they both close the menus and put them on the table. "I have to confess something," Sam says.

"What's that?" Kinsey leans forward her arms folding on the table.

"I already knew you were married and about your kids and where you are working. Good for you by the way. Making partner in the firm is huge. I sort of stalk your social media every couple of years or so when I get nostalgic." He pushes back in his chair, his right hand playing with the utensils wrapped in a cloth napkin. Sam looks relaxed and she can't help but notice the twinkle in his eye when he catches her gaze.

"How did you find me? I only have my married name on social media."

"There aren't that many Kinseys in the world you were pretty easy to find."

"Oh." She isn't sure how else to respond. She is flattered that he remembers her and thought about her as she thought about him. At the same time, he has never actually reached out to her, both knowing it's a terrible idea. They had been together for ten minutes now and the magnetic pull that had always been between them is in the air again. Kinsey can't help but feel the energy and excitement and she can see it in his eyes he feels it too.

The server comes back with their drinks, and they place their order. "So, what are you doing for work now?" Kinsey changes the subject.

"I started my own firm." Sam beams proudly.

"That's amazing! Congratulations." She leans back and smiles. "Well, I would say we have both done well for ourselves."

"Thanks, looks like we both set the world on fire as we planned." Just not together she thinks. "Do you ever keep in touch with anyone from school? Or our internship?" Sam asks.

"Only Fiona. She's married with three kids. She and Gabe lasted a year before calling it quits. What about you?"

"Marcus and Justin work for me, and Gabe and I hang out sometimes. Mostly at the driving range or a local pub. I keep trying to poach him, but he is happy where he is and doesn't want to "ruin our friendship." Sam makes air quotes and Kinsey laughs.

"Do you ever hear from Becky?" even after all these years saying her name leaves a bad taste in her mouth.

Sam laughs, "You hated her so much!"

"I did not," she protests half-heartedly then a smile crosses her face as she gestures with her finger and thumb, a breath apart, "Well, maybe just a little." Sam laughs even harder and she joins him then sobers quickly, "No, seriously have you kept in touch."

"Well…" he says and her eyes widen, "No, I have no idea where she is or how she is doing and I don't care."

Kinsey's hand rests on her heart feeling relieved, "Good to know."

Their lunch is set down in front of them and they pause to put it together. "Is there anything else I can get you?" The server asks.

"Actually," Sam holds a finger up and looks at her, "Do you still like mayo on your burger." Her eyes light up, smiles, and nods gratefully that he remembered. Turning to the waiter Sam puts in the request.

"Thank you," she tells him as she removes the tomato and onion, and he holds his burger open for her to place on his.

"You're welcome," Sam says as he closes his burger and then hands over his pickle spear. Smiling she takes it. The waiter returns with herb mayo, and she thanks him. They eat in comfortable silence for a few minutes when Sam takes a drink. "So, what do you do in your spare time these days?"

Kinsey laughs, "Spare time? What's that? Between working, running the boys around for their after-school activities, and maintaining the house. Plus, with Grayson gone four days a week for work, I'm in charge of it all while he is away. Then trying to spend time with him when he is home." The charge in the air changes at her mention of her husband, both of them feeling it. She kicks herself for bringing him up. "What about you?"

"I have season tickets to the Yankees."

"That seems like fun."

"Yeah, I usually take the girls but sometimes use them to impress clients or go with friends." He doesn't mention taking his wife unless he included her as part of the girls, but somehow, she doesn't think so. They continue talking finishing their meals and ordering refills for their drinks. It is like old times with how they become so comfortable with each other.

Finally, he pushes back in his chair, "You look amazing," he tells her, his eyes not leaving hers.

She swallows hard feeling a blush coming on strong, her neck and cheeks warming at his compliment, "Thank you. I could say the same about you."

"Are you training for a marathon?"

She laughs, "You could say that," she said coyly.

"Really? Which one?"

She bites her lip and leans forward. He follows suit shifting closer to her. "My husband has a fantasy he would like me to carry out." She waits but he doesn't ask any questions. She can see the slight tick in his jaw joint. If she hadn't known to look for it, she would have missed the subtle movement. She surges forward, "He wants to watch me... with another man...He envisions us going to a hotel bar picking someone and seeing if they are willing. Then wants to go to the room for him to watch us. I really don't want to."

"Then don't," Sam practically growls, his eyes locking on hers their faces much closer than before. Heat rushes up her neck covering her entire face.

She surges forward, "We have a good marriage and a great life this is something he has been asking for. I've stalled as long as possible. I told him I wanted to lose weight and get back into shape. I've accomplished that."

"Clearly," he seems aggravated.

"Anyway, I don't want to have sex with someone else. I was thinking what if I could get someone," she waves her hands in the air. "I've already been with to agree to go along with it. Grayson can't know or it won't work. No strings attached, no feelings. Maybe he won't even go for it when it's right in front of him. Or he will regret it after and never want to do it again."

"What if he likes it and wants you to do it all the time? Then what?"

"He told me I won't have to do it again if I don't want to."

"You've been fighting him on this for how long now?"

"A while," she admits.

"And you think he will stop once he gets his fix?"

"I don't know. I hope so."

"Why are you telling me this?"

Kinsey looks at him and he meets her eyes, "You know why."

"I'm married."

"I know, but you already cheated on her once with me. I won't tell her. It's not an extra number for you or me."

"Christ, Kinsey." He finally leans back in his chair. She pushes back in her seat and watches him. She can see a range of emotions cross his face as he rubs his hands over his eyes, possibly to hide them from her. "You know it's more complicated than that. It might look simple to you on paper but this is our lives you are messing with. You know, no good can come from this."

"I know," she whispers ashamed she even brought this to him.

"I can't," he says with a deep sigh his hands hitting the tops of his thighs.

"I get it," she stands. Digging through her purse she pulls out the card for the hotel bar and places it on the table in front of him, "I will be here at eight o'clock on Friday night if you change your mind." Flipping through her wallet she pulls money out for her portion of the bill but he waves her away.

"I've got this."

"Are you sure?" At his nod, she says, "Thank you. Just forget I ever asked. It was nice seeing you, Sam. Take care," then as quickly and gracefully as she can she starts to walk away.

"Kinsey, wait." Sam takes her wrist. It feels like a volt of electricity shoots up her arm. She looks down to where his strong fingers wrap around her, then to his face. An expression she can't place is there, but he says nothing.

"I have to go." Kinsey pulls her hand out of his grip and practically runs from the restaurant.

Chapter Twenty-Eight

♥

When Kinsey returns to work, she finds a grinning Trish. She is looking at her watch indicating Kinsey has been gone far longer than the customary hour lunch. Kinsey does not have a good poker face and Trish's smile turns to concern as she follows her work wife into her office.

"What happened?" Trish asks as soon as she closes the door behind her friend.

Kinsey tosses her purse on her desk and then slumps down in her chair, "He told me no," she groans, "And now he knows what I'm going to do, and now I'm humiliated-no mortified. I should have never opened that door with him."

"You were gone a long time. Was it awkward? Did you have a tough time bringing it up?"

"Lunch was great, we just fell into step like we had never stopped talking to each other. Then I had to open my big stupid mouth and ask him to sleep with me. I won't tell your wife, I said. Who says that?"

"Mistresses," Trish offers up lamely, and Kinsey's eyes snap up to meet hers. Both women burst into laughter. "Listen, this is probably for the best. Now you can just sleep with some random hottie and be done with it. Enjoy yourself, take the hall pass and run with it."

"I guess," Kinsey says gloomily.

"I'll trade with you if you want," Trish offers.

Kinsey smiles, "Thanks, but I think Grayson would notice."

Trish shrugs good-naturedly, "Well, I offered."

Chapter Twenty-Nine

♥

Friday night Kinsey walks through the door of the bar. She sees Grayson on the right, sitting at a booth, he arrived twenty minutes earlier. Looking around the room she takes in her options. The bar, a large black granite oval, stands in the center of the room surrounded by tables, the wall lined with black leather booths. An older gentleman sits at the end of the bar towards the right, and she moves on. Two younger guys are next watching the game on TV. A couple of women are nearby. A good-looking man is sitting in a booth, and she smiles at him. He smiles back as a woman slips by her and takes the seat across from him.

At the end of the bar is a man with a wedding band. She continues around the backside of the bar. Ugly. Not going to happen. Hate his hair. Don't like his nose. Gross. Kinsey knows she is being picky but none of them are Sam. She sighs as she chooses a seat that has two empty stools on either side of her. She can't see Grayson, but they had said they would give it an hour before calling it quits for the night if things didn't seem like they were going to happen.

"What can I get you?" the bartender asks her setting down a coaster in front of her.

"I'll take a Lemon Drop Martini please."

"Coming right up."

"May I join you?" she hears a man's voice over her shoulder. Swiveling on her stool she sees a nice-looking man and she smiles. She isn't sure how she had missed him on her sweep of the room. The front door opens catching her attention. Sam is standing just inside, his gaze finding her instantly.

Turning back to the stranger she tells him, "I'm sorry I'm waiting for someone." Sam slides into the stool next to her.

"I'm sorry I'm late," he tells her.

"You came," tears sting her eyes.

He swivels towards her, "Of course I did."

Kinsey's beverage is placed in front of her, and the bartender asks Sam what he would like to drink. He orders a draft IPA. "I'm Kinsey," she holds her hand out for him to shake.

He takes her hand in his much larger one, "Nice to meet you. I'm Sam."

Sam's beer arrives and he takes a drink, "You took off your wedding ring," she observes.

"Yup. So did you."

"I did. The plan was to lure someone in first then see if they were game."

"How were you planning on luring someone in? You know asking for a friend," he jokes.

"Well," she leans in close exposing her cleavage which she knows his eyes dart to. She cups her hand around his ear and leans close to whisper. Her other hand rests on his upper thigh. "I want you inside me." She licks his ear and then pulls away.

"Damn you're good."

She can't help the grin that spreads across her face, "Thank you." Kinsey crosses her legs making sure they rest up against his thigh. Leaning towards him he meets her halfway. "Your thighs feel rock hard."

His hand rests on her neck pulling her forward this time whispering in her ear, his face burying in her hair, "That's not the only thing that's rock hard." His lips brush her neck. He pulls away but not far.

"Touché," she allows.

She whispers in his ear, "Do you remember the time you fucked me in your car?"

He whispers back, "No." She pushes back to look at him. His lips go to her ear, "I remember not getting the chance to fuck you. If we hadn't been interrupted, you have no idea what I planned to do to you." Kinsey swallows hard. Holy. Fuck. She is going to enjoy tonight way more than she should be allowed. Grayson walks by and watches her face.

Shame roars through her body feeling the heat of it down to her toes. Her crossed legs have migrated between Sam's thighs as they are fully facing each other. Her hands are holding onto one of his forearms brushing the bristly arm hairs while her other hand is resting on his upper thigh. Sam still has one hand around her throat the other arm is draped casually across the bar. "What's wrong," Sam asks sensing her stiffening.

She looks at Sam the way they used to look at each other, conveying a message she hopes he receives. "Where is he?" he asks, his voice hard. Kinsey now feels him tighten up.

"He just moved to a booth on this side of the bar where he can watch us." Sam picks his drink up from the bar and takes a long drink.

"Which one is he?" Sam is already scanning the room.

"Over my right shoulder in the booth." She watches horrified as Sam raises his beer in salute to Grayson. Turning she sees her husband lift his in response, no expression on his face. Turning back, she looks at Sam.

"What are you doing?" she hisses.

"I'm telling him I'm in," his gaze leaves Grayson and focuses in on her, "That I am going to fuck the shit out of his wife."

She picks up her glass and downs the rest of her beverage. The bartender magically appears and before she can ask for another one Sam orders shots of Tequila. At least Grayson is sitting behind her and can't see her face but she knows he can see Sam's. "You can still bail at any time, you know?"

Kinsey looks up, "What?"

"We can call this whole thing off if you want to." The bartender slaps the two shots down in front of them. They pick them up, she is ready to shoot hers back when he stops her. "We should make a toast."

She thinks about it. "To getting to finish what we started, once upon a time."

"Hear, hear," he clicks his shot glass to hers, and they down the drink.

They put their glasses back down on the bar and she asks if she can have another martini. "Coming right up," he tells her.

When he is out of earshot she looks to Sam, "You know what I never got to do?"

"What's that?" he asks before taking a swig of his beer.

"Suck your dick."

He almost loses it. She is lucky she isn't wearing his beer. He grabs a nearby napkin to cough into. She laughs as she gently taps his back. When he recovers clearing his throat, he tells her seriously, "You're going to be the death of me Kinsey." Her face splits into a grin. She remembers the last time he had told her that. If she didn't know any better, she was beginning to think he wanted her to be the death of him.

"I'm going to the ladies' room," she announces. He stands and helps her down from her stool. She knows he is watching her leave just like she knows Grayson will follow her. He is right behind her slipping into the private bathroom with her.

Locking the door behind them Grayson takes her in his arms and kisses her. Hard. "You're so fucking hot." He tells her. He is turned on by watching her and Sam at the bar. Part of her, no all of her, is aroused by Sam. She puts that into her kiss with her husband. "Are you ready to go upstairs?" She nods. "I'll meet you at the elevators."

"Okay," she agrees, and he kisses her again before leaving. She uses the restroom, washes her hands, and returns to the bar where Sam is waiting for her.

"Showtime," she tells him without sitting back down but she does pick up her glass and downs as much alcohol as she can. Sam pays the tab with cash, smart. He ushers her out of the bar his hand on her lower back.

Grayson is standing at the elevators as promised. The three of them stand in a line, Grayson, Kinsey then Sam. The doors are gold and shiny. She can see their reflections staring back at her. Her eyes find Grayson's looking straight ahead, when her eyes shift to Sam's, they meet hers in the reflection. The door dings and opens breaking the spell. Once inside Grayson presses the button to their floor.

Sam pulls Kinsey into his arms. Her hands rest on his chest, she can feel the warmth and comfort his arms are offering her. His head dips down and she accepts his lips on hers for the first time in decades. His hands are now on her ass, he knows that is a huge turn-on for her. Her tongue mingles with his, her hands slide up around his neck. Kinsey reaches up on tiptoes pressing her breasts into his hard chest. He pulls hard on her hair breaking the kiss, and leaving her chin jutting forward in the air. He bites her chin then works his teeth down her neck and she cries out. He remembers all her weaknesses and it makes her want to cry.

The elevator comes to a stop as three drunk guys stumble inside. Sam and Kinsey separate. "Awe man is this elevator going up?" one of them asks.

"We need to go down." Another clarifies.

"The elevator is going up," Grayson confirms holding the door for them to get back off.

"Dude, we have to get off," the third one says. All three of them make their way back into the hallway and off their elevator.

When the doors close Sam leans down and whispers in Kinsey's ear, "Dude I need to get off," she giggles at the joke. She turns to Grayson, feeling guilty, and finds he isn't looking at them. Is he changing his mind? At this point, she is not sure what it would do to her if they didn't go through with this plan. She has been denied so many times with Sam in the past. Tonight, she wants Sam to finally make her cum and cum hard, like multiple orgasms hard.

The door opens for their floor and Grayson steps out first, turning down the hallway. Sam and Kinsey follow at a much slower pace. Sam reaches for her hand and she clings to it. She feels like she is having an out-of-body experience.

They turn a corner and continue down the hall. At the end on the left Grayson puts the key to the door and opens it. He closes the blinds of the windows along the wall. Grayson had splurged for a suite. They walk through the living room towards the bedroom. At the other end, double doors stand open revealing a king-sized bed with a fluffy white comforter and pillows piled high. Grayson takes a seat in the high-backed chair in the corner facing the bed.

"I'll be right back," Kinsey excuses herself and slips into the bathroom. She feels guilty leaving Sam alone with Grayson, talk about awkward. She is freaking out and needs to calm her nerves. She turns the water on to hear something other than silence.

Chapter Thirty

♥

Kinsey watches herself in the mirror as she takes off her clothes revealing the black lingerie underneath, which she picked out online and ordered. She hadn't shown Grayson hoping to surprise him. The water is hot, so she turns it to cool testing with her finger to confirm the temperature. She cups the cool water and splashes her face with it her hands going down and around her neck trying to cool off. She is petrified. She has gone from not wanting to do this at all, to wanting this to happen more than anything. The guilt she feels about lying to her husband and not picking up a stranger is eating her up inside.

She has a minor freak-out moment then puts her hand on the doorknob, turns, and pulls. Sam is only a couple of feet away he has been standing there watching the door. The look on his face is priceless as he takes in her attire. Looking past him, she can see Grayson doing his own appraisal. A small smile touches his lips and she knows he approves.

Her attention returns to Sam because he is pursuing her. He picks her up and her legs wind tightly around his hips. He pushes her back up against the wall and kisses her. Kinsey kisses him back. She yearns for him to be inside her right now. He had told her one time that he didn't rush and that he enjoyed giving pleasure. Knowing him she knew that to be true, but they hadn't had time on their side. They had to steal moments when they could. Now they had all night.

He takes her hands and presses them above her head with one hand his fingers entwined with hers. The other hand is cradling her ass cheeks. He licks the inside of her upper arm and then nibbles her elbow. It does something to every nerve ending in her body and she whimpers. "I'm only getting started," he whispers in her ear, her nipples hardening at his promise. As if sensing they need attention, he hikes her up higher on the wall bringing her breasts to his face. His long tongue licks her through the fabric his eyes watching her for a response. He bites down on her nipple and then sucks hard on it, her body arching towards him.

When he sets her on the ground, she pulls his shirt up over his head. He tosses it to the floor towards the end stand. She circles his body her hand running across all the peaks and valleys of his upper torso. When she is standing in front of him again, she drops to her knees. Normally, she would just unzip his jeans, but she wants to play with him as he has done with her. Her hands rub his erection through his jeans, his hands bury themselves in her hair. Kinsey wraps her hands around cupping his ass, his hips thrust towards her face. Her eyes look up the length of him, his intense stare intensifying her pleasure.

Using her teeth, she grazes every inch of him from the base of his manhood to the tip of the jeans. Going back down again she repeats the move down his shaft toward his balls. She remembers asking him once if he liked his balls sucked and he had told her he did. She presses her tongue from his balls to the tip of his dick through his jeans. This time her teeth undo his button and zipper. Using her hands, she gently removes his pants, her lips kissing his thighs as they are exposed. Her hands travel down the back of his thighs, then calves feeling the muscle and wiry hairs, helping him step out of them. He kicks his shoes off, and she discards them to the side as well. Kinsey looks at his socks, she had never seen his feet and now it is a must. She pulls his socks off. His feet are just as sexy as the rest of him.

Starting with his feet her hands run back up the length of him. Kinsey blows her hot breath through his underwear not touching him. Looking back up at him she sees his jaw is clenched tight. Good, she is getting to him. She smiles a wicked grin at him, and he raises an eyebrow at her. She slides his underwear off careful not to touch him.

He stands straight in front of her in all his naked glory. She teases him and plays with him before finally taking his length into her mouth. She beams as she watches his head roll back in pleasure. He lets her have full control as to how much she fits into her mouth at once, and what pace she wants to work at. She moans knowing she is satisfying him.

Sam pulls her to her feet and kisses her, as his hands roam her body. His penis presses hard into her belly. Still kissing her he turns her and guides her toward the bed. "Get in," he tells her. She is quick to respond laying down in the middle of the bed, her head propped up on a pillow as she waits for him. Anticipation building, he saunters to the foot of the bed grabbing both her ankles and pulling her down towards him. Lifting one foot he kisses it through her stocking, then her ankle down her calf, and inner thigh. He unclips her stocking and removes it slowly. He repeats the process for her other leg.

Once removed, he stretches her closer to the edge of the bed kneeling in front of her. Oh god. The lacey panties she is wearing have a slit in them, so they are not required to be removed. She feels his hot breath there like she had done to him earlier. He licks and sucks on the joint between her thigh and womanhood on both sides. Kinsey's back arches off the bed begging him to take her in his mouth, "Please," she whispers her hand going to rest in his curls the other clutching the bedsheets.

Sam's eyes heavy with emotion hold her gaze, "Watch me." She is already nodding her head in agreement. His tongue fucks her, diving as far as he can go, in and out, in and out. Holy mother of God. He is worried about her killing him? This may well be the death of her. Sam moves to her clitoris this time slow and methodical making her want to crawl out of her skin for more. As if sensing when she is ready to break, he gives her more, licking, sucking, and biting.

"I'm going to cum," she tells both men. In her peripheral, she can see Grayson stroking himself through his pants.

"Cum for me," Sam commands. He sucks on her hard feeling her legs quiver on either side of him not letting go. She does though, she lets go of everything, and her orgasm shakes her making her cry out both hands now clutching the comforter.

Her whole body collapses and he gives her a final lap of his tongue. Wiping his face, he stands. Kinsey scoots back towards the pillows crooking her finger at him to follow her. He does follow her on his hands and knees until his body is over hers. They kiss, hands meandering over body parts reveling in each other. Her hand finds his dick and she caresses him, his tip wet with pre-ejaculation fluid she uses her fingers to spread it down his shaft.

"I want your dick back in my mouth," she tells him.

"Yeah?"

She nods, "I want you to straddle me and fuck my face." His eyes darkened as he pictures what she wants him to do. Eager to do her bidding he gets on his knees and scoots forward. Kinsey opens her mouth and takes his hard dick inside. This time, she lets him rock his hips back and forth as deep as he wants down her throat. He holds onto her head pulling her forward onto his cock. Her hands grasp his ass cheeks encouraging him forward. She watches as he licks one of his fingers and then leans back between her bent knees to play with her. Every time she tries to please him, he reciprocates, and she just laid there while he had gone down on her.

"Can I fuck you now?" he asks.

She nods, "Condom is on the end stand." He crawls off of her to retrieve protection. Tearing the foil packet, he slides the rubber over his erection. When he turns around, he finds Kinsey has gotten on her knees and elbows, her ass in the air for him. Positioning himself behind her on his knees he guides himself inside her and then grasps her hips with both hands.

She gasps at the expanse of him. He waits for her to grow accustomed to his size before moving slowly. Kinsey spares a glance to Grayson. He has pulled his dick out and he is stroking it watching her getting fucked by another man. "His dick is so big," she tells him. When they had roll played in bed, he had responded by asking her if she liked it, if she was a naughty girl. Now, he is silent, and she is relieved. She doesn't want Sam to see them interacting. Kinsey needs to concentrate on the amazing fucking she is receiving.

Sam's thrusts grow more persistent. She can hear his balls smacking against her as she grinds herself against him. One of his hands reaches around and rubs her clit causing her to cry out. "Yes, you feel so good," she tells him. "Don't stop."

"I couldn't even if I wanted to," he tells her truthfully. He winds his hand around her long locks and pulls her up off her elbows, her back resting on his chest. One of her hands reaches out to hold the headboard for support the other behind his head. She turns her neck to face him and they share a kiss while he continues to thrust inside her and his fingers play between her thighs.

"Is it okay if I choke you?"

"Seriously?" Kinsey asks.

He nods solemnly, "It will heighten your experience, I promise." He nibbles on her neck. "I'll stop whenever you want me to, if you're close to passing out, or when I make you cum again." She likes the sound of that, well maybe not the passing out part.

"Okay," she agrees.

He kisses her again his hands pulling her breast from the confines of the lace pinching her nipples and rolling them between his fingers. She gasps, then finds his hand squeezing her throat applying slight pressure with his thumb and forefinger. Everything begins to tingle. She can feel the solid length of his cock pulsating inside her. Her nipples scream for attention. As promised, Kinsey can feel her climax building as she struggles for breath. Of all things holy, she has never felt this good in her entire life. He is nibbling on her ear now sending a new wave of sensations as he continues to plow her from behind.

Sam removes her hand from the headboard, and she falls forward, her face pushing into the mattress. He readjusts himself behind her bending one leg to gain leverage, he still has a grip on her throat. Pain sears across her ass as she realizes he has just spanked her. That's when her body releases coming across her in waves. Her pussy clamps around his ridiculously sized manhood and he releases her throat.

He waits for her to regain her composure before pulling out of her. Kinsey is heartbroken. Is it over? Sam rolls her over and grins down at her satisfied expression. "I'm not done with you yet," he warns.

"Promises, promises," she teases.

His thumb finds her clit and her body jumps in response to being touched, her lips are swollen with desire. He spreads her legs and guides himself inside her again. Now she can touch him and she explores with her hands and her mouth as he lays on her. Gladly accepting his weight, he rests the majority of it on his elbows.

Now tender he removes a lock of hair from her face and searches her soul with his eyes. Her mouth opens slightly, and small moans and gasps escape as he continues to thrust inside her. Her hips move with his, her thighs cradling him.

Sam is observing her, and she returns his gaze steadily. Kinsey wonders what he is searching for and if he has found it. All the years they have spent apart melt away. It's like they were speaking but no words are uttered. They express how much they missed each other. Her hand cups his face and he kisses her, slow and sensual. They make love for hours.

Kinsey is sore, her muscles tight in places, but her whole body feels like mush at the same time. And one thing is for sure, she is one billion percent satisfied. Now fully nude she wraps herself in the hotel robe as she watches Sam get dressed.

Kinsey walks him to the door. They stop when they reach it. He has one hand on the door when he turns to look at her. Kinsey's breath catches in her throat. Sam's other hand reaches for the bathrobe belt and pulls her closer to him. He leans in for one final kiss goodbye.

"Thank you for coming," she whispers.

"How could I not?" he asks.

"I do appreciate it," she gazes up at him. Sam's hand comes to rest on her neck his thumb rubbing across her throat.

"I know."

"Goodbye, Sam."

"Goodbye Kinsey," and then he is gone. The sadness she feels is instant at the separation. She knows this will be the last time they see each other but deep down knows it's for the best.

Kinsey takes a shower. When she returns to the room, Grayson is waiting for her. They make love like they never have before. No, that's not true, they always made love. Grayson fucks her. It's like he wants to erase away the memory of Sam. As good as it is with Grayson, and she cherishes him, there is no way she will ever forget her fleeting time with Sam. That is something that she will tuck away deep down inside her.

She will tell Grayson if he ever asks that she doesn't want to do this again-that it isn't for her. After witnessing what she did with Sam he might find that hard to believe seeing how much she had enjoyed herself.

Chapter Thirty-One

♥

The following morning, Grayson brings her a cup of coffee in bed. Originally, they had planned to spend the night in the hotel but after Grayson had showered, he had suggested they go home.

Sitting up, Kinsey accepts the steaming cup from him, from the comfort of her bed. He is already dressed. "I'm thinking we should go to the park today with the boys. We can bring a picnic and a soccer ball?"

Kinsey takes a sip, "Sure," she agrees. She watches curiously as he paces their bedroom. He comes to kneel by her side and her hand rubs the side of his short haircut.

"I love you," he tells her his eyes meeting hers.

Smiling she responds, "I love you too." He isn't going to discuss last night she realizes. They hadn't talked about what she had let another man do to her, with his permission, last night and she isn't going to be the one to bring it up. She's relieved, they will move past this becoming closer and stronger as they did after a fight. No one likes to fight but if you come out on the other side understanding your partner better and willing to offer forgiveness or ask for it and receive it you can move forward.

She gets up and starts the shower, her muscles are tender from last night's excursion, and she smiles at the memory. Grayson leaves her alone while she gets ready to wake the boys. Now that they are teenagers, they felt they could stay up till midnight and wake up at noon. She wonders if other parents allow this or drag their kids out of bed too.

Going into the kitchen she sees what she can scrounge up for lunch. Slicing some ham off the bone from the fridge she cuts up some sharp cheddar cheese. She takes out the loaf of Italian bread and makes four sandwiches wrapping them in tin foil. Kinsey washes some grapes and puts them in a plastic baggie. She adds baby carrots and ranch dressing in separate containers. Looking around for dessert she finds brownies and cuts them up adding them to the pile. Going to the fridge she pulls out four cold water bottles and then thinking better of it, adds a couple of extra remembering they are going to kick the soccer ball around.

Aidan comes down first rubbing his eyes a hoodie covering most of his head. "Good morning sweetie," Kinsey greets him. She gets a grunt in response. Ethan comes bounding down the stairs the total opposite of his brother.

"Morning Mom," he swings by kissing her on her cheek. "Dad says we are going to the park today?"

"Yes, I've made a picnic and we can bring the soccer ball."

"Why can't we just have fast food?" Aidan wants to know from inside the pantry.

"Because this is nicer." Kinsey walks to the living room, takes the blanket off the back of the couch, and folds it up. She lines the cooler with ice packs and puts the food in the middle and the blanket on top.

Grayson enters hugging her from behind and kissing her cheek. Ethan smiles at her and Aidan flops down in the nearest chair breaking off pieces of a pop tart and guiding it to his mouth. Kinsey smiles as she observes him, he is her personality, not a morning person, serious at times. Ethan is like his dad, easy going and always has a smile on their faces.

The day is perfect. She brings a book to read while her boys play in the park. The picnic is delicious and even Aidan compliments her. Afterward, her sons join a nearby group playing spike ball, and Grayson curls up with her on the blanket. He rests his head in her lap as she runs her fingers over his scalp, and they lay together in comfortable silence.

Chapter Thirty-Two

♥

Monday morning, Grayson sends flowers to Kinsey's office. There is a note that reads, "You are the only woman for me. I love you to the moon and back. Forever Yours, Grayson." Kinsey holds the note to her chest.

Hours later she gets a text from Sam. "I can't stop thinking about you." Kinsey ignores it. A half-hour later, "I'm serious Kinsey. I need you. I need to be balls deep in you right now."

"Sam, you need to stop. This was a one-time thing. Please let it go."

"If you don't come to me, I will find you."

Shit. "Fine. When and where?" She needs to end this with him. He tells her noon and gives her the address of a parking garage.

When Kinsey steps out of her SUV and locks eyes with him across the aisle, she knows she never had a chance with him. Fuck. She is going to screw his brains out and like it. It is already a foregone conclusion, and he knows it too.

"A mini-van?" Kinsey asks as she locks her door and strides across the parking garage towards him. Sam is standing outside and opens the sliding door for her.

"It's all the rental place had on short notice. I thought it might offer more room?"

She climbs inside and sits in one of the captain's chairs. She can see he has already put the back seats down into a makeshift bed. Sam gets in after her and closes the door. "Thank you for coming."

"Sam, we can't do this. This is crossing a line. It's one thing to do what we did but you are talking about an affair."

Sam looks dejected. His elbows are on his knees, and he puts his head in his hands, "I know! I just can't stop thinking about you."

Kinsey touches his upper arm and feels how tense he is, "Trust me, I know, I keep replaying the whole night over and over again in my head. It was amazing."

He looks up at her, "I can still taste you." Kinsey pulls back her hand and swallows hard. "I can still feel your lips around my cock." Her lips are suddenly dry, and she finds herself licking them, "I can still feel myself inside your sweet pussy clenching me, milking me." She is instantly wet. Their breathing is becoming more labored as they refuse to break eye contact from their intense stare.

She isn't sure who moves first but they are off their chairs on their knees kissing, their hands rough on the other's body. Clothes are being violently ripped off. Once naked, he picks her up and drives into her as her back hits the cushions. Kinsey's feet prop against the back of both headrests of the captain's chair. They fuck hard and fast. Her hands are on his ass encouraging him on. His hands are also on her ass to bring her to him. Sam's full weight is on her his head nestled against her neck.

Grunts and gasps are bouncing around the close confines of the mini-van meeting their ears and the beautiful music they are making together. A one-of-a-kind symphony, a concert for two. "Sam!" the urgency in Kinsey's voice breaks through the sex fog.

Pausing his thrusting he leans on one elbow looking down at her, "Are you okay?" he asks and the concern in his voice almost breaks her.

"You aren't wearing a condom."

He grins and looks down at their joined bodies then back at her, "Oh, yeah. I've had a vasectomy. I can't get you pregnant."

"Okay good. Carry on."

He laughs good-naturedly and she joins him. He kisses her sweetly, the nature of their lovemaking changing. Her feet come off the chairs and her legs wrap around his thighs. "I liked it when you choked me the other night," she says softly.

"Oh yeah? Do you want me to do it again for you?"

"Do you like being choked?" She asks instead.

"Sometimes," he allows.

"Can I choke you?"

Sam smiles, "Yes, but let me take care of you first because I will cum when you do that to me."

He is always thinking of her pleasure first. "Okay."

Sam shifts her up further on the cushions and comes to his knees. One hand clamps around her throat and his thumb starts stroking her clit. Her mouth forms an O as her body begins to move with the rhythm of his thrusts.

He is slow and deliberate in his thrusts and it is driving her mad. She wants more, harder, faster. Sam knows what he is doing to her. When he is fully inside her, balls touching her ass, his fingers work ferociously at her clit. Then stop abruptly and slowly pull out leaving her whimpering. His dick slams back into her giving her what she wants, and his fingers go back to work bringing her closer to orgasm then denying her as he pulls out and discontinues his play with her sensitive nub. Kinsey bucks her hips in protest. He stops his hands leaving her neck and her clit. He presses her thighs into the cushions spread wide for him. "Please, Sam," she begs. "I need to cum, please make me cum." She is desperate.

He pulls out of her altogether and she cries out until she feels his mouth on her sex. Her eyes roll back into her head as he snacks on her. Her body is quivering desperate to reach her orgasm. "Please fuck me, Sam. Please!" She gasps the last as he has her clit in between his teeth licking at lightning speed. Her body twists away from him the sensation overwhelming but he follows her not allowing her to escape.

Before she is finished with one orgasm, he is back inside her again immobilizing her to the cushions. He is kissing her lips as she tries to gain control of her breathing, but she can't as he slams into her tight convulsing pussy. "Shit. Fuck. Oh, God. Yes!" she screams each word. A second climax joins the first and overpowers it. She knows the van is rocking and anyone walking by could guess what is happening inside but she doesn't have any other care in the world other than finishing each other off.

He rolls her so she is now on top giving her the power and he sees her trying to recover before taking over. Kinsey's hips rock forward, grinding on him, her hands flat on his chest. She lifts herself off him and takes him in, over and over again. Her hands circle his throat and apply a steady pressure as he had done to her. "Fuck," whistles through his teeth.

Sam's hands grasp her hips as his hips thrust up impaling her in quick succession until he ejaculates inside her. Kinsey collapses on top of his chest and his arms wrap around her. They lay tangled together as their breathing slows. Her fingertip draws a lazy circle around his nipple.

"I was going to leave her," Sam says.

"What? When?"

"Twenty years ago. Do you remember the last phone call we ever had?"

Oh God, she does remember she had called to talk to him about Grayson. Her heart soars at the news, then plummets, but he hadn't, "What happened?"

"I cried."

"What?" She sits up to look at him. Sam is looking away from her like he is reliving the day.

"I hung up the phone. Went to the bathroom, locked myself in a stall, and bawled my eyes out. I left work early and drove around in circles. When I went home, I was going to tell her it was over. She beat me to the punch she told me she was pregnant."

It feels like a knife stabbing Kinsey through the heart. Life isn't fair. She lays her head back on his chest, "Did you tell her about me?"

"No. I…"

"What?" she wants to know what he is choosing not to say.

"I knew I missed you, but…" he trails off again. This time she waits. "I didn't expect the void you left after I got a taste of you again."

A tear slides down her cheek. "I know what you mean," her voice breaks.

"I love my girls," he tells her as he plays with her hair.

"I couldn't imagine my life without my boys. What are we going to do?" They understand that the boys and girls include their spouses.

"I don't know," he tells her honestly. They lay there for a while both deep in thought. Kinsey moves first putting her clothes back on. She needs to get back to the office and away from him.

Sam sits up and watches her dress while he puts his clothes on. "When can I see you again?" He asks.

She pauses tucking in her blouse. "Are you serious? We can't see each other again. This was it. Last time was supposed to be it. Maybe we just needed some additional closure, but we can't do this again."

"Please," he takes her hand and kisses her knuckles. "I promise. I will behave. I just want to talk to you. Like we used to. I miss our talks. Don't you?"

She softens, "Of course I do."

"Listen, I have an apartment in the city. It's not much I just keep some clothes there when I need to spend the night in the city for a late night at work or an event. It's not a family home or anything mostly business. Let's meet there once a week for lunch. I'll bring us takeout and we can talk. Scouts honor."

"You were never in the scouts," she grins at him.

His lopsided smile does her in, "Correct, but honestly please meet me."

"Just to talk?"

"I swear."

"Fine," she agrees and is rewarded with a kiss.

"Sorry," last time, "It was a thank you."

She finds her phone on the floor and pulls up her calendar. "Okay, I can do the 14th."

Sam is looking at his calendar, "No that's not going to work I have a meeting I can't move. Also, that's already two weeks away."

"Well, I can try for the 28th or… tomorrow."

"Tomorrow. I vote for tomorrow."

"Text me the address. Can you do one?"

"I'll be there ready with food." They finish getting dressed and climb out of the van. "Can I have a hug before you go?" Sam asks.

Looking around to make sure no one is in the vicinity she leans in when the coast is clear. They stand there for a long while. He strokes her hair, and she rubs his back her face pressing comfortably against his chest.

Kinsey pulls away and walks back to her SUV. When she climbs inside, he is still standing where she had left him. He smiles and holds a hand up as she drives by. What has she done?

Chapter Thirty-Three

♥

Sam's apartment is luxurious even though it's roughly a thousand square feet. Vaulted ceilings with an electric fireplace lined with dark grey slate from the floor to the top of the second floor. The kitchen is on one wall. The cabinets are black with a white and grey marble waterfall island. A round glass table with four upholstered chairs is near the large windows. On the left is the living room, with a sectional couch and a huge television. In between the kitchen and front door is a black metal staircase leading up to a loft. She can see the bed through the metal horizontal banister wires. The ceiling is an industrial mixture of wood, steel pipes, and concrete.

A brown paper bag is on the table when he invites her in. "I'd give you the tour, but you can see everything from here. The bathroom is upstairs off the bedroom," he points towards the loft upstairs.

"It's nice."

"Yeah, it does in a pinch. Have a seat. Can I get you something to drink?" He walks to the refrigerator opening it for her to see the options.

She laughs, "You have my favorite drink from college?"

"I do. Why?"

"I haven't drunk that in years."

"Oh," Sam seems deflated, he has clearly gone out of his way to purchase this specifically for her.

"I want one now though." He grins as he reaches in and pulls her out the juice filled glass bottle and a soda for himself. They walk to the table. She opens the bag and starts pulling out food. Sam has ordered Thai food, one of her favorites. Spicy rice, fried ravioli, paradise beef, and chicken fingers. "This is amazing. Thank you."

"Thank you for coming."

They eat family-style reaching over each other's arms using the wooden chopsticks that came in the bag. They are talking, they can't stop, tripping over their words trying to get the past 20 years out. Kinsey drops a ravioli on the table and before she can pick it up, he has snatched it up with his chopsticks. He has a twinkle in his eye, and she grins at him.

"What do you plan on doing with that sir?"

"Feeding it to you."

"Oh yeah?" Kinsey leans across the table and opens her mouth wide. He slowly moves it to her lips then at the last second pops it into his mouth. "Hey! That's not nice!" He is laughing and now choking on the food in his mouth. "Serves you right." She tells him. "I know CPR but I'm not sure I would use it on you."

"You took an oath," he says once swallowing, merriment still in his eyes.

"I'm not a doctor. I took no such oath." Looking at her watch she groans. "I need to get back to the office. This was so much fun. I just need to use your bathroom before I go." He stands with her. She heads up the stairs her heels clicking loudly on the stairs. Her eyes try and avoid the bed as she locks herself in his bathroom.

It's a full bath, with a glass-enclosed shower with tile. She uses the restroom and washes her hands after flushing. When she comes out, she half expects Sam to be waiting for her on the bed but as promised he is behaving downstairs picking up their lunch.

Walking downstairs she pulls her coat off the back of her chair and puts it on. "Thank you so much."

"Of course," he turns to her after putting the leftovers in the fridge and throwing the trash away. "Give me a sec and I'll walk you out." He takes a paper towel wetting it before wiping the table.

"Who trained you?" she wants to know. Instantly regretting her question.

He grins at her, "My mom."

Relief washes over her, "I need to thank that woman for raising such a great man." He blushes, his head ducking in embarrassment. He throws the paper towel away and washes his hands. Sam walks her to the door.

"Am I going to have to wait to see you until the 28th?" Sam asks.

Kinsey pulls out her phone checking over her schedule, "That just got booked today. I might be able to do eleven o'clock next Wednesday?"

"Done."

"You sure?"

"Already entered."

"Great, I'll see you then."

"It's a date." She ignores his words. He holds his arms out for her and she accepts the hug he offers. He has the best hugs, feeling safe and secure in his arms. Leaving she isn't sure how to feel. Sam didn't try to make a move on her once. That's what she wanted so why does she feel so rejected? They had a lovely time.

At the end of the hall, she turns around. She isn't sure what she is doing. Her heart is thudding so loud in her ears that she can't hear herself think. Her hand is raised but before she can knock Sam is opening the door.

"Did you forget something?" he asks surprised midstride one hand on the door.

"Yes," she breathes as she barges back into his apartment. She takes his face in her hands and he slams the door shut behind her as their lips collide.

"Kinsey," her name is sweet on his lips.

"Sam," she sighs into him. She drops her purse on the floor and he helps her remove her coat as she tugs off his. She kicks off her shoes and he does the same.

"Let's not rush this," he tells her.

"Okay." Taking her hand, he leads her to the stairs. He tugs off his wedding band and she follows his lead doing the same with hers. He places them on the countertop.

"I want it to only be the two of us up there." She nods in agreement. His fingers entwine in hers and they make their way upstairs. "Lay down," he commands.

Kinsey starts to undress, and he stops her, "Just lay down clothes and all." Confused, she does as he requests. He climbs into bed towering over her she welcomes him her body cradling him. "Do you have time? I want to make this last as long as possible."

"I don't," she tells him, "But I'll make time."

"Good," he kisses her breathlessly. He is growing hard against her leg. Her hand reaches between them cradling him through his pants and he moans rubbing his body against her. She repositions herself underneath him, so his erection is situated against her opening and they start rocking against one another. Kinsey's panties are soaked through with her arousal. She tugs at his tie loosening it before pulling it over his head.

His hand is kneading her breast through the fabric of her blouse and bra. She has managed to get the top couple of buttons undone on his blue shirt. Kinsey nibbles on his collarbone as he continues to rub against her. Taking her chin in his hand his lips meet with hers again. They kiss and kiss and kiss some more. Rolling him over, she takes control. Straddling him she rolls her hips against his. His hands grasp her hips grinding her against him.

Kinsey slowly starts unbuttoning her blouse her eyes lock on his which are heavy with desire. He watches her, biting his bottom lip, the gesture has her cumming in her pants. Gasping and falling forward slightly she uses her hand to brace herself on his chest. Her orgasm rocks her body, and he feels it. Grinning he crooks his finger at her. Falling forward onto him he kisses her senselessly. His hands roam across her back and her ass. She bites his lower lip, and he calls her a minx. She bites him harder.

He sits up so they are facing each other in bed, her still on his lap, and he bites her neck, "Don't leave a mark," she warns. He licks where he had just bitten.

"I want to claim you as mine." The thought sends shivers down her entire body causing her to whimper. "I fucking love the sounds you make when I'm pleasuring you."

She gasps, "Oh God." He is turning her on so much. Their lips meet again this time more savagely. Kinsey rips at his shirt desperate to get it off and feel skin-to-skin contact.

"Slow down," he pleads.

Kinsey takes his wrist in her hands and pulls his fingers to her lips. Watching him she sucks on his pointer finger. She feels him twitch under her and she grins in satisfaction. She licks his palm and nibbles on his wrist as she undoes his cuff. He allows her to remove the sleeve. Applying kisses up the length of his arm she watches the hairs on his forearm stand up. His head turns to watch her. Placing her hands gently on his jaw she draws his lips to hers again. Sam rolls her over, so her head is now at the foot of the bed.

Sam finishes untucking her shirt from her pants and unbuttons it one-handed while he watches her watch him. She has a silky camisole underneath. His large palm, fingers splayed starts at her stomach and roams up her chest. Kinsey is kissing his forearm that is next to her head.

Sam's lips are now on the bare skin of her stomach. They take their time, kissing and teasing, and removing articles of clothing. When they are both fully naked, he studies her body. Her breast once perky and round look more like ski slopes from nursing twins. Her taut stomach has a scar from the boy's C-section. "You're beautiful."

She laughs at his compliment wishing he had seen her back in the day when her body had been young and vibrant. "Don't laugh at me. You must know how beautiful you are." She is shaking her head vehemently. Sam takes her chin in his hand stopping her. "Look at me. You are a beautiful person. Here," leaning down he kisses her lips. Pulling back his hand moves from her chin to her breastbone holding it over her heart, "In here." She smiles at him as his finger slips inside her pussy, her back arching up to meet him, "For sure here."

Their lovemaking turns serious as he plays with her. Her fists wrap around the bedsheets. "Sam?"

He leans over her his fingers still inside her and kisses her neck, "Yes, my love?" Her body squeezes his fingers at his words.

"I need you to," she is having difficulty articulating what she needs as he begins to play with her clit.

"Yes?" he is still sucking and licking her neck, "tell me what you need, and I will give it to you."

"I need your cock inside me right now," and just like that his fingers are gone, and his hard shaft is buried deep inside her. She gasps at the sudden change.

"Your wish is my command," Sam growls as he moves inside her. Her arms and legs wrap around him urging him on. They find a rhythm then he changes it or the position they are in. They are on the bed, off the bed, up against the metal railing, the view of the New York skyline spread out before them.

Hours later, they lay sated in bed their bodies entwined. Sam has wrapped them in sheets and the comforter is now somewhere on the floor. "It's sad to say but we had more willpower at age 22."

Sam laughs, "I guess you're right. I can't believe this is real. That you are real." She rolls toward him kissing his chest.

"It's surreal. I never thought this day would come."

Downstairs she finds seven missed phone calls, two voicemails, and twenty-nine texts, mostly from Trish. Shit. She texts her back without reading any of them. "I'm so sorry I think I must have gotten food poisoning."

"Oh, no. That's not good. Are you okay? I thought you were dead."

"I feel like garbage. I don't know if I'm going to make it in tomorrow either. I'll text you in the morning."

"Okay, feel better!"

Kinsey feels guilty for lying to her friend but feels she covered pretty well. "Do you want to play hooky with me tomorrow?" She asks over her shoulder to Sam.

"I'm down."

Chapter Thirty-Four

♥

The next day Sam opens the door of the apartment for her. He gestures for her to come in. The second the door is closed he is wrapping her up in his arms. Their lips are fused together as he walks her to the kitchen island setting her down on it.

She has chosen to wear a skirt today for better access. He takes advantage, hiking the skirt up to her hips. Kinsey also chose not to wear any panties. Sam wraps his arms around her thighs pulling her bottom to the edge of the countertop. She grips the edge of the granite her legs positioned over his shoulders as his mouth licks her insides.

She closes her eyes and bites her lower lip. When he is done pleasuring her orally, he stands up straight. "I've been daydreaming of doing that to you in my kitchen since lunch yesterday." He pulls his t-shirt over his head and starts to unbuckle his jeans. She pulls her sweater off and unclasps her bra. She eases the skirt off her hips but when she reaches for her heels he asks her to, "Leave them."

"Yes, sir." She scoots away from him planting herself in the middle of the long island. Kinsey crooks her finger at him and he easily hops up on the marble. He is on his knees his cock standing at attention. She gets on her hands and knees to face him. She takes his dick in her hand and her mouth starts stroking him. He grunts in satisfaction, and it makes her moan in pleasure. Sam fists a handful of hair and smacks her ass with the other hand. That hand reaches over the top of her as he guides his middle finger inside her.

"Lay down," she commands.

He does as she says. She straddles him in a reverse cowgirl. Squatting on her heels she takes the full length of him inside her bobbing up and down on him. Her hands are on his thighs for support. He is running his hands all over her. Cupping her ankles and sliding up her calves and thighs and across her ass cheeks. She works harder and he is meeting her with every thrust his hips working with hers.

"I want you to touch yourself," he tells her.

"Yeah?" she looks over her shoulder at him and he nods encouraging her. She licks the fingers on her right hand and touches her clit exposed and sensitive still from yesterday's pleasure. Her hand rubs back and forth vigorously. She sits up straighter unable to concentrate on moving her hips but it doesn't matter because he is still thrusting inside her. Both hands are on her hips, to guide her on his shaft while she cries out in ecstasy.

"I want to see your face when you cum," he tells her. She spins on him still buried deep inside her. Changing positions, she is on her knees now. She rolls her hips, grinding against him. Sam sucks on his thumb his eyes watching her then he takes over pleasuring her clit. Kinsey's mouth is slightly ajar. Her hands come to rest on his chest her nails digging in. Her left hand reaches up and grabs her breast squeezing it. Rolling her nipple in between her finger. His free hand does the same to her other breast and she throws her head back in desire.

She shifts again getting up on her heels her legs bent she is able to move up and down with ease. Their rhythm increases in speed again, tensions building. "I want to kiss you," she tells him.

He sits up easily they are sitting facing each other on the countertop in the middle of his kitchen. Her thighs lay on top of his, his arms encircling her, one on her back the other cupping her bottom. Sam's lips capture hers as he pulls her towards him. She touches his body, the peaks and valleys sending a thrill through her. She gives in to the kiss, wanting to stay in this moment forever, their bodies joined. Her fingertips wander over his smooth back.

"Tell me what you want," he whispers.

"I want you."

"You have me." Music to her ears. "I'm all yours." He tugs on her hair pulling her face away from his so he can look into her eyes as he fucks her and tells her, "I'll do whatever you ask of me."

Kinsey studies him. Does he mean sexually or with anything? Does he mean that if she were to ask him right now to leave his wife he would? She is too afraid to ask. The last time she made herself vulnerable and asked she had been rejected. She can't do that again. Does she want him to leave his wife? What about Grayson? Is she willing to leave him? What would that do to her boys? What about his girls? Would they ever forgive themselves for destroying their families? So, what are they doing now? There has to be an end game. She has been refusing to deal with it because of the ramifications.

"I have to go," she pushes away from him jumping down off the countertop.

"Kinsey, wait." He jumps down off the island. She is already picking up her clothes off the floor and heading for the door trying to put distance between them. He stands in front of her blocking her way, his hands holding her upper arms. "What did I do?"

"What are we doing Sam?" The question is not lost on him.

He steps closer to her, "I mean it, Kinsey. I will do whatever you want." He cups her face. She wants to believe him. She wants to trust him. Her heart cannot take another rejection from him. "Ask me," he says softly. Tears in her eyes, she opens her mouth, but the words won't come out. He kisses her cheeks, where apparently tears have fallen. Sam kisses first one cheek, "Ask," then he kisses her other cheek, "me."

She can feel herself losing her resolve, she wants to be in his arms more than anything else. "Leave her." She manages to whisper.

"Okay," the words are out of his mouth as she asks the question. Zero hesitation. The clothes in her arms fall away dropping at their feet.

Kinsey throws her arms around his neck and their lips meet, crashing together. Their mouths stretch wide as he crushes her to him. Picking her up he carries her in front of the fireplace he lit before she got there. Gently he sets her down on the shaggy white rug coming to rest on top of her.

They make love until both are fully satisfied. Afterward, he grabs a throw blanket from the couch and wraps them up in it.

"I want you to come to my house," Kinsey said.

"I don't think that is a good idea at all."

"Yes. I want you to see how I live. We won't have sex there. We haven't been introduced into each other's lives to know if that is something the other wants."

He sighs, "Do you want to see my place?"

"I would but only if you are willing to show it to me. I want to know where you sleep at night. How your house is decorated. Grayson is gone for the next two days and the boys will be in school if you want to come over tomorrow morning? Say nine to be safe?"

"Okay, text me the address."

Chapter Thirty-Five

♥

Kinsey is waiting for Sam. Her heart is racing in her chest. She spent all last night cleaning her house. Her house is clean just not always tidy. The boys and Grayson leave articles of clothing and personal items, strewn about the house like one day there will be a scavenger hunt for random items they need at their fingertips. She knows she won't be opening any closet doors that's for sure.

Her heart lurches inside her chest as she sees him pull up to the curb. She has the curtain pulled to one side as she watches him turn off the ignition and unbuckle his seat belt. The door swings open and he unfolds himself from the car. Standing he is wearing sunglasses and he is checking out her neighborhood looking across the street before turning his attention to her home.

He spots her in the window a smile appearing on his face, his hand lifting in a wave. Moving away from the window she hurries to the front door. Opening it she sees him jogging up the front stoop. He is dressed in a suit and tie. Sam removes his sunglasses as he approaches. Opening the door wider she steps aside, "Please come in." He crosses the threshold, and she quickly closes the door behind him. His cologne wafts around her, the smell is intoxicating.

"Hey," she breathes out.

He rewards her with, "Hey yourself." A small laugh escapes her relieving some of the tension she had built up. "Do you feel like a criminal?" he asks her.

"Kind of," she admits. They are standing in the wide central hall. There is a coat closet behind him on his side of the hallway. The swinging door for the kitchen is on her side. Straight ahead twenty feet or so is a grand staircase that curls to the right. Halfway between them and the stairs is a living room to the right and a hall table to the left. Another set of doors leads to the kitchen.

They don't hug or kiss, both feeling like it's inappropriate. She walks him through the house, and she watches him as he observes her home. He doesn't say much, and it has her on edge. When they get to her and Grayson's bedroom, they are both standing at the foot of the bed looking at the perfectly made bed that she had only done for today. Typically, Grayson rolls out of bed first and she never has the time to take care of it.

"What side do you sleep on?" Sam asks.

"The right." Sam turns to smile at Kinsey. "What?" she asks confused.

"I like to sleep on the left."

"Good to know," she grins back at him.

"Are you ready to see my house now?"

She nods and he holds his hand out for her to take. Her lips purse. "Not here," she tells him and he withdraws.

"I'm sorry."

"It's okay. I'm just a little paranoid."

They walk back downstairs, and she checks out the window sending him out first then waiting five minutes before joining him.

Chapter Thirty-Six

♥

Kinsey is not prepared for Sam's house. They make the long drive into Connecticut. They are mostly going against the traffic, but she can see why sometimes he would choose to stay in the city. Pulling off the highway he drives down a handful of long windy roads.

Slowing down, he turns right and stops on a patch of cobblestone. A large stone wall surrounds a house lined with a black wrought iron gate. Rolling down his window he presses a series of numbers into the digital panel allowing the gates to open. Kinsey notices a camera at the top of the stone pillar looking down at them and her eyes widen.

"You have security cameras?"

"I disabled them this morning."

She breathes out a sigh of relief, but warning bells keep going off in her head. This was not well thought out. The rest of the driveway is paved, and it winds its way through a manicured lawn and trees. "You don't mow this do you?"

"No, we have gardeners."

"As in plural more than one?" He gives her a sheepish apologetic shrug. Pulling up to the house he drives them under a two-story portico. Running around to her side of the car he lets her out.

"I gave the staff the day off so no one should be here."

"Staff?"

"We have a housekeeper and a cook."

"Ah-ha." What else do you say in response to that comment? Sam is leading a different life than hers. Walking up the stone staircase Sam opens one of the twelve-foot tall arched, glass with black wrought iron detailing swirled through the panel door.

Inside the expansive foyer is warm honey oak hardwood floors in a herringbone pattern. The walls are all white. No family photos line the walls just expensive-looking artwork. Sam walks her through the home. It's beautiful. For as large as the spaces are it feels homey. Then Kinsey realizes all the furniture is white. The couches, the upholstered bar stools, and the chairs around a glass table.

"Do you actually eat at that table? Or sit on those couches? Is this what your house looked like when you moved in and had babies? Toddlers?"

He laughs, "We do. I watch the football games right there." He points to the white couch in front of the large flat-screen TV above the fireplace. "I make breakfast for the girls in the kitchen on the weekends when they are home and awake before noon."

"Your girls sleep half the day too?"

"Yeah, didn't you?"

"Not really. My dad would say don't waste a beautiful day."

Sam smiles at her, "That's sweet."

He shows her his study which has wood paneling and books filling every nook and cranny of the room. It looks out to the side yard which has rolling hills and trees, old stone walls sectioning off areas that used to be farmer's fields.

"The property is beautiful."

"I like it. Most nights I take long walks to clear my head of the day. That or I take my boat out."

"Wait, you have a boat?"

"We actually have a few."

"A few!"

"Well, her dad owns a massive yacht. We have a baby yacht, and a rowboat for the pond out back, but I own a sailboat. That one is my baby."

"Can I see it?"

"I would love to show it to you someday, but it's at the marina and there are too many people I know there, and taking you onboard the rumor mill would be burnt to the ground by the time we got back."

She sighs, "I get it." He continues the tour through the eight-bedroom ten-bathroom mansion.

"This is my room," he opens the door for her to walk in. She stops outside the bedroom door now unsure she wants to see the marital bed.

"Come on," he coaxes gently. "You said you want to see where I lay my head down at night. You can't chicken out now."

"I changed my mind."

"Fair enough," he closes the door.

"Do you want to see the pool?"

"No, I want to go."

"Okay. We can do that." They leave the house, and they are silent in the car on the drive back to the city.

He holds his hand out to her palm facing up and she laces her fingers through his. This small simple gesture calms her fears and puts her at ease. "This was a bad idea." He stiffens at her words. Did she mean seeing each other's houses or being together?

"I feel like that was so wrong on so many levels. I'm sorry I asked you to do that. I know you didn't want to." She waits for the "I told you so speech," but it doesn't come.

Instead, he lifts her hand and kisses her knuckles, "You were curious and that's okay."

"Ugh! We all know curiosity killed the cat!" He laughs a deep rich sound, and she can't help but smile at him. He gives her a wink and she melts.

Chapter Thirty-Seven

The wife 22 years ago...

Diane is wealthy, not just rich, but WEALTHY. Her dad owns not one but multiple pharmaceutical companies and makes hand-over-fist money. Diane graduated college four years ago, at the top of her class, she is smart and planning on taking over her dad's corporation when he retires. She has just gotten back from vacation in Greece. She is used to getting anything and everything she ever wants.

One day she is tanning in her favorite red string bikini on her dad's yacht when she sees a few young men board. She is on a lounge chair on a level above them. Lowering her shades, she takes them all in. One is cute, he is laughing with the other two. They are here to clean the decks. She hates when they come on board because they are always so noisy, and she likes to sunbathe in peace.

Rolling onto her back she closes her eyes and tries her best to ignore them. Sometime later, she gasps as cold-water splashes across her bare abdomen. "Oh shit, I'm so sorry are you okay?"

"What the hell?" she rants, sitting up. The one she had thought was cute is standing next to her chair.

"The bucket slipped out of my hand. I didn't mean to, I'm so sorry." He says again as he holds out a towel for her to dry off with.

Lifting her sunglasses onto her head she leans back on her elbows pushing her breasts forward. She has one knee bent and the other lying flat.

Her fingernails and toes are painted in matching red. "You made the mess you clean it up," Diane says in a haughty tone.

Instantly, he straightens, the towel down by his side, "I don't want any trouble. I need this job. I can't get fired."

"You won't get fired. That is unless you don't clean up your mess." She watches as he contemplates his options. She is frustrated that this isn't an easy decision for him. She is giving him access to her incredible body and he is turning her down. He seems like a challenge, and she instantly wants more. She is going to see if she can fuck him before his shift is over.

Resigning, he bends over and wipes the water droplets off her stomach. "Lower," she says seductively. He looks to see if she is serious. She chews on her lower lip and bats her eyelashes at him. He wipes down her thighs. "You missed a spot," she taps her finger on the narrow red triangle that is covering her womanhood, "I'm wet here too." Her double meaning not going unnoticed. He takes in the mammoth engagement ring on her finger.

"Who is the lucky guy?" he nods his head towards her ring.

"Brock Hamilton the fourth." She loves saying her fiancé's name. It drips with affluence.

His hand glides the towel back up her thighs applying a little pressure between her legs and rubbing in a circular motion, "When's the big day?"

"At the end of the summer," Diane says casually as if she isn't turned on. "Thank you. You may go now." She dismisses him as easily as she had paid attention to him. He removes the towel, and she flips over to sun herself giving him a view of her tight ass.

He carries on with his business working around her cleaning the deck. At one point she peaks through one eye and sees he has removed his shirt to work. He has a nice body. Diane is planning on how she can get him alone and deep inside her.

She is listening for him and it's quiet. Opening both eyes, she doesn't see or hear him. Sitting up she looks around, he is gone. Why didn't he at least say goodbye? Diane hurries down the stairs and to the side railing.

The guy is on the pier with his co-workers heading towards the parking lot. "Excuse me!" she calls. The three men turn around.

"Yeah?" the one she had been talking to asks.

"Could you come back here? There is something I need to show you."

"Is there a problem?"

"No." The three of them start walking back. "No, they can go. I want to show you." He looks at the other guys, and they shrug their shoulders.

"They're my ride."

"I can get someone to give you a lift home." He looks reluctant to come back and she worries for half a second that she may not be able to pull this off with this one. Usually, guys are falling all over her. She watches as he says goodbye and jogs back up the plank.

He stands in front of her, "Did I miss a spot?"

"You did in fact. Follow me." She leads him downstairs and through the narrow hallway toward her bedroom.

"I was told we weren't to go in the bedrooms." She ignores him and continues down the hall until she reaches her room. Opening the door, she waits inside her bedroom, and he is standing just outside, not crossing the threshold.

Reaching for him, she hooks her fingers in the top of the waistband and tugs his shorts. He allows her to pull him into her room. She shuts and locks the door behind him not losing eye contact with him.

It sends a thrill down her spine that he holds her gaze. She licks her lips and his eyes dip to them, but he doesn't move, his arms are down at his side. Diane takes the hand that isn't holding onto his waistband and unties the string of her bikini behind her neck. Slowly she pulls the strings down exposing her perky breasts.

"Do you like them?" He nods, "Do you want to touch them?" He nods again, "Go ahead, and don't be shy." Both hands come up cupping her. His fingers are calloused from arduous work. All of the men she has been with had never needed or wanted to do manual labor, they paid people for that. He is rolling her nipples bringing them to life.

Diane takes a step closer and slips her hand down his shorts. She is surprised by how big he is, she isn't expecting that. "What do you want from me?" he asks surprising her even more.

"I thought it was obvious. I want you to fuck me."

"What about your fiancé?"

Leaning forward she has to lean up on her tiptoes to kiss him. She is still stroking his cock. He allows the kiss. Pulling away she says, "He never has to know. Besides, I'm not married yet." She says with a shrug.

"You don't even know my name. Christ, I don't know yours."

Exasperated she pulls away from him. "Fine. Go." She ties her bikini back up. He turns to leave. The nerve of this guy, no one, ever, has turned her down. Without thinking she slips in front of him her back pressed against the door. They are a breath apart.

"I'm Diane," she juts her chin forward.

He grins, "I'm Sam. Was that so hard?"

"Yes," she grinds out causing him to laugh, a deep sound that vibrates through her.

"You're pretty when you frown," he tells her his finger slipping past her bikini bottoms finding the "wet spot" he had missed earlier. She didn't realize she was frowning but stops, her face softening, as he works her body into a frenzy. Clutching his broad shoulders, she gasps and spreads her legs for him. "Do you have condoms, Diane?"

She nods her head, "In my bedside stand."

"Convenient," he agrees. She pulls his shirt up over his head and then quickly goes to work on his shorts. He removes both pieces of her bikini as he kisses her. Picking her up, he throws her onto the bed. Taking her ankles, he spreads her wide his mouth giving her attention in between her thighs. Her eyes roll into the back of her head. She usually likes to be in charge in the bedroom, but it is clear he is taking over. Diane is used to a certain caliber of man and Sam does not fit the mold. For one thing, he is far too young for her. Any guy who says, "I can't afford to lose this job," is not in her inner circle.

Oh my God, what is he doing now? A guttural noise that is not at all ladylike escapes her lips. Her experience in life so far had been a mostly in-and-out type of situations. Even Edwardo, the tennis coach she occasionally played with had been quick romps at the club. She had slept with him because she had heard Latin lovers were intense. While it felt good, yes, she hadn't found it to be the case.

Sam moves up her body caressing every inch of her, pleasuring her with his fingers and tongue simultaneously. Sam takes his time with her as if he has nowhere else to be, which is probably the case. She hands him the condom when it is time, and he puts it on himself. He has his way with her flipping her into all different positions, some she had never experienced before.

Afterward, she is a hot sweaty mess. Her perfect dark locks are matted to her head and stick to her shoulders and back. Diane tries not to pant as she regains her breath. Sam rolls out of bed and starts putting his clothes back on. Where is he going? Yes, she had plans to kick him out, but she hadn't dismissed him yet.

Taking the phone off the hook on her nightstand she makes a call, "Can you have Milton pull the car around? I need him to take an employee home. Thank you."

"Good luck with the wedding," he tells her then ducks out of her room. Diane pulls a cigarette and lighter out of her drawer. Lighting up she takes a long drag. Releasing the smoke into the air she flops back down on the bed.

A couple of weeks later, she sees him again. She had planned to avoid him altogether but after having mundane sex with Brock last night her mind wanders to the man-child that had made her cum three times in a row. Diane puts on a white dress with yellow sunflowers deciding to go for demure rather than sexy although the halter top and no bra help in that department. She timed it just right to arrive when they were leaving.

They are walking down the dock when she brushes past them. He grins when he sees her, and she smiles back. "Hey Diane."

She lowers her sunglasses as if just seeing him they circled each other. "Sam? Isn't it?"

His smile tells her he knows what she is doing but doesn't call her out on it. "Yeah, that's right."

"I was just going to take the boat out. Care to join me?"

Sam looks at the guys and tells them he will catch up with them later. Then follows her on board. Diane tells the captain she would like to go out. "Please drop the anchor then take a break below deck for a couple of hours."

"Yes, ma'am." He tips his hat at her.

Diane walks out of the room and asks Sam if he is hungry or thirsty. They dine outside and drink champagne. She asks him questions and he tells her about his family and how he is up to his eyeballs in debt for student loans that's why he has three jobs. He works at the college bookstore, cleans boats with his friends, and bartends nights and weekends.

"When do you have time for fun?"

"I'm having fun right now," he tells her.

"You know what I mean. Do you have a girlfriend?"

Sam laughs, a deep rich tone that warms her, "I don't have time or money for a girlfriend." She can see that. She bites her lower lip thinking and raises an eyebrow at him now that he is staring at her lip.

"Have you gotten rid of your fiancé yet?" he asks her.

She leans forward her breast pressing into his tanned muscled arm and licks his neck then takes his earlobe in between her teeth, "Not yet."

"Are you planning to?"

She straddles him and his hands wander up her thighs and find her bare ass under her dress. She shakes her head, "Now why would I do that?"

He shrugs but doesn't answer. She kisses him and passion ignites between the two of them. They don't undress she just unzips his shorts and together they wiggle them down to his thighs. This time he is prepared and has a condom in his pocket putting it on, he is instantly inside her.

Sam slips her breasts out of the confines of her dress as she rides him. He pulls her off his lap and sits her forcefully on the table in front of him, plates and glasses tumbling over. He lifts her skirt and buries his head in between her thighs. Diane's hands curl in his hair pulling him closer and urging him on.

She looks up to see the captain leaving his post. He has set anchor and is retreating to his room as he was instructed. For a minute, his eyes lock on hers and she moans letting him know that this other man is pleasuring her. He gives her a small salute with his hat and moves on. This isn't the first man he has witnessed her having sex with. Diane thinks he gets off on her escapades, he never mentions it and she admires his discretion.

Sam fucks her on the table then bends her over the railing drilling her from behind, still not removing their clothes. Afterward, they collapse in a heap on the deck floor. "I need a cigarette," Diane pants, "Do you want one?"

"No thanks," he frowns. Getting up she goes to search for one while he removes the condom and pulls his shorts back up.

"There is a trash can over there." Diane points as she lights her cigarette.

Sam wraps it in a napkin before throwing it away. He starts to pick up the mess they created when she waves it away. "Don't do that. I have people for that."

He gives her a look, "I'm one of those people." Sam continues to clean up the mess.

"Don't be silly," she says as she blows out a puff of smoke. "Really, just leave it."

"I don't feel comfortable with that. We made the mess we should clean it up and not leave it to others."

She takes another drag from her cigarette, "Whatever." She sits and watches him but doesn't offer to help. "Where do you live," she wonders aloud.

He finishes picking up the mess before telling her, "With my family."

"When do you plan on moving out?"

"After college."

"What are you studying again?"

"Finance and business."

"So, you like money?"

"Who doesn't?" he asks as if that is a stupid question.

"What do you hope to accomplish after school?"

"I want to open my own firm one day and be a Fortune 500 company. I've applied for a paid internship for next year. I should be hearing soon if I got in. It's competitive, but I feel like I have a pretty good chance. If I get it, I will just be doing that for my senior year and not need to go to class."

"Impressive."

"What does your fiancée do?"

She perks up at the question, "He is a defense attorney. He is on track to be the youngest partner at his firm."

"Sounds like you are all set."

She shrugs, "I guess."

"Having second thoughts?" Sam asks.

She is silent for a moment as she continues to smoke, "The sex isn't that great."

"Ahhh…" he says slowly, "So, you are slumming it with me?" he asks not mad.

Smiling she admits, "Pretty much."

"Too bad I didn't come from money, right?"

"Yes, that would have been super helpful." Smiling she cocks her head to the side.

"What?"

"You are easy to talk to."

"I'm pretty easy to fuck too."

Laughing, she tells him, "That's an understatement."

"Is it now?" His voice is husky.

"Do you have a cell phone?" she asks suddenly changing the subject.

"No."

"Hmm…" Diane ponders his response.

"Why do you ask?"

"I guess in case I need to reach you to… talk."

"Or to fuck."

"Yes, that too."

"Are you sure you want to marry this guy? Besides sex being lame, what other qualities do you like about him?"

"He is good-looking. Comes from the right family. He has political ambitions my dad approves of."

"Do you do anything together? How does he make you feel when you are with him?"

"He makes me feel important."

"Okay, but is it because he makes you feel that way or what he can do for you that gives you that feeling?"

Frowning she ponders his question, "I don't know. I thought we were perfect for each other. We run in the same circles. I've known him for years. I hate his mother though." Her hand clamps down on her mouth, she hadn't meant for that tidbit to come out.

"It's okay, I don't know anyone you know it's not like I'm going to tell anyone."

Diane visibly relaxes. "That's one of the things I like about you."

Chapter Thirty-Eight

♥

Diane can't stop thinking about the things Sam had said. Is he right? Is she marrying Brock for the wrong reasons? She loves her engagement ring. Diane holds her hand out in front of her admiring the sparkle from the large rock. The entire wedding is planned and paid for. She has sixteen bridesmaids and a five-hundred-person guest list. Once the doubt has entered her mind, she can't let it go. Her dad is going to lose his shit if she calls off this wedding. She starts to realize that she on the other hand won't lose her shit if she calls things off.

One morning she wakes up and finds Brock dressed for work and sitting at their kitchen table. He is reading the paper and drinking his cup of coffee. Sitting down he barely glances up at her. "Brock, I think we should talk."

"Hmm, huh," still not looking at her. At her silence, he finally puts down the paper. "What's up Buttercup?"

She will not miss that nickname, "I think we should call off the wedding."

Brock cocks his head to the side a slight frown on his brow, "What? Why?"

"I don't think we are right for each other. I mean on paper sure we make perfect sense. Are you in love with me? Am I who you want to spend the rest of your life with?"

"I thought when I asked you to marry me, I was answering those questions. Where is this coming from?"

"I've been thinking-"

"That's dangerous," he chuckles.

She purses her lips together, but surges forward, "I'm serious. We aren't right for each other and we will just end up divorced and you can't have that if you are going to get into politics. I'm trying to save us both."

That piques his interest. "Well, it seems like you have made up your mind for the both of us. I will send someone over to collect my things. I can stay in a hotel for tonight until I figure out what I'm going to do next."

Standing, he takes his coffee cup placing it on the countertop. "Good luck with whatever you are looking for, Diane." He takes his keys off the hook and leaves their apartment. No fighting, no sadness, it's done. Leaning back in her chair she looks out the window. Well, that was easy.

Diane wants to call Sam and tell him she did it, but he doesn't have a cell phone. He can't afford it. Tapping her fingers on the table she debates her next move. She wants to thank him but she isn't sure how.

Two weeks later there is a knock at her door. She has work spread all over the kitchen counter as she sits on a high stool drinking wine. Standing she heads for the door. It's late and she isn't expecting anyone. Looking through the peephole she sees Sam. Smiling, she opens the door wide, her expression freezing on her face because he doesn't seem happy to see her.

"Sam!"

"What the fuck did you do?" he demands as he storms past her, uninvited to her home.

"What do you mean?" she closes the door behind him.

"You paid off my student loans."

"It was to thank you. I called off my wedding with Brock. I thought you would be happy."

"Those were my bills, my responsibility." His finger angrily jabs into his chest with each syllable.

"It was a drop in the bucket. I would have spent more on a divorce."

"It wasn't a drop in the bucket to me! I will pay you back," he assures her.

"You don't owe me anything." she holds her hands up in defense. "I was trying to be nice. Maybe now you can afford a cell phone so I can call you."

"You know this isn't normal right? You don't just buy friends."

"Friends? Is that what we are?" Diane asks curiously.

"I'm not sure what we are, but we aren't to the point where we pay off each other's college debt."

"Do you want a drink?" she asks throwing him off.

"What?"

"A drink. I'm having wine but I might have a six-pack of beer lying around. I also have hard liquor or wine."

Sam deflates, "I guess I'll take a beer." She walks to her fridge and pulls a bottle out for him. He is looking around her apartment with awe on his face. She likes he isn't from her world and doesn't take everything for granted. He takes the beer from her outstretched hand and opens it. She returns to the kitchen island to retrieve her wine.

"Why don't we sit down?" She leads him to the living room and they both take a seat on the couch.

"So, you broke off your engagement? How did that go?" he asks.

"Actually, better than expected. He didn't put up much of a fight and he has already cleared out all his stuff. He is probably relieved if not just a little pissed, I was the one to pull the trigger. My dad took it worse than Brock did."

"What did your dad say?" Sam wants to know before taking a pull from his beer.

A huge sigh escapes her, "Oh you know…I've disappointed him. What are people going to think?"

"Wow, you would think he would be happy you weren't making a big mistake?"

"That's not how my dad thinks. Plus, he is pissed about all the money he spent on a wedding that now isn't going to happen. It's fine. He will get over it."

They talk into the night when he finally gets up to leave. Putting down her empty wine glass she stands to block him. "Leaving already?" she asks her hand resting on his chest.

"Sorry. I'm just not in the mood tonight."

She frowns, "Why?"

"Just let it go, Diane." He manages to maneuver around her and head for the door.

"I will not. We just had a nice night and now you want to leave?"

He rakes his hand through his hair. "You emasculated me today." He looks down at her.

She is taken aback, "When did I do that?"

"When you paid off my student debt. That was my responsibility, and I don't appreciate you handling it for me like it was no big deal."

"It wasn't a big deal," she shrugs.

"It was a huge deal!"

She softens, "I'm sorry," she takes his hand in hers and gives him her best puppy dog eyes, "Forgive me?" Her lower lip is in a pout as her big eyes blink up at him. His eyes narrow a frown on his face as he glares down at her. Diane can tell he is pretending to be mad and a slow smile spreads across her face.

"Why are you smiling?"

"Because you forgive me."

"Says who?"

"I can just tell. You don't want to, but you do."

His glare intensifies and she giggles causing him to break. Her phone starts ringing in the kitchen. Letting go of his hand she runs to answer the call. It's past one in the morning and way too late to be getting a call. Flipping her phone over she sees her dad's number.

"Hello?" worry in her voice. The conversation takes less than thirty seconds, "I'll be right there." Hanging up she turns and finds Sam has followed her into the room.

"Everything okay?"

"I need to go to the hospital."

"I can drive you."

"Thank you. I just need to grab my purse and put on my shoes." Diane goes to her front closet and pulls out what she needs. "My stepmom is in the hospital."

"I hope it's nothing serious," Sam says as she locks her door.

"She is having a baby."

"Oh," is all he can think to say.

In the car, Diane plays with all his presets getting an idea of what type of music he likes to listen to. Hard rock, soft rock, country, hip hop, and folk music. She pulls a face when she gets to the last preset. Sam smiles, "My brothers like to mess with the buttons. It's a thing we all do to each other."

"How many brothers do you have?"

"Two."

"Any sisters?"

"No just three boys. What about you, any brothers, or sisters?"

Diane looks out the window and Sam wonders if he has hit a sore spot. After a moment she responds, "My parents only had me. They divorced when I was seven. My mom moved on quickly and the new husband didn't want kids, so I didn't fit in the picture anymore."

"I'm so sorry Diane."

"About what?" she asks. "I got to go live with my dad. Well, that was until he got remarried. Then I was shipped off to boarding school. My dad had two more girls with his second wife. They got divorced after ten years. I don't see my sisters much. My mom got divorced and remarried when I was thirteen. She has two boys with him. They are brats. My dad's latest wife is younger than me by four months."

"Yikes," Sam offers.

Diane scrunches her nose at him. "I know, right?"

"Yeah, that's not cool. And she is having a baby right now?"

"Yup. I get another sibling who will want nothing to do with me."

Sam takes her hand bringing her knuckles to his lips. "I want something to do with you."

She smiles at him, "Is that so?"

He wiggles his eyebrows at her, and she laughs. He pulls into the parking garage of the hospital, and parks. Unbuckling, she assesses him, "You're coming in?"

He pauses, "Oh, I'm sorry. Of course, it's a family matter." He pulls the seatbelt back over his shoulder and clicks it into place.

Diane places her hand on his forearm stopping him. "I would like you to come inside. I was just surprised you wanted to."

Diane paces the waiting room for the next three hours intermittently flipping through old magazines not reading any of them. Her dad walks in looking younger than Sam pictured. The man's face split into a grin. "It's a boy!" he announces.

Diane jumps up and hugs him around the waist. "Congratulations!"

"Finally, a boy. Someone to take over the family business." Her stiffness is instantaneous.

"Excuse me? You told me I was taking over the company. I've been working for you since I was sixteen years old. You promised me I would take over. I'm your second in command. He is in diapers!"

"Whoa," her dad tries to placate her, "I apologize. I was just excited about having a boy. It was a slip of the tongue, my mistake. Maybe you can show him the ropes when he grows up and you can run the company together?" Her silence is answer enough. "Well, I have to get back in there. Thanks for coming down."

Diane stands there seething, her fists clenched at her side, her heart racing. She jumps when Sam comes to stand by her looking at the waiting room door. "You okay?" he asks softly.

"Not really. He calls me down here in the middle of the night. Acts like having a boy is the end all be all. Threatens to take away everything

I've ever worked for in one second. I've been here for three hours and doesn't even invite me in to meet the little shit."

Sam laughs, "Do you want to head down to the nursery to see if he is in there?"

Looking at him her eyes wide, "We can do that?"

He shrugs, "I would think so but what do I know?"

"Okay, let's go do that." They ask a nurse for directions. Standing on the outside of the glass they look at all the little bundles laying in plastic bins on rollers. One of the nurses comes to the window.

"Which one are you looking for?"

"Sterling," Diane responds. The nurse smiles and heads to retrieve the infant. She scoops up the sleeping baby and holds him up to the window.

Diane instantly softens towards the little shit. "Awe, he's so cute." She puts her hand to the glass, "I'm your big sister, little guy. I'm going to show you the ropes."

When they are walking in the parking lot hints of the sun are happening on the horizon. "Are you hungry?" Sam asks her as he opens her door.

"Starving actually."

"I know a 24-hour diner close by. Do you want to go?"

"Sure."

She orders an egg-white veggie omelet and black coffee. Sam gets chocolate chip pancakes with home fries and chocolate milk. After breakfast, he drives her home. "Do you mind if I smoke in your car?"

"I'd prefer it if you didn't."

She raises an eyebrow at him but places the pack of cigarettes back in her purse. When he stops outside her building to let her out, she looks at him. "Do you want to come inside?"

"I need to get home and sleep. I work tonight."

"How far do you live from here?"

A big yawn escapes him before answering, "Forty-five minutes or so."

"Just sleep here. You're exhausted and so am I and I don't want to have to worry if you got home or not."

He looks at his watch, "Alright, thanks."

They crawl into bed. He has stripped down to his underwear and she is wearing a silky nightgown. Sam spoons her and they fall asleep within seconds. Several hours later they wake up and make love.

Diane asks him to come by after work that night. "I'm not going to be done until two in the morning."

"So?"

"You want me coming here that late?"

"Sure."

"Can I ask you something?"

"What's that?"

"Would you consider quitting smoking?"

She is smoking in bed next to him now. Blowing out a puff of smoke she frowns at him, "Why would I do that?"

"Because it's bad for you. I like you and wouldn't want anything bad to happen to you."

She smiles, "That's sweet." She takes another drag.

Sam picks at her sheets, "And when I kiss you it kind of tastes like an ashtray."

"Well, that's not as nice," she blows out more smoke.

"Will you think about it?"

"I don't want to," she pouts.

"I know."

Chapter Thirty-Nine

♥

That night when he comes back, she is rubbing her eyes when she opens the door. Sam is holding a box of Nicorette. Half-asleep she pulls her sleeve up she is already wearing a patch. She is rewarded with a kiss that turns into more.

Sam moves in with her. He gets into his internship for the fall semester. She takes him out to celebrate. He comes home excited mentioning a woman named Kinsey. Then never again. A week later Sam is in the shower when his phone starts to ring. Being nosy she flips it over to see who it is. The dread she feels is undeniable. It's Kinsey. Debating for another ring she answers the phone. When she hangs up, she deletes the call from his history.

Sam starts to become quiet around her, pulling away. Diane tries to spice things up and when he does have sex with her, she feels the other woman's presence. It's like he isn't aroused by her but by the fantasy of another woman.

Diane tosses and turns all night. Sam had texted her that he received his letter of intent to keep him on at the firm for next semester. She only prays that the girl he is falling in love with at the office doesn't get one too. He tells her that he and the others are going out for drinks to celebrate after work.

Diane feigns sleep when he comes home. She hears him tiptoe into the room careful to not turn on the lights and quietly removes his clothes before slipping under the sheets.

The next morning, she notices the cut on his hand but isn't sure how to bring it up and he doesn't offer an explanation. His coat is dirty, she just sends it off to the dry cleaners. She surprises him at Christmas with tickets to Aruba for two weeks.

They have the best time, and she silently pats herself on the back. This is just what they need, time away just the two of them the way it used to be. Sam sleeps most of the first two days. Poor thing is exhausted she thinks. Diane plans excursions around the island, and he starts to come out of his funk. The smile she fell in love with makes a return and she parades around him in all the new lingerie she bought especially for this trip. She feels invigorated and renewed when they return home.

Things are somewhat normal after he returns to work, and she lets her guard down. She was anxious about going to the retirement party. Would she run into the woman that held her man's heart? What would she do? Claw her eyes out? It was a strong possibility. She often daydreamed about their confrontation if they ever had one. She is almost giddy when the emergency phone call comes in as they are leaving for the night.

"I'm so sorry," she apologizes to Sam and instantly regrets the reprieve she had hoped for when she sees the relief in his eyes. Fuck.

Hours later she is still on the phone doing damage control with her team when Sam walks through the door. He is home earlier than she would have expected. She has had time to contemplate the pros and cons of not going tonight. On one hand, she didn't think she could come face-to-face with the woman that is pulling Sam away from her. At the same time, she wishes she would have been able to flaunt how much Sam belongs to her.

Sam walks straight for the fridge and pulls out a beer. Twisting off the top he throws it away as he takes a long drink. Frowning, she watches him. She has missed something in the phone call when she realizes there is a pause on the other end. "Sorry guys what was that?" They repeat the problem, and she does her best to concentrate as she watches Sam. He looks up at her and smiles and it makes her visibly relax until he mouths, "I'm going to take a shower."

She plasters on a smile and nods at him. She is still in the black cocktail gown she had planned to wear tonight her heels are long gone and she is pacing the kitchen floor barefoot. She decides to get out of the dress now. Underneath she is wearing a matching lace bra and thong and waits for him to return.

After the shower, he comes out looking refreshed in his boxers, his body tempting, scattered drops of water still on his chest he had missed with the towel. He rinses his empty bottle at the sink and places it in the recycling bin under the countertop. He approaches her from behind, wrapping his arms around her, and gives her a big squeeze kissing her neck. "Guys I've got to go. Let's regroup in a half-hour for a report."

"Make it an hour," he growls into her ear.

"Actually," she corrects, "Let's make that one hour. I want to hear good news." Hanging up she throws the portable phone onto the couch turning to face him. Leaning up on her tiptoes she kisses him. He is savage in his attack on her, and she welcomes it. She wraps her legs around his waist as he picks her up. He is already rock-hard. She tries not to think about the fact that he is coming home from seeing her. She wants to believe it's her that he wants and desires and not his pent-up sexual frustration. She full-heartedly believes he has not physically cheated on her yet. Emotionally? That ship has sailed a long time ago. The day he stops having sex with her is the day she needs to worry.

He places her roughly in the middle of the marble-topped coffee table. He has brought a condom with him; he is never without a condom. She is fairly certain his mom ingrained it in his brain at a young age, no glove no love. Her ankles are around his neck as he drills into her. It's fast and hard, him grunting over her before he is releasing himself inside her. Standing he still has his boxers barely down over his ass cheeks.

Sam leaves to clean up and she sits up on the coffee table. "I should have scheduled the follow-up call for fifteen minutes. I thought you wanted an hour," she is grinning as she teases him.

He has an overconfident grin on his face as he stalks her, "Oh you thought I was done with you?"

"Weren't you? Felt like you were done!" she squeals out the last word as he bends over wrapping his arms around her waist and throwing her over his shoulder. He slaps her bare ass as he carries her to their bedroom. Throwing her down on the bed he goes down on her for the next half hour until she is begging him to be inside her again. Reaching for the condoms on his nightstand he fulfills her wishes making her late for her next phone call.

Hours later she is sitting up in bed clicking away on her laptop as Sam sleeps naked next to her. He is laying on his stomach his face turned towards her. She loves him so much. Diane pushes his hair gently away from his features and sighs. Don't ever leave me she thinks. She has been abandoned by everyone she has ever known at some point or another. It's the reason she has such a tough exterior. She has to be otherwise she will crumble. Sam is the reason she had finally started to let go and let him in. Letting him in on the big stuff in her life. Maybe it was a mistake? She shakes her head.

She is going to call her dad in the morning and have him call his contact at Sam's company and make sure they don't hire him at the end of the year. It's the same call she had made last summer to get him the internship in the first place.

Chapter Forty

♥

Things are better with Sam after graduation but in the fall, she notices a change again. Months later he comes home from work the look on his face tells it all. This is it; he is going to finally leave her.

"I'm pregnant," she blurts out.

"What?" The shock on his face is unmistakable, "How? Aren't you on birth control? I use a condom every single time."

She shrugs forcing a fake smile on her face, "Aren't you excited?" His eyes dart to her stomach. His shoulders drop, defeat taking over.

Diane had lied. She isn't pregnant. She doesn't even want to be pregnant. The one thing she knows for sure is she isn't willing to lose Sam. Not to her. Not to anyone.

It becomes clear Sam isn't planning to sleep with her anytime soon either. He wards off all her advances. Desperate times call for desperate measures. One night she gets him drunk, so much so that she has to drag him to bed. His arm is slung over her shoulders as she supports his weight on her tiny frame. He flops onto the bed fully clothed and when she tries to help him out of them, he rolls over pulling the covers over him.

The comment he makes is so faint she thinks she imagined it, but no. The words play on repeat in her head. "Not going to happen." He knows and he is calling her bluff. Not directly to her face of course. She needs a plan of attack. She can pretend she has a miscarriage. No, he would mourn the loss of the baby that never was, but he would leave her. Sam would pack his things and go to the woman he had fallen in love with. Diane is sure of it. If he finds out she lied and was never pregnant he will never forgive her.

Her only hope is to become pregnant. She listens to the soft snoring beside her. There is a lawyer at her company that has the same coloring as Sam. He's had a crush on her, and it would be easy enough to sleep with him. The strings involved in that affair would be too messy. She needed something without a paper trail. Or at least a paper trail she could buy off.

A sperm bank is an answer that hits her like a lightning bolt. Sitting up straighter in bed she starts to ponder the idea. She could pick out someone that looks like Sam. They would be anonymous, with no one to come knocking on the door. She would make sure they were intelligent and had no health concerns. Feeling confident in her plan she snuggles under the blankets.

The following morning, she dresses as if she is going to work. Kissing Sam goodbye, he groans out, "Love you." Still feeling hungover from the night before.

"I love you too," She cups his face. I'm going to make us a baby.

Diane walks confidently into the sperm bank. "Yes? Can I help you?" The woman behind the receptionist's desk asks.

"Yes. I'd like to see your list of donors please," Diane is pleasant, at the same time confident with her request.

"Of course. Name?"

Diane is taken aback. She doesn't want a paper trail. "Why do you need my name? Aren't they just a number? Just give me a number."

"I'm sorry do you have an appointment for today?" The receptionist asks. Diane sighs in frustration. She wants to ask the lady if she knows who she is, but she clearly doesn't and she doesn't want her to.

"Can I help you?" Another woman has come out of her office.

The receptionist turns to her boss. "She doesn't have an appointment, and she wants to see our donors without giving her name."

The boss looks over at Diane before a warm smile touches her lips. "That's okay Karen. I've got this. Would you like to come with me?" She asks waving Diane towards her office.

Diane follows the woman and has a seat across from her desk when she gestures with her hand. Closing the door behind them she takes a seat on the other side of her desk. "Now Ms. Sterling, how can I be of assistance?" Diane's stomach tightens, busted. "I'm sorry I'm being rude I know who you are and haven't introduced myself. I'm Tara McFadden, I'm the director of this facility. I've seen your article in Forbes and I have to say I admire you."

"Thank you. I appreciate that."

"So, what can I help you with today? Are you looking to become a mother?"

"Yes."

"Wonderful!" Tara exclaims. Clicking on the computer she looks up. "I can arrange a consultation for you in about eight weeks," Tara beams at Diane.

"Eight weeks?" Diane sits back in her chair. "I was hoping for much sooner."

Tara starts typing and clicking her mouse ferociously. "I can maybe move some things around and get you in about 4-6 weeks but really that's the best I can do."

"And after the consult how long does it take?"

"Generally, we can have you conceive within the year sometimes as early as six months."

Diane is already shaking her head, "This just won't do. I need to get pregnant today."

Tara's sharp laugh is cut off by Diane's cold look. Clearing her throat Tara apologizes, "I'm sorry. I really am but that is going to be impossible."

Diane stands and Tara follows her lead. Diane opens her purse and pulls out stacks of hundred-dollar bills wrapped in paper indicating the amount of each packet and lines them up on the director's desk. "How impossible? I don't care how the money is split or if you would like to keep it all to yourself, but I need this to happen today and I need you and your staff to sign a non-disclosure agreement." She pulls copies of the legal documents from her purse. She had her lawyer draw them up this morning for a hefty fee.

Tara is silent for a moment as she takes in the thousands of dollars piled on her desk and the formidable woman standing in front of her. "Double it and I'll see what I can do."

"Done," Diane tells her confidently.

"I will pick out some applicants personally for you. Any features or traits you are looking for?" Diane gives her the must-have list and is left to wait while her donor list is compiled. It's imperative this work.

It's not as simple as Diane had hoped. Tara gives her an ovulation test to take home with instructions. "The second that says you are ovulating I want you to call me. This is my personal number. You call me and we will get you in here." Tara hands Diane a business card.

"How long will this take?"

"No longer than a month."

"I really can't wait that long."

"We will have a better success rate if you are ovulating. Hopefully, it will be sooner rather than later. Only time will tell."

Three days later Diane is ovulating. She calls Tara immediately and tells her to meet her at the office. She has the procedure done with donor #52796. Miraculously, Diane conceives on her first try.

Her daughter Quinn arrives early thankfully with help from an herbalist. Sam hasn't proposed like she thought he would, and she doesn't push. Sam falls instantly in love with their daughter. He is the best father doing diaper changes and two a.m. feedings. He sings her to sleep and rocks her in the chair they bought for her nursery.

Diane gets post-partum depression. She has a tough time connecting with the baby. Sam is there for both of them. He finds her a therapist and is patient with her.

Seven months later 9/11 happens. Diane is home that day because Quinn had a fever, so she hadn't dropped her off at daycare. She hasn't heard from Sam since the attacks started and she is pacing as Quinn screams. She is bouncing her up and down on her hip and if her daughter wasn't crying, she would be the one in tears.

The keys in the lock catch her attention and Sam flings open the door to their apartment. They lock eyes, "Oh thank God," she rushes to him, and Sam envelopes them both in a hug.

"Are you okay? Is Quinn, okay?" Sam asks running his hand over the two of them making sure they are physically fine. He crushes them to him again.

"We are okay. Are you okay?"

"It's crazy out there." He tells her.

"I know. I've had the news on all morning. This is so scary. Do you think we are safe in this building?"

Sam starts to undo his tie as he walks to the windows checking out the skyline, not a cloud or plane in the sky. "I think they have issued a no-fly zone right now and grounded all flights just to be safe. I need a drink." He turns to Diane, "Do you want one?"

"That would be great thanks."

They sit in front of the TV for hours watching the horror of the day unfold. With the Tylenol and the fact that Daddy is home holding Quinn, their baby girl has drifted off to sleep. They don't eat, just drink and watch the news. That's all that is on anyways no regular scheduled programming. The terrorist attacks are on every channel.

Finally, at one in the morning, they lay their daughter down to sleep. They stand albeit a little unsteady on their feet and watch her. Once they leave the room, they close the door softly behind them.

"I was so scared," Diane tells him.

"Me too." They are standing close together in the hallway. His hand comes up slowly as if asking permission to touch her. They have been living together and co-parenting, but they haven't had sex since before Quinn was born.

Diane steps closer. His hand cups her face and he bends down to kiss her. It is explosive like the first time. She pulls at him, and his hands are cupping her breast. Before she knows it, her yoga pants are off, and he has turned her around, so she is facing the wall. He pushes inside her, and she frowns. He isn't wearing a condom. That is her last conscientious thought because this feels amazing.

She tells him so. His grunting confirms he feels the same way but she doesn't want to break the spell. At one point she cries out and Quinn stirs from inside her room. They freeze and she is afraid he will pull out of her, but he doesn't. He just clamps his hand around her mouth and proceeds to have his way with her.

Diane's body shakes from her orgasm and when he comes, he doesn't pull out. She turns to look at him. He doesn't explain himself just removes his hand from her mouth, kisses her, and then slaps her on the ass. "Come on let's take a shower before bed."

Six weeks later she finds out she is pregnant. "I think we should get married," he tells her. It's not the proposal she had wanted but she takes it.

They plan the wedding of her dreams with all the bells and whistles she had been envisioning since she was a child. Sadie is born a month before the wedding. Quinn and Sadie are in matching gowns and are pushed in a stroller down the aisle as their flower girls. They move to Connecticut. Her dad hands over the reins of the company to Diane. Her father dies of a stroke three months later.

Diane feels like she is a super mom, and head of the PTA she is there for all their moments. As much as she didn't want children, they have become her entire world. Diane is also a boss running a multi-billion-dollar company and having it all. She plays tennis three days a week and swims on opposite days. She has nannies for the kids, house cleaners, and a nutritionist cook, a massage therapist on retainer that comes to her house, two gardeners, and a pool boy. She runs a tight ship her schedule is planned to the minute of every day.

When Sam starts spending more time in the city, she is too busy to notice. When he stops having any interest in her naked body or her advances on him, she starts to question. When her phone asks her if she wants to become friends with Kinsey Wells she knows. How did this happen? When did this woman come back into their lives?

Diane starts digging and immediately finds proof of his infidelity. She thought they were past all this bullshit. She is so mad she is seeing red. She isn't sure how she should proceed but she isn't going to take this laying down.

Chapter Forty-One

♥

Kinsey Present Day

Kinsey comes out of the elevator in the parking garage to hear someone's car alarm going off. Walking towards her car she hears shattering glass and shouts. Rounding the corner, she sees a woman with a baseball bat confronting the security guards running toward her. The woman swings the bat wildly and it lands soundly on the hood of her SUV! What the hell?

The woman turns and spots her, she charges Kinsey but is quickly overpowered by two security guards. "Stay away from my husband!" she screams at her. Kinsey jumps at the verbal assault.

She takes in the other woman's appearance. She is wearing fitted jeans, flats, and a collared shirt with a teal sweater over it, looking stylish. Minus the other woman's smaller frame and darker chocolate brown hair, Kinsey looks similar to the woman. Kinsey isn't sure how she feels about this realization. Is she the 2.0 version or vice versa?

Kinsey watches horrified unable to move from her spot, as they drag Sam's wife, kicking and screaming out of the garage. Walking slowly towards her vehicle she assesses the damage. Both headlights are shattered, a large indent is on her hood, and she was keyed all the way around. How is she going to explain this to Grayson? "You remember that guy you let me have sex with? Yeah well, we've still been at it and his wife found out and she is sort of pissed."

"Mrs. Wells-" Kinsey gasps, clutching her chest at a male voice so close to her, "I'm so sorry about your car." Kinsey swivels to see one of the guards has returned. "If you follow me this way? I can have you fill out a claim. The company will pay for the repairs." She lets him lead the way in a daze.

"Do you want to press charges?"

"No," she said quietly, and she can feel the guard's silent judgment.

Kinsey dials Sam's number, "She knows," she says simply.

There is a brief pause on the other end of the line, "How do you know?"

"She came to my work with an aluminum baseball bat and took out her frustrations on my car."

"Jesus, are you okay?"

"Yeah, just a little shaken up. I didn't press charges. My company is supposed to take care of the damages because it happened on their property. How did she find out?"

"I don't know. Where are you? I'll come pick you up. I want to see you."

She knows it isn't a good idea, but she agrees anyway. When Sam pulls up to the curb, she hops in his sleek car an upgrade from the beater he had in college. He holds her shaking hand rubbing his thumb over her knuckles helping to soothe her nerves. Sam drives them to a quiet residential neighborhood before pulling over.

Unbuckling, he reaches for her, and she does the same. She breathes him in, her whole body begins to shake again. "What if Grayson finds out? How am I going to explain the damage to my car?"

Sam is rubbing her hair, "Maybe you should tell him about us."

Kinsey pulls back to look at him, "You're serious? And tell him what exactly? That I-" she stops herself before confessing she had fallen in love with him. She tries again, "That we've known each other since we were twenty-one? That you had a girlfriend you refused to leave for me? That I moved on with him and when his fantasy involved another man, I immediately thought of you. That after we saw each other again after over twenty years we still can't keep our hands off each other. That should go over really well."

"I'm in love with you Kinsey. I loved you then and I never stopped loving you."

Her heart speeds up. The declaration is exhilarating and twenty years too late, "Why didn't you ever tell me?"

"I was scared. I know that is a lame excuse, but it is true. I was going to tell you but then I found out I was going to be a father. I couldn't abandon my daughter or her mother."

Chapter Forty-Two

♥

Kinsey walks into her house exhausted from the day. Sam has just dropped her off because her vehicle is getting towed to an autobody shop. She hangs her bag on the hook on the wall and stops short when she sees Grayson's bag. He isn't supposed to be home until tomorrow. She immediately thinks about the boys.

"Grayson!" Kinsey hollers as she walks past the empty living room.

"In here!" She follows the sound of his voice, pushing open the kitchen door. Grayson is at the kitchen table he looks up when she enters. "Are the boys…?" Her voice trails as she realizes he is not alone. A dark-haired woman also sitting at the table turns to face her. It's Diane.

Silently, Diane stands and walks through the door closest to her into the hallway. Grayson won't look at her and she is avoiding him just the same. The tension is palpable, a heavyweight in the room. She realizes now they may have just witnessed Sam drop her off at the front door through the large kitchen window. Kinsey is finding it hard to breathe. She takes a seat at the table, her legs no longer willing to hold her weight.

Kinsey notices Diane left a business card on her kitchen table. She is infuriated that woman was in her household. Then remembers that she had once toured the other woman's home. Neither speaks until they hear the click of the front door latching behind Diane.

"Do you want to explain to me what the fuck is going on?" his quiet calm voice has her shaking more than if he had screamed that question at her. What is she going to tell him? How is he going to take it? How much does he already know?

Grayson sits down at the table next to her and she can't even look at him. The guilt she feels is overwhelming. Tears sting her eyes that she has hurt the man she loves. The one she had given her battered and bruised heart to so he could mend it with his kindness and generosity. His head is bowed, and he is holding his face with his hands his elbows resting on the table.

"I'm dying Kinsey," the words are so light she doesn't believe what she just heard.

"What? Are you serious?" She touches his forearm, and he flinches away from her. His hands are now down on the table. He looks at her and realizes his eyes are bloodshot. He's been crying. Did he cry in front of Diane? "What do you mean you are dying?" Maybe it's a metaphor and he is talking about his heart he can't possibly mean... A large lump forms in her throat as she searches his face for clues.

"I have stage four pancreatic cancer."

"Oh, God. How long have you known?"

"Six months."

"Six months! How have you known for six months and not told me? What about treatment?"

"When I first found out it was stage one. I took one day out of the week for a month for chemo treatment. I was lucky and didn't lose my hair. It would knock me out so I would rent a room and sleep it off until the next morning. Work knows."

Work knows, plays over and over again in her brain. "Who else?"

"I haven't told a soul. I just wanted us to live our lives. I wanted us to love each other for the time we have remaining."

"How much time," she croaks out tears unabashed running down her cheeks.

"Most patients don't make the year," her chest constricts, and she can't breathe, she is holding in the giant sob that desperately needs to escape her lungs. "Almost no one makes it five years. When I found out I thought of you and the boys. I don't want to leave you. I thought you might have a hard time moving on. I don't know why but I got this thought into my head that if you were with another man with my permission, it would be easier for you."

She feels like her brain is fragmenting into tiny little pieces. "So that whole thing was because you are sick? Because you are..." she can't say the word.

Grayson is nodding his head and finishes for her, "Dying."

"Oh my God. What have I done?" She pushes the chair away from the table needing to stand immediately. "I didn't want to do it!" Kinsey screams at him, her arms flailing as she paces back and forth. "You forced my hand. You should have just told me! Why the fuck didn't you just tell me!?" She is sobbing now at this point her legs give way and she collapses on her knees to the floor. Kinsey sounds like a wounded animal. Guttural cries are ripping at her throat. She is holding her stomach rocking back and forth.

He stands and she thinks he is going to comfort her. Instead, he says, "I'm going to a hotel tonight. When I get home tomorrow night, I want you to have made a decision. Me or him." Grayson snatches his keys off the countertop and walks out.

She cries some more. She cries because her husband is dying. She is crying because he's the one that allowed another man into their marriage. Yes, she is the one that invited the only other man she has ever loved into her bed. She takes full responsibility for that. Not only that but the fact that she let it continue after the fact. That was a betrayal of her marriage. But she would have never in a million years done that if she had known the truth. What was he thinking? She is devastated.

Kinsey isn't sure how long she lays on the cold tile floor, but she is aware of the fact that the sun is going down outside, and her muscles are stiff. Looking at her watch she realizes the boys will be home from soccer soon. Picking herself up off the floor she starts to make dinner. Grayson isn't even supposed to be home tonight, so the boys won't know any different.

She takes Diane's card off the table and puts it into her pocketbook out in the hall. She goes into the downstairs bathroom. Her appearance is atrocious. Her hair has come out of her updo, her make-up streaked down her face, and her eyes and nose are red and puffy from all the crying. Washing her face, she tries to remove make-up and reduce the appearance of bloodshot eyes and a puffy face. Taking her hair down and running her fingers through the strands she assesses herself, not much is helping but she looks somewhat better.

Dinner is almost ready when the boys come barreling into the kitchen. They are carrying their sports bags which smell like feet. Both of them have their sweaty soccer socks in hand they know need to make it to the laundry room ASAP.

They each kiss her on the way by. "Mom, you, ok?" Aidan asks her. Ethan stops to access his mom to see what his brother is referring to.

"Yeah, I'm fine. I just think my allergies are kicking in tonight."

"Me too actually," he says. "Do you want some Claritin?" Aidan asks as he drops his socks off before opening the cupboard where she keeps, Advil, Tylenol, Vitamins, and Claritin.

"No thanks, sweetie. I already took some," she lies. "How was practice?"

"It was good," Ethan responds to her before picking up their backpacks and placing them where they should be in the hallway on the hooks.

"Go wash up before supper." She tells them and they hurry upstairs. Fifteen minutes later the boys are out of the shower, their hair wet and sweatpants and t-shirts for bed on. They sit down as a family and have dinner. The boys talk about their day.

They start on their homework as she clears the dishes. She doesn't sleep all night. Crying she thinks about her options. Tossing and turning Kinsey throws off her covers and gets dressed. She can hear the boys playing their video games still even though it is past ten and their bedtime. Ignoring it for now she slips out of the house. Not having a vehicle, she hoofs it to the nearest subway stop and rides it until she reaches her dad's apartment. Climbing the stairs, she wonders if he is even still awake. Inside the building, she takes the elevator up and knocks softly on her dad's door. After a minute or two, it is flung open. "Kinsey, what's wrong, Sweetie? Come in. Come in," Pierce beacons her inside. The fireplace is going in the living room. "You look like you could use a drink?"

She nods and he heads toward the kitchen as she takes off her coat and settles on the couch. Pierce comes back with two glasses of red wine and hands her one before sitting next to her. They are silent for a long time while she takes sips from her glass staring into the flames. Finally, tears stinging her eyes she looks up to her dad, the one true constant in her life. She puts her glass on the coffee table and he follows suit. They face each other one knee bent towards the back of the couch the other foot planted firmly on the ground. "Grayson is dying."

"Oh my God," he gathers her into his arms and whispers while she sobs. "I'm so sorry Sweetie." He rubs her back while she tries to regain control of her emotions. Wiping her tears, she finally pulls away.

"Stage four pancreatic cancer." Her dad swears and it makes it feel more real. "It gets worse...." Kinsey can see the concern in his eyes. How can it get worse he is thinking? "I did something..." she isn't quite sure how to tell her dad she had an affair with a married man no less. "I didn't have all the facts and I'm not saying that excuses my behavior, but I still did what I did." She is talking in circles now and she can see she is losing him. "Do you remember Sam?"

Pierce leans back his arm now resting on the back of the couch, "Ahhhh, Sam. I remember him. The one that got away."

"What? No, we were just friends." Her dad's eyebrow shoots up and she looks ashamed. Taking her wine off the coffee table she takes a sip. "Anyway, I've made a mess of things and I don't know what to do."

"Yes, you do," he tells her softly, "You just don't want to. You are breaking someone's heart either way, including your own." Tears stream down her face as she listens to her dad's wisdom.

"It's not fair," she whispers.

"The cruel reality is life's not fair."

"It's a stupid rule," she grumbles, downing more of her wine.

"I agree."

Her dad drives her home, and she finds the boys have finally logged off for the night and are passed out face down on their pillows. In her room, she strips down and gets into her pajamas again before crawling into bed. She tosses and turns until the sun hits her windowsill. Kinsey hasn't slept a wink, but she has a plan.

Rolling out of bed she knocks on both boys' doors before opening them and turning on their lights. "Rise and shine," she calls as chipper as she can. Returning to her room she showers before getting into a robe and doing a second wake-up call as her boys are still passed out in their rooms. This time they stir and fight for the bathroom. Kinsey returns to her room confident they will be ready to leave for school on time.

They meet in the kitchen. Ethan has started her coffee and it is ready in her travel mug. She adds cream and sugar. The boys are eating at the kitchen table when she sees the bus pull up outside. "Bye Mom," they shout as they grab their bags and run out the front door.

"Bye! Love you! Have a great day!" Slam! The door is shut forcefully behind them.

She pulls out her phone and texts Diane, "This is Kinsey Wells. I'd like to talk. Can you meet me at Sal's cafe at noon?"

"I'll be there," is her immediate response. Step one.

She heads off to work. Trish sees her coming and the smile on her face freezes when she sees Kinsey's appearance. Standing, Trish beats her inside her office. Kinsey takes a seat at her desk. "What the hell happened to you?" Trish asks after closing the door behind her.

"Grayson has cancer."

"Oh my God! Kinsey, I'm so sorry. Is it bad? That's a stupid question. Of course, it's bad." She is still standing at the door unable to decide what to do.

"I'm giving my notice today," Kinsey wants Trish to hear it from her first.

"No!" she rushes forward, "I'm sure the company will give you as much time as you need off. Don't quit."

Kinsey is already shaking her head, "I've made up my mind."

Trish collapses in defeat in the chair across from Kinsey's desk. "This is just so sudden." she is staring at the floor in front of her.

"He's known for six months."

Her head snaps back up, "What? No. Kinsey, I'm so sorry." Kinsey is all cried out for now. She is numb. Trish helps her write her letter of resignation, effective immediately. Her friend helps her pack up her office. Years of her life were spent working to this point. Coming through the door Trish says, "You can't forget your mug. I found it in the breakroom."

It's the mug Sam had bought for her so long ago. She had always kept it at her work never bringing it home. "You keep it," she tells a shocked Trish.

"I can't keep this. This is your favorite mug. You have had this as long as I've known you and that's a long time. You've had a relationship longer with this mug than most marriages." Kinsey's smile is sad. Trish's analogy is not lost on her. "Please?" Kinsey asks. It has to be all or nothing with her. She can't bring it home and she can't throw it away. It will make her feel better knowing her friend has it.

Trish assesses the mug sensing her friend needs this from her. "Okay. I'll take good care of her."

"Thank you," Kinsey breathes out her appreciation.

"Of course."

After the morning of packing up, she asks Trish if she can arrange a courier to take her stuff home later that evening. "Absolutely." They hug. Trish has already agreed not to say anything for a couple of days about her leaving and Grayson. She isn't ready for goodbyes quite yet.

Kinsey texts Sam, "Can you meet me in the park outside your building at three?"

"Yes," is his immediate response.

Next, she heads straight for the Apple store and gets a new phone number. She deletes every social media account she has. After that, she arrives at Sal's cafe. Diane is already there waiting for her. She has a cup of coffee she is stirring. Kinsey doesn't feel like drinking anything but orders her usual anyway to have something to hold during this conversation.

Settling in the chair across from Diane feels like she is facing off with a lifetime nemesis. She feels bad for her. Kinsey hadn't wanted her to ever find out yet here they are.

"Thank you for meeting me," Kinsey says. Diane is silent, only a manicured raised eyebrow is her response. "I've known Sam for a long time," Kinsey begins.

"I've known him longer," Diane's voice is frosty.

"I get that."

"Did you know he had a live-in girlfriend all those years ago?"

Kinsey is ashamed, her face flushing, her eyes dropping to her tea, "I did."

"It didn't stop you from flirting with him though, did it?" Kinsey shakes her head. "I knew about you. When you called and I answered I knew you were the one." Diane confesses.

Shocked, Kinsey's eyes meet the other woman's only to dart away quickly. "Nothing had even happened with us."

"Yet," the other woman fills in for her. "He had already changed so I knew something was up."

"I love him."

"How convenient for you. I love him too. So where does that leave us?"

"I wanted to let you know that I won't be a problem going forward."

Her brow furrows, "I think it's a little late for that don't you think?"

"I didn't want any of this to happen."

"Well, it has, and you've made quite a mess of things. You've clearly won," Diane tells her.

"I don't think destroying two marriages is a win."

She shrugs and takes a sip of her coffee. "We all had a hand in it. I took the win when I was handed it all those years ago."

Dread starts to creep in, "What do you mean?"

"I conceived on purpose." It's as much of the truth as Diane is willing to part with at the moment.

Why is this woman giving her ammunition? "You had no right! He had chosen me!" Kinsey hisses at her.

"You had no right!" Diane yells back her fist hitting the table causing Kinsey to jump in response. The woman isn't wrong, Kinsey had known he was in a relationship, and she had pursued him aggressively. The effect Diane's next words have on Kinsey is as harsh as if she had slapped her. "We were engaged."

"You were engaged?" Kinsey whispers.

"Yes." Diane lies.

"I had no idea."

Diane hides her smug grin as she takes another sip of coffee. "How could you?" Diane asks not helpfully.

"I'm sorry for everything. All of it. Then and now."

"Your apology is useless to me. You know you aren't even that pretty." Kinsey smiles at the other woman. It's clearly meant to hurt her because she is hurting. Diane is a classic beauty while Kinsey is more the girl next door, subtle. Also, Diane clearly knows her husband believes Kinsey is beautiful, so the insult doesn't land. "What am I going to tell my daughters?" Diane asks when she doesn't get a rise out of the other woman.

"Nothing. You don't have to tell them anything. I'm bowing out. I'm leaving. Please don't make this worse than it has to be."

"Do your boys know?" Diane asks and her blood runs cold.

"Don't," Kinsey begs.

"Why? Don't you think they should know what kind of person their mother is?"

"What about your daughters?"

"What about them?"

"Did you tell your oldest she was a bargaining chip used to keep her dad tied to you for life when he had wanted to leave you?" The look on her face says it all, "I didn't think so. Listen, I've apologized. You can either take it or leave it. I really don't care but I've said my peace and now if you don't have anything to add I'll be on my way." Kinsey stands up from the table.

"You may go," Diane dismisses her like she is one of her employees. Kinsey walks out of the coffee shop and throws away her five-dollar tea untouched.

The next stop is the real estate office. She puts her home up for sale and schedules an appointment with a moving company and the photographer so they can get it on the market ASAP.

Now the hard part. The part she has been dreading all day. She meets Sam in the park. She had wanted to get there first but as usual, he is waiting for her. Sam rushes to her. "What's the matter?" he asks the second he sees her. It's been an emotional 24 hours since she last saw him. She backs away, with her arms up in defense, as he tries to take her in his arms. "Kinsey you're scaring me. What happened last night? Did you tell Grayson? You should have called me."

"I can't do this anymore."

"Yes, you can," he tells her.

"I've already made up my mind. There is nothing you can do or say that will change how I feel. I only ask you to give me the same courtesy I gave you when you finally told me it was over and move on."

Sam staggers backward, "Wow. Are you going to play it like that? That's not fair and you know it. We were kids then. I was young, stupid, and impressionable. Don't compare what we have now to what we had then. It's different and you know it. I love you, Kinsey."

She desperately wants to repeat those words back to him, so she is biting her tongue inside her mouth to stop herself. "Please don't contact me or my family."

"You are a coward, Kinsey."

"Takes one to know one Sam." She turns and walks away.

"Kinsey wait!" Sam shouts jogging to catch up with her. She doesn't stop so he walks next to her. "Can you just please tell me why?"

"I chose him. It's as simple as that. Please don't make this harder than it already is." He stops walking and as much as it kills her to do so, she keeps a steady clip until he is out of sight.

Chapter Forty-Three

♥

    Kinsey is walking down the stairs when Grayson walks through the front door. She is halfway down, and he is in the middle of the hallway, his bag at the door. They stop and stare at each other. Each tries to figure out what the other has to say. Grayson has dark circles under his eyes, and he looks ashen. "Well?" his voice croaks and he clears his throat.

    She knows what he is asking, "I choose you."

    A noise neither recognizes escapes his lips, "I thought I had lost you."

    This breaks her heart, "You could never lose me. You're my person." He rushes to her she meets him her arms wrapping around his neck, his arms winding around her back crushing her to him. He was the one that had picked up the pieces all those years ago. He has loved her and no one else. He has been an amazing husband and an incredible father. Last night when she had been tossing and turning, she had thought of all their moments. Meeting him in a bar, his pilot's uniform, him carrying her home that first night in the snow, him showing up unexpectedly at her door, the first time they had made love. The proposal, the wedding, their honeymoon in the Maldives islands, the christening of their home the day they bought it, his unwavering strength through IVF treatments, and the birth of their miracle boys. He has been there through it all, never wavering, strong and steady, his love for her deep. Grayson is her reality while Sam was her fantasy. The problem with fantasies is that you wake up to find they aren't real.

"I thought I had lost you," Grayson whispers again. The pain she feels inside her chest is overwhelming. She knows she has to tread lightly any wrong comment or gesture can be misconstrued.

"Never," she lies. He will never know how close he came to losing her, but maybe he does realize and that is why he was so scared of her decision. Instead of more words, she kisses him. They haven't made love since the night he had watched her with Sam. Grayson is her person. The kiss deepens and he starts tugging on her clothes and she follows suit. They don't make it past the stairs, half their clothes still on as their bodies join together. When they had christened the house and even over the years never had they made love on the stairs. It was something they made fun of in the movies now it was the most urgent need for both of them.

The stair tread is digging into her back but rather than move she runs her hand over his cropped hair, the familiar sensation of the tiny hairs tickling her palm makes her smile. He is still inside her. "The boys will be home soon. I think we should order pizza tonight. What do you think?"

He is kissing her collarbone, and he murmurs, "Hmm" They collect themselves and their clothes and go upstairs.

In their bathroom, in their post-coital cleanup, she tells him, "I have a plan. I've made several decisions and I'm not sure how you are going to take them."

"Okay…" he says hesitantly.

"I quit my job today."

"What? Why?"

"Hear me out. I'm also putting the house on the market." He starts to interrupt, and she holds her hand up. "We are going to sell the house and move to San Diego so you can be closer to your family. The weather is better out there. You don't want another New York winter. We can transfer your records. Dad has already made a call and has a new oncologist lined up for you. The boys aren't going to be happy about leaving their friends, but I think it is best for all of us." He is quiet as she finishes her update. "What do you think?"

"It's a lot to take in."

"I know. I didn't sleep last night."

"Me either." She runs her fingers over his hair she can tell.

"Have you thought about how we are going to break the news to the boys?"

"That's all I can think about."

As if on cue they hear the front door open and slam behind the kids. "Showtime," she says without much enthusiasm.

"Let's eat before telling them anything," Grayson suggests.

Kinsey is nodding, "Good idea. I don't think anyone will be in the mood to eat after the news."

"I'm sorry," he says.

Kinsey cocks her head to the side, "For what? For being sick? Yeah, how dare you." Grayson laughs and she smiles sadly at him.

"It's not going to get any easier the longer we stay up here."

"Are you sure?" she asks hopefully.

"Pretty sure I'm afraid."

She sighs dramatically making him smile again. He holds his hand out to her and she takes it like a lifeline. They walk downstairs and smile at the spot on the stairs they just were. As if sensing her thoughts Grayson looks at her and wiggles his eyebrows.

"Hey, Dad," Aidan calls out.

"Hi, Aidan. How was school today?"

"Stupid," Aidan allows.

Grayson smiles as Ethan enters the hallway, "How was practice?"

"Coach sucks, he made us run extra laps because some kids weren't paying attention to the drills."

Kinsey releases Grayson's hand as she hugs both boys in greeting. "We were thinking of pizza for dinner tonight. What do you guys think?"

"Yes, please," Ethan says.

"Can we get the bacon cheeseburger pizza?" Aidan asks.

"Of course. Ethan, do you want the white pizza with chicken and broccoli?"

"Yeah, thanks."

"Why don't you boys go clean up?" Grayson suggests. They run up the stairs racing for the bathroom.

After the pizza is scarfed down and paper plates are thrown away Grayson asks for them to join him in the living room. Kinsey wants to throw up. She is not ready for this news, and she envies the boys at this very moment in their ignorance. Kinsey will not want to be in their shoes in a minute when their world will be shattered.

"What's going on?" Ethan is already starting to sound cautious.

"Please have a seat," Grayson directs them to the couch. The boys sit side by side. Instead of sitting in the chairs across from them, Grayson sits on the coffee table facing them. She watches as the boys exchange a look. Their twin sense is kicking in.

Kinsey sits down next to Grayson facing the boys. "Your mom and I have some stuff to talk to you about."

"This sounds serious," Aidan is frowning. Grayson takes a deep breath.

"Are you getting a divorce?" Ethan asks.

This takes them both by surprise, "What? No," they answer in unison as they exchange a look of their own.

"I'm sick," Grayson dives in before any more guesses can be thrown their way. "I have stage four pancreatic cancer. The prognosis isn't good." Tears start to well up in Kinsey's eyes as he breaks the news a little gentler than he had with her but really there is no good way to tell people you are dying.

Aidan leans forward and vomits on the carpet at their feet. Ethan jumps up. "I'm sorry," Aidan starts to cry.

Grayson reaches out to his son, "It's okay, don't worry about it." Aidan launches himself into his dad's arms. Ethan is standing awkwardly next to them, and Kinsey jumps up and walks around the coffee table her arms open. Ethan immediately takes her up on her offer of comfort.

The smell of vomit on the floor is overwhelming. "Guys let's take this conversation somewhere else," Kinsey suggests.

Grayson and Aidan stand, "I'm sorry," Aidan murmurs again.

"Sweetie, it's okay," Kinsey tries to reassure him. "I'll clean it up later." He leaves his dad's arms, and she accepts him into her embrace with one arm still holding onto Ethan with the other. Grayson's arms encircle his family unit.

They finally separate and she guides them out of the room. "Let's go to our room," Kinsey suggests. They climb the stairs in silence. Inside their bedroom, the boys crawl into bed with them. They sit cross-legged facing each other.

"When did you find out?" Ethan asks.

Grayson takes a deep breath before answering, "Six months ago."

"What?" Ethan and Aidan's response is explosive.

"Did you know about this?" Ethan demands looking at Kinsey.

Grayson places a hand on Kinsey's knee, "Your mother just found out."

"I don't get it," Aidan is picking at the comforter avoiding eye contact, "Why would you keep this a secret?"

"I'm sorry. I really am. I thought maybe I could beat it on my own. I didn't want our family bubble to burst. I realize now I took something away from you and that is time. Our time is so precious on this Earth." He takes Kinsey's hand, "Your mom and I have decided that we want to spend as much time as we can together, so we are both quitting our jobs and moving to San Diego."

"Hold up!" Aidan shouts, "What about our friends? We have a life here! We are in the middle of our soccer season. We could go to the state championship this year and you want us to miss it?"

"I know it's a big ask," Kinsey chimes in for the first time, "but New York winters are tough and it's going to be hard on your dad. I thought-"

"We thought," Grayson interjects.

She turns to smile at him, and he squeezes her hand in solidarity, "We thought it would be best for your dad to be around his family as well. We are going to sell the house."

"We can't even keep the house? This is bullshit!" Ethan explodes.

"You're right this is bullshit. This whole thing is bullshit. I agree. None of this should be happening, but it is. We never expected your dad to be dying at this stage in his life or yours."

"You're dying?!" Aidan shouts. "You said you were sick. You have cancer, people get cancer, but they have chemo or some shit. Then they get better. You never said you were dying."

Ethan looks at his brother, concern etched on his face, as he sees the pain he feels on his twin's face. "Yes, I'm dying. Pancreatic cancer is aggressive and I'm already in stage four. Most patients don't live five years." Grayson is speaking but Kinsey is watching tears stream down her boy's cheeks, and it breaks her. She knows what it is like to grow up without one parent.

"So, you might be around for our graduation?" Ethan asks.

"I'm hoping to make it to Christmas," Grayson says truthfully.

"Merry fucking Christmas to us," Aidan says. Neither parent say a word about his foul language, it is justified in this case.

"Let's make a list!" Kinsey claps her hands together.

Ethan frowns, "What are you going grocery shopping?"

Kinsey jumps off the bed and opens her nightstand pulling out a pad of paper and pen before getting back in bed. "No, let's make a list of all the things we want to do together."

"Never have pizza again," Aidan says.

"Okay, no more pizza," Kinsey puts it at the top of the list.

"I want to drive the coast," Grayson says. "I'm from California and I've never done it."

"Perfect," Kinsey adds to the list.

"Can we go see an NFL game?" Ethan asks.

"Good one," Aidan approves of his brother's pick.

"Yes," Kinsey adds it to the list. "How about game night once a week?" They all grumble but don't tell her not to add it to the list, so she does.

"Aidan, what about you?" Grayson asks.

He is tapping his finger to his chin deep in thought, "How about swimming with sharks?"

"No," Kinsey says but is immediately vetoed by Grayson and Ethan.

"Hell yeah," Grayson says and high-fives his son across the bed. For the first time since breaking the news he smiles.

"We are doing that first," Ethan says, "You should move that to the top of the list."

Kinsey is relieved that this plan of action is helping. They continue to add things to the list and circle around the conversation about Grayson's illness. They tuck the boys in that night something they haven't done since they were little.

Meeting back in the bedroom they are emotionally and physically exhausted. It's past eleven. The boys never got around to doing their homework. When she had suggested they stay home from school the following day they had both refused wanting to say goodbye to their friends.

They get into their pajamas and crawl into bed. Kinsey scoots to his side of the bed to rest her head on his chest. His arms encircle her, and she listens to his heartbeat and more tears come as she realizes that one day his heart will stop, and he won't be here for her to hold anymore.

"I'm sorry," Kinsey whispers scrunching his t-shirt in her hands. "I'm sorry for bringing Sam into our lives." Grayson tenses beneath her.

"Don't ever mention him again," he says stiffly. "I forgive you because I'm partially to blame for even suggesting it, but I don't want to waste another breath talking about him. Just to be clear I'm devastated and hurt over what you did but, given the circumstances I want to move on with what time we have left together and have it just be the two of us." Her heart constricts in her chest as she remembers removing her wedding band when Sam had wanted it to be just the two of them.

"Well, if it wasn't for Trish none of this would be happening either." The second the words are out of her mouth she wishes she can take them back.

Moving up on his elbow he looks down at her. "What do you mean? Does Trish know what we did? Why would you tell her that?"

Kinsey bites her bottom lip, "You know I wasn't fully on board with the idea, and I was stressed about it, so she asked. She is my best friend!" Kinsey's voice is rising in self-defense but realizes it and lowers it as she continues, "She is the one that suggested I pick someone I had been with before to make it easier. Trust me I didn't want to do that either, but I also didn't want to pick up a random stranger. So, like I said I'm sorry it was a stupid idea."

Grayson grins down at her, frowning she asks, "What?"

He laughs, "I'm actually a little relieved."

"Why?" she asks still confused.

"I thought that you might have been in touch before this and been having an affair the whole time or at least immediately thought of him as your go-to. I know it's stupid, but it makes me feel a little better knowing it was Trish's idea. Remind me not to send them a Christmas card this year." Kinsey relaxes. "Let's drop it now," Grayson suggests.

"Deal," Kinsey rolls over and he spoons her from behind. She must leave Sam behind for good this time.

The next day the photographer comes to take photos for the real estate company. The house goes on the market that evening. Kinsey calls a moving company, and they move out that weekend having one last brunch with her dad on Sunday morning. Pierce drives them to the airport afterward.

"Call me anytime day or night," Pierce tells his daughter as he hugs her fiercely on the curb of JFK terminal drop-off.

"I will. Thank you, Dad, for everything."

Pierce hugs the boys and Grayson. They have a direct flight and Grayson's parents pick them up from the airport. They haven't broken the news to them yet. His parents think they are on an impromptu visit. They have plans to tell the whole family tonight at dinner.

Chapter Forty-Four

♥

On Monday they enroll the kids in school. They still want them to have some semblance of normalcy. The boys talk to the team's soccer coach, and he invites them to practice to see if they will make the squad and they are both happy when they do.

Grayson and Kinsey unpack personal items but put the rest of the furniture into storage. A week after settling in, Kinsey makes a phone call to find out about swimming with sharks. She has it booked for this weekend before hanging up the phone. "Okay, we are all set," she tells Grayson when she gets off the phone.

He looks up from the lounge chair he is relaxing in. Grayson had treatment this morning and is recovering on the back deck. They have a scan scheduled next month to let them know if any of the cancer is shrinking. "What are we all set on?"

"Swimming with sharks," she says cheerfully.

He sits up straighter in his chair. "Seriously? We are doing it?"

Kinsey sits in the chair next to him. "Yes. I said we would, so we are doing it."

He smiles, "Good. I'm glad." Grayson reaches for her hand, and she takes it. The air is warm with a slight breeze, and they watch the waves crashing on the shore.

That weekend they have a great time, and she makes sure to capture the moments with her phone. As much griping as the guys gave her for a game night it becomes one of the household's favorite days of the week. She buys a new game each week. Her family is super competitive, and games become intense. They laugh and joke and smack talk each other. It's the rare occasion when cancer isn't as present in their lives.

Kinsey books seats for the San Francisco 49ers including a hotel room for the weekend. They fly up on Friday night after practice and go out to a fancy restaurant. On Saturday they go on a tour of the famous prison Alcatraz followed by lunch at a bistro then a trolley tour of the city. The next day is the game and Kinsey has scored seats close to the 50-yard line. "How did you manage this?" Grayson leans in to ask.

She pats him on the hand, "Money, lots of money." The 49ers win the game in overtime. They spend another night in the city and fly back Monday morning after breakfast in the hotel lobby.

Grayson and Kinsey attend every soccer game and cheer the boys on. Kinsey has bought a camcorder and records every game. She has started to capture other smaller moments at home. Grayson starts doing a lot of writing. "What are you up to?" She asks one day.

"You'll see," he says as he folds the paper and seals it in an envelope. He places it in his bottom right drawer. She has a sad feeling she knows now what his letters are. A way to say a final goodbye beyond the grave. Kinsey walks to him at his desk and kisses the top of his head. He wraps his arms around her waist, and she holds him tight.

At Thanksgiving, they are given a miracle. The scans come back clean. He is in remission, thank God. They celebrate, her dad flies out and Grayson's whole family comes for the holiday meal. Spirits are high as everyone rejoices in the news. This reprieve from death. When they go around the table to give thanks, Grayson is at the top of everyone's list.

Aidan brings his new girlfriend to dinner with the promise to go to her parent's house for dessert. Their nieces have also brought along significant others and the boys all retire to the living room for more football.

Kinsey is in the kitchen with her mother and sisters in laws cleaning up. "He looks good," Rosemary leans over as she dries a pan. Kinsey looks into the living room Grayson is standing behind the couch talking to his brother-in-law, and she smiles.

"He really does," Kinsey agrees.

They continue with their weekly game nights and still try to live every moment to the fullest. Christmas is magical. Christmas Eve is spent with the whole family at Rosemary's house. Christmas day is just for the four of them. They spend the entire day together which has a feeling of being special. She has a rule this year that they need to make one present that they give to each other. She makes hot chocolate for everyone, spiking hers and Grayson's, and turns on Christmas music in the background while they open presents. They sit around and tell stories about when the kids were little. Grayson tells a few stories from his childhood she has never heard before. They take a stroll on the beach after dinner. Grayson and Kinsey hold hands as the boys run ahead picking up shells and launching them back into the ocean.

"I love you," he tells her.

"I love you too, Grayson." He stops her in her tracks like he had done so long ago on the streets of New York when they were going to the bodega to get movie snacks. Her hand goes to his chest and his lips lean down to capture hers.

"Ewww," the boys say. Laughing they pull apart.

"Just wait until you find the love of your life and tell me how gross it is," Grayson tells them, and she grins up at him. He winks down at her and her heart melts. He is her person.

Two nights later Grayson jumps from the bed running to the bathroom. Kinsey's heart begins to pound, as she throws the covers off and follows him. The door is ajar, and she can hear him retching before she gets there. Opening the door, she stands there, dread creeping deep down her spine. The look he gives her when he is done, his eyes meeting hers, is panic.

"No!" she whispers. "No," she says again before joining him on the floor. They cling to each other. "Are you having any other symptoms?" She asks, fearful of the answer.

"My back has been tight the last couple of days, but I didn't want to say anything," he confesses.

"Grayson," she admonishes, "I'll call the doctor right now." She tries standing and he pulls her back down.

"Let's wait until morning." Grayson kisses the top of her head, "Things aren't going to change that drastically from now until then. Let's try and get some sleep." He flushes the toilet and washes his mouth out with water from the sink before ushering her back to bed. They lay in each other's arms neither one sleeping worried about what the morning will bring.

She calls the doctor the second they open that morning and gets him in immediately for scans. Kinsey drives him to the hospital before the boys are even out of bed. When they get home she says, "Go wake the boys."

"Are you going to tell them?" he asks.

"Nope. We are going on a road trip. It's Christmas vacation, and we haven't done your drive up the coast. I think now is a perfect time." She doesn't add that it's the last thing on their bucket list and this may be their only opportunity for a while to complete it. Grayson understands this and without a word goes to wake the twins.

They hop in the SUV and Grayson drives. She has packed snacks and drinks and some games for the road along with the camcorder. She films him driving and the boys have fallen back asleep in the backseat mouths hanging open.

The drive is breathtaking. The boys wake up around lunchtime and they stop at a roadside diner. "Let's make it interesting," Kinsey says. The boys stop eating to listen to her game plan. "We should come up with a point system for any wildlife we may see on this trip. Obviously, the more exotic an animal is the more it's worth."

"You're on," Aidan says.

Ethan grins, "You're going down," he tells his brother with all the confidence in the world.

"You both might want to take a backseat because your old man fully intends on winning."

"Why don't we put a wager on it?" Kinsey suggests.

"I want a PlayStation," Ethan declares.

"Whoa!" Grayson says, "That's a serious prize. Hmmm," he ponders. "I think I would like to go skydiving with the family if I win."

"I'm out," Kinsey says.

"I want your car," Aidan says.

Grayson laughs, "Mom's SUV?"

"Hey now. No one is taking my vehicle," Kinsey chimes in.

"No, I want dad's convertible," Aidan says confidently. Grayson has an old muscle car he had bought to restore but it never happened. It was sitting in the garage under a dusty tarp.

"Oh, shit!" Ethan laughs at his brother's absurd request. "I thought my request was ridiculous."

"Deal," Grayson says and shakes first Aidan and then Ethan's hand. Both boys' mouths are hanging open in surprise. A grin starts to spread across their face before they are rocking in the booth seat and high-fiving each other. That isn't enough for their merriment, so they start hugging and clapping themselves on the back. Grayson and Kinsey share a look and a sad smile, luckily the boys don't witness the exchange.

That night they pull over to watch the sunset. The boys are running around on the beach. Grayson and Kinsey are sitting above them in the sand dunes. Grayson's phone starts to ring. Pulling it out he looks at it. It's the hospital. She sees the number over his shoulder, and he puts the phone back into his pocket. They are calling the same day with the results. They both realize what this means but if they don't answer they can stay in their protective bubble a while longer.

They spend the rest of the week enjoying the views of the coastline before returning for New Year's Eve. The boys have asked to go to a friend's party, and they agree to let them go. They know this will be the last bit of fun they will have for a while.

Scans come back and it's not good. Grayson takes a turn for the worst and ends up in the hospital. After a week he asks to go home. They send him home on hospice putting a hospital bed in their bedroom. At night she wheels him closer to her and lowers him so she can reach in between the slats just to touch him, his hand, or arm.

Three days later the nurse tells her it's time for everyone to say their final goodbyes. Kinsey calls his family and they all come to stay the day. Rosemary and Fred spend the night in the guest bedroom. The nurse orders the pain meds that will take the pain away but they also know this is the end.

Grayson dies shortly after midnight surrounded by his family. Her dad comes out for a couple of weeks. Trish flies out with Tom for the services. Kinsey and the boys continue to live in San Diego. At the reading of the will, letters Grayson had written, are passed around to everyone. Kinsey inherits everything except a PlayStation he had bought for Ethan, and the keys to his convertible are handed over to Aidan with five thousand dollars to help with the restoration project.

At home when Kinsey retreats to her bedroom and opens her letter it is blank inside. Did he have nothing to say to her? Had he never really forgiven her for what she had done? It eats at her.

Kinsey and the boys start seeing a therapist. Aidan starts having anxiety attacks. Covid hits making it worse. All of them are quarantined inside and the boys are remote learning. After about six months she decides to try and get a remote job. She does and it helps take her mind off things.

Rosemary comes to see her one day they are out on the back deck drinking wine. "How are you holding up?" she asks.

"Could be better, could be worse," is Kinsey's customary response.

Rosemary smiles sadly, "I hear you."

"How are the boys?"

Kinsey sighs, "They are back in school so that's helping."

Rosemary nods, "Good. Good." She takes a drink as she stares out at the waves.

"What are you not saying?" Kinsey asks her. In the past year and a half, she has gotten to know her mother-in-law much better.

Smiling Rosemary turns to face her, "Fred and I were talking…about you…"

"Were you now?"

"And we both thought that maybe…"

"Spit it out, Rosemary."

"If you want to take your wedding ring off, you can. If you want to date, you have our blessing-not that you need it. Mind you."

Kinsey starts playing with her engagement ring twirling around her finger. "It's only been a year…"

"It's been over a year and if you aren't ready, you aren't ready and that's perfectly fine. We just wanted to let you know that we don't want you to worry about us or what we think. I also think Grayson would have wanted you to move on eventually and not be alone forever."

Tears sting Kinsey's eyes as Rosemary hits the nail on the head. Grayson didn't want her to be alone. Forever looking after her. "I'm not ready," Kinsey whispers.

Rosemary puts her glass down and holds her arms out to her, "I'm sorry sweetie. I didn't mean to upset you," Kinsey stretches out next to her and takes her hug. Rosemary really has been filling the mother's void in her life. Rosemary rubs her hair soothing her. "You take as much time as you need."

Chapter Forty-Five

♥

During the boys' senior year. Ethan approaches Kinsey, Aidan by his side. "Mom, we need to talk."

Her heart immediately feels like it's in her throat. "Is everything okay?"

"It's great," Aidan tells her.

"We got our college acceptance letters today."

She grins, "You did? That's great."

Ethan hands her the paper. Looking it over she sees, "Congratulations you've been accepted for the fall semester…" Her eyes flick up to the letterhead when she realizes why the boys are so nervous to tell her. New York University. "You guys applied to NYU? When? Are you planning on going? Why wouldn't you tell me?" She stops to take a breath.

Aidan laughs, "Yeah mom we want to go. We didn't know if we would get in and we didn't want to worry you if it wasn't an option, but we both really want to go. We miss New York and our friends and grandpa and it's your alma mater." It's the school she was attending when she met Sam, her heart constricts.

"We want to take a road trip to get there too. We are finished with dad's car. That's what we plan on driving," Ethan adds. Even though Aidan had "won" the car he had asked his brother if he would help him restore it. Ethan had readily agreed, spending hours at a time in the garage.

"What? No way."

"Mommm," Aidan whines. "We are adults now. You can't stop us." Kinsey folds her arms across her chest frowning at her boys ganging up on her.

Ethan puts his hand on Aidan's chest pushing him gently aside, "You could absolutely stop us, but we would really like to do this. It will be a good bonding experience for us."

She feels herself softening and the boys can sense it too. "I don't like it."

Aidan grins sensing her wavering, "We will text you every night."

"You will call me every night and text me several times a day and send me proof of life photos."

"Thank you, mom," Ethan says.

"Deal!" Aidan agrees and they wrap her up in a hug.

Kinsey goes overboard shopping for the boys' dorm room. She ships everything to her dad's apartment. He calls her a week later, "I think you have a problem."

"I know! I can't stop," she laughs, and he joins her.

Chapter Forty-Six

♥

Kinsey flies out in October to visit Aidan and Ethan during parent weekend and decides to stay for a week. The campus organizes a bunch of events for parents and students. During the week she visits her dad, and they plan a lunch date with the boys Friday afternoon after their classes. Kinsey is walking toward the large circular water fountain on NYU's college campus. The air is crisp, the leaves are turning vibrant shades of red and orange with a smattering of yellow thrown in for good measure. The sun is shining but not adding any warmth.

She sees a man walking toward her. There are several people around, but her eyes are fixated on him. He doesn't see her, not yet. Her heart rate increases and her palms are instantly sweaty. Kinsey had wondered if they would see each other again. What it would be like.

He spots her, stopping dead in his tracks. This makes her smile, now he is smiling. The magnet turns back on. They speed up, he starts jogging. They are running as they crash into each other. Their arms wrap around one another, and they stand there taking in the feeling of being in each other's arms again. It's like they never left. Except they have, time and time again. Grandfather time never on their side.

Kinsey is afraid to let go as if he might disappear. Sam must be feeling the same because he is also reluctant to pull back. He doesn't remove his arms but searches her face. "You're here," he whispers as if he has had this moment before and been disappointed by an illusion.

Kinsey grins at him, "I am."

He finally pulls back letting her go, "Let's go to lunch. Catch up?"

"I can't I have plans right now."

"Tonight?"

"I'd love to."

"Great-" he is interrupted by her phone ringing in her pocketbook.

Looking at it she sees Aidan's name on her screen, "I'm sorry. Do you mind?"

"Not at all."

"Hello?"

"Hi, mom. Where are you? We are here already."

"I'm coming. I'm almost there."

"Okay, love you."

"Bye, I love you too." She is watching him as she hangs up and she can see the guarded look on his face at her words. Wanting to put him at ease she tells him, "That was Aidan. I'm meeting them for lunch with my dad." She watches as the light enters his eyes and his shoulders relax. "Here," she holds her hand out to him, "Give me your phone so I can give you, my number. You can text me the time and address of the restaurant and I'll meet you there."

He digs his phone out of his pocket and hands it to her. The phone wakes up and she sees a picture of him and his daughters. The phone is locked. Kinsey holds it back out to him. "Do you want to put in your password?"

"The number is 083198," Sam says. She plugs in the number and the screen opens. The number he said to her is repeated in her head. 08. August. 31. 31st. 98. 1998.

"Your passcode is the day we met?"

"It was a memorable day." She smiles up at him. He hadn't forgotten her. "How could I forget?" He answers her even though she hadn't asked the question. "When did you get a new number?"

"The day I told you it was over," he is already nodding his head as if that is what he had been suspecting all along.

"That would explain why you never answered any of my calls or texts."

"You texted me?" she asks but she knows it's true which is why she had gone to such great lengths to distance herself from him.

"You don't think I would let you go a second time without a fight, did you?" The love she sees in his eyes is overwhelming. Kinsey fights back the tears trying to regain her composure she looks back down at his phone, finds his contacts, and puts her information in.

"I'll see you tonight." She tells him.

"Can't wait," his fingers brush hers as they exchange the phone.

Kinsey isn't aware if her feet even touch the ground as she makes her way to her lunch obligation. She hears none of the conversations around her as her boys talk with their grandfather telling him all about NYU and the roommates, parties, and classes they are taking. She does take in their enthusiasm and is happy they are finally getting closer to normal. Since losing their dad it has been tough on all of them.

The boys being back home and seeming like their old self makes her feel a sense of guilt. Kinsey stands by the decision she made three years ago. She can't help but think about her future, will Sam be in it?

Sam texts her as if on cue, telling her to meet him at seven and the name of the restaurant, nothing more nothing less. She looks up the restaurant it's in NoHo a small intimate Italian/Spanish restaurant.

After lunch, with her dad and the boys, she goes shopping. Nothing she has packed for this trip will do for her date with Sam tonight. She is nervous. Was he wearing a wedding band? She hadn't looked. Why hadn't she looked? Did he notice she no longer wore her wedding band and engagement ring? She didn't think so. What did this mean? Will this be a real date? Is he still married? Is she willing to walk away if he is? Will she fight for him? What if he tells her he chooses his wife? What if he will continue to have an affair with her but does not leave his wife? Would she be willing to do that? Does she want to be that person? What if that is the only way to have him? She groans in frustration at the thoughts racing through her brain when a saleswoman asks her if there is anything she can help her with.

"I need a dress that says..." she stalls on the words… "everything."

The woman smiles. "Got it."

Kinsey tries on everything the woman brings her and they are all perfect. Each one is more stunning than the one before. The perfect "little black dress" with one arm and shoulder bare, the other covered, fitted with an uneven hem. A red lace one is next. Followed by a burnt orange one she would have never picked off the rack, but it looks fantastic on her body and with her dark coloring. The saleswoman is reading her expression as she comes out. "I'm not sure these are what you are looking for. Can I just try something?

"Of course," Kinsey returns to the dressing room and removes the dress. There is a knock on the door. Opening it a crack she takes the pile of clothes including shoes into the room. The woman has picked out a cream-colored sweater dress. Kinsey slips it on. It's cozy and hugs her body in all the right places. There is a soft leather jacket in pale pink. The zippers are gold with a belt hanging loose on the back and sides. Animal print booties she slips on. Looking in the mirror she likes what she sees. Walking out of the room the woman is giving her an appraising look.

Turning around she goes to a couple of racks and returns with gold dangly earrings and a long gold chain to add to the outfit. Kinsey puts them on. The woman takes a caramel bag off the rack and hands it to her. Kinsey puts it on her shoulder and turns to the mirror. The outfit is perfect. It doesn't scream that she is trying too hard which the other dresses clearly were. "I'll take it all."

"Perfect. Whenever you are ready, I'll take you at the register."

Kinsey gets a manicure and pedicure going with a desert taupe. She can get in for a last-minute hair appointment for a shampoo and style. The woman blow-dries and curls her hair. She twirls two locks, from her temple and bobby pins them to the back of her head leaving the rest flowing but it's just enough out of the way for her earrings to be noticed. When she finds out the salon also does makeup, she shows them her outfit and they give her a natural glow with pinks and a smoky brown for her eyelids.

At her dad's house, she gets into her outfit. Pierce gives a low whistle when she walks into the living room. "Going out tonight?"

"I am."

"Do you plan on coming home tonight?"

"Dad!" She is shocked that her dad is so observant. She gives him a kiss on the cheek, telling him, "Don't wait up."

He grins at her. "I'll see you tomorrow?" He isn't stating a fact only asking her if she will be home by then.

"I'll call you," she allows.

"Don't do anything I wouldn't do." He calls after her.

"Can't make any promises. Goodnight, Dad." She walks out the door with a huge smile on her face. She gets a ride there. The car pulls up to the restaurant. There are multiple tables outside and awnings that come out to offer protection from the elements. The door is open wide, and servers are busy hustling and bustling through with platters of food.

Kinsey squeezes past people and into the restaurant. The room is cozy inside. A bar is on the right and wooden tables with mismatched chairs are filled with patrons. On the left is a bookcase filled with bowls of all different shapes and colors. The wooden wide-planked floors look original to the building.

The hostess greets her, "Do you have a reservation with us today?"

"Yes. It's under Anderson," Sam is suddenly behind her his hand resting on the small of her back.

"Oh, hi," Kinsey greets him her head turning to the side.

"Sorry, I'm late," he apologizes. "Have you been here long?"

"I just got here, and you aren't late."

"Your table is ready," the hostess announces.

"Great," Kinsey tells her and follows her to another room where wine bottles are everywhere the ceiling and the walls. A brick wall with three arches and wrought iron gates lines a portion of the wall on one side.

Their table is small tucked into the corner with little glass jars housing real candles that make a beautiful glow on the table.

Sam holds out a chair for her and she takes a seat, "Thank you."

"My pleasure." He settles in the seat to her left.

"Your server will be right with you," the hostess informs them.

"Thank you," they say in unison. She notices he isn't wearing a wedding band. Her heart rejoices at the news. She is cautiously optimistic. Did he take it off for this evening?

Sam immediately notices her glance, and he holds his hands up, flipping them on both sides as if to show he isn't hiding it anywhere else. "Divorce has been finalized for a couple of years now."

"I'm sorry to hear that," Kinsey offers him condolences on the end of his marriage.

"I'm not. It was a long time in coming. It should have never happened in the first place. She knew that so she didn't fight me too hard when I asked her for a divorce."

"How are the girls?" Kinsey asks, worried that Diane went through with her plan to tell them about Sam's infidelity.

"Girls are good. Quinn works with her mom. CEO in training. Sadie is a senior at NYU, that's how I ran into you. I had stopped in to say hi. She just went through a bad breakup, and she is having a hard time with it."

"Breakups are the worst," Kinsey agrees. The sadness in Sam's eyes hits her.

"So do you want to tell me why you aren't wearing a wedding band either?" his head nods to her folded fingers on the tabletop.

Their waitress picks that time to arrive. "Hello. My name is Eileen. I will be your server this evening. Have you dined with us before?"

"No this is my first time," Kinsey responds, and Sam is shaking his head no.

"Okay! Well, welcome." She pours them each a glass of iced water, "Can I start you out with some drinks?"

Sam orders them a bottle of wine, and bread with olive oil to dip. "Of course, I'll put that right in for you." She gives them a rundown of the specials before leaving.

Kinsey glances over the menu not ready to talk about Grayson. Sam, understanding also peruses his choices. After making her selection she sets the menu down and Eileen is back with their wine. She opens it at the table and pours them each a glass. "I'll be right back with your bread."

True to her promise she returns with a wooden board, looking like a flight of beer except it has three olive oil decanters, and three small white bowls to pour them into. Each is labeled with the flavor. Once she is gone Kinsey leans forward crossing her arms on the table, "Grayson passed away."

"Kinsey," that one utterance says it all. He is broken for her. Sam reaches across his corner of the table, takes her hand and squeezes. She squeezes back. "I had no idea. I'm so sorry for your loss. You don't have to talk about it if you don't want to."

"It's fine. He was sick when everything went down, he just hadn't told me until he found out about us. I couldn't leave him, not like that. He needed me. The boys needed me."

"I get it. Trust me I do."

"I know you do." He had always put his girls first. "I had to make a clean break with you. I got off social media. Put the house on the market, quit my job, and left it all behind. Including you."

"You definitely disappeared off the face of the Earth."

She laughs letting go of his hand as she continues with her story, "We went to San Diego so we could be near his family. He went into remission at one point, and we thought for maybe a second, that he had beaten the odds. We had a memorable last Christmas but after the New Year, he took a turn for the worst. It happened quickly after that. I was gutted."

"I can imagine," He rubs his hands over his face. "I'm sorry for what I said when we last saw each other."

"Which part?"

"Calling you a coward. You are the bravest person I know."

"I'm sorry too."

"Don't be. I was a coward. I have been for a long time. Diane paid off my student debts before we even started dating."

"What? Who does that?"

"Right? I'm not wrong that's weird. I felt indebted to her. Her parents were both neglectful. Her dad treated her like shit. I felt bad for her, and my hero complex wanted to save her. One day on the golf course her dad told me if I ever left her, I would be sorry. He would destroy any business contact I had ever made."

"Wow," Kinsey is getting a clearer picture of why he had refused to leave Diane.

"I know that is no excuse, but I was a dumb kid and I felt like I was in an impossible situation. I didn't know how to advocate for myself."

"Well at least I have a why now. I can't even tell you how torturous it was for me when we were in college. It was so frustrating."

"Make no mistake about it. I wanted you. More than anyone or anything I've ever wanted in my entire life."

Her hands come up to cup his face drawing him closer as she firmly plants her lips on his. What was supposed to be a quick chaste kiss deepens. He reaches for her across his corner of the table. Realizing they are in a public place they separate both, half out of their chairs. They laugh, returning to their seats.

Their waitress is standing next to the table her pen and pad in hand and a smile on her face, "Are we celebrating a special occasion tonight?"

"Yes, we are," Sam tells her. "Today is the first day of the rest of our lives."

Kinsey's hand presses against her chest over her heart, "Awe," she and the server say in unison. "Dessert is on me," Eileen winks at them.

"Thank you," Kinsey says.

"Are you ready to order? Or would you like a couple of minutes." Kinsey picks up her menu ready to order but Sam says he needs another minute. "No worries, take your time." Eileen walks away.

Sam grins at Kinsey, "I can't see the menu." He pulls out a pair of reading glasses and puts them on. Kinsey grins. "What?" he asks self-consciously.

"I didn't think you could get any cuter."

"I'm glad you think so," he grins at her before returning to his menu, "That's better."

They put their orders in. Kinsey rips a piece of bread off and dips it in the olive oil. Sam takes a drink of wine. He sits back and appraises her as she pops the bread in her mouth smiling and chewing. "What?" she asks after swallowing.

"Do you want to be my girlfriend?"

"Yes. Yes, I do."

Chapter Forty-Seven

♥

Sam takes her to his place. In her mind she pictured the apartment they used to meet at but that isn't where he is living. "I needed a place where the girls could come visit me," he explains as he unlocks the door. Inside he gives her a tour. It's modern no clutter, not a white wall or piece of furniture she can find. Walls worth of floor-to-ceiling windows line the apartment that is set up high in the New York City skyline. Twinkling lights from surrounding buildings cast a romantic glow into the apartment. He turns on soft lighting not overpowering the ambiance outside. He has a terrace, a lovely open space with outdoor furniture, and potted plants.

There are three bedrooms and two bathrooms. His bedroom is tucked in the far corner of the apartment on the opposite side of his girl's bedrooms. This room too has an L-shaped wall of windows. The room has varying shades of grey. A large closet and bathroom are off the room.

"I have something to show you. It's why I was late to the restaurant."

"Oh, please. Being on time is not late."

"Not according to my dad," he lets her know and she smiles. Taking her hand, he leads her back to the living room. "Can I get you a drink? A white wine? A lemon martini? Shots of tequila?"

Kinsey laughs, "A white wine would be lovely. Thank you."

"Have a seat," he gestures to the couch. Sitting he hands her a white box with a red satin bow tied prettily around it. "This is for you."

It is heavy in her lap, "What is this?" she asks curiously.

"Just open it," he urges her. She slips off the bow and removes the top and finds stacks of paper. She begins reading, "Kinsey. Please don't do this. I need you in my life. I will fight for you. I will fight for us. I'm not scared anymore. I don't care what anyone thinks. I love you and I'm willing to prove it." Her fingers run over the text reverently. Sam has printed out all the texts she didn't see over the past three years. Kinsey keeps reading, it's a lot of begging for her to respond. He tells her that he asked Diane for a divorce and how she took it. He talks about work and people he knows. Sam talks about his girls and how mad they are at him. He wishes her a happy birthday. Talks about his divorce. Tells her about the hard days. Tells her he loves her. Asks her to give him another chance. Pages and pages of text are all documented for her to read.

He returns with her wine and sits quietly while she removes her shoes, tucking her feet up underneath her while she reads and drinks. She would have caved she realizes and that would have been devastating for Grayson and the boys. She would have never forgiven herself for not being there in the end.

After an hour of reading, Kinsey is about three-quarters of the way through his text. Sam moves positions to sit next to her on the couch. He stretches her legs out on his lap, and she gets cozy her head nestling against one of the pillows. He pulls a blanket over her.

"Thank you," she murmurs still thoroughly engrossed in the text manuscript. He starts massaging her feet and she glances up at him. "That's amazing." She bites her lower lip.

He leans forward unable to help himself to a kiss. Her arms wind around his neck pulling him closer. Sam's hand slides from her foot down between her thighs. Pages start to slide off her lap landing scattered on the floor. Neither even acknowledge the fact.

"If you're not ready, I understand. I can wait," he pulls away speaking directly to her his hand cupping her chin.

His thoughtfulness is overwhelming. Kinsey's hands hold his face as she searches his eyes. God, she loves that face. She has known that face for over half her life. She wants more than anything else in the world to make love with him right now. Feelings she doesn't understand start to bubble up without her consent. Much to her horror, she begins to cry.

Sam removes his hand immediately from between her thighs. He hugs her tight as she cries. "I'm sorry."

"It's okay. Please you have nothing to apologize for," he wipes her tears off her cheeks as she sniffles.

"I don't know what's gotten into me. I haven't been with anyone since Grayson died."

"You were my last."

"Seriously?"

"Scout's honor."

"That's a long time. Have you dated anyone?"

"I tried. Quinn set me up with someone. She was nice enough. We went out a couple of times, but nothing ever developed." Her eyes narrow she should not be jealous of this other woman, but she is. He laughs, "Trust me. I was waiting for you. I guess you haven't gotten to that part. I tell you all about her."

"Move," she uses her foot to push him away from her and reaches for the scattered pages on the ground. Laughing he helps her pick them up. She grins at him, and he grins back. They are both on their knees on the floor. Reaching for his face she brings his lips to hers. He pulls her closer some of the papers getting crinkled under her.

She can feel his arousal against her thigh, "Let me finish this then I'm all yours," her promise has him scooping up the pages and getting them into neat piles. She laughs and helps him try to get them back in order. She puts the pile aside she has already read and moves to a chair much to Sam's dismay with the remaining pages.

As promised, she reads about his dates with Cheryl. She tries to speed-read through those, but something catches her eye. This one is a long text, and she sees words like sucking and pulsating. He wrote her a sexy text. She swallows hard as she reads the whole thing. Sam describes in detail what he is going to do to her body. She is instantly wet and desperately wants the real deal.

Glancing over at Sam on the couch, she sees he is on his phone scrolling. She puts down the remaining pages and walks to him. Looking up he asks, "All done?"

"Nope." He looks around her to see the pages set aside, "I'm horny." Her hand reaches for him, and he takes it putting his phone down. Kinsey straddles his lap her dress rising on her thighs. "I've gotten to the part where you tell me all the things you are going to do to me and I want that to happen."

Sam brushes her hair, so it is down her back, "You do? Do you?" Kinsey nods fervently. "Hmm, where do I want to start with you?" He is building up her anticipation. "I could kiss you."

"That's always a good place to start."

"Seems kind of obvious," he tells her, and she smiles.

"Right," she plays along, "wouldn't want that."

"I could touch you."

"You could," she allows, "but where?"

He folds his arms bringing one hand to his face his finger tapping on his lips, "That is a very good question. I could start here," his hands cup her breasts, "but I know you like it when I touch you here." He removes his hands from her chest and slides them around cupping her ass.

"I do like that," she agrees.

"I could go for the gold and touch you here," his hands come around to touch the top of her thighs his right hand going under her dress. His whole hand palms her pussy through her panties and she moans rocking her hips toward him. "I feel like I'm in a dream," he confesses.

"If we are, I don't ever want to wake up."

"Agree," his voice is rough with emotion as his fingers push her panties to the side and rub them between her folds. She bites her lower lip and moans. "God Kinsey. Do you know what you do to me?"

"I have a pretty good idea because the feeling is mutual." Her eyes are heavy with passion as he plays with her like she is an instrument meant to be stroked.

Leaning forward she licks his neck inhaling his cologne. "Bite me," he commands, and she does, sinking her teeth into his neck, her hand cupping the opposite side of his neck. The hand on her thigh reaches around cupping her ass again. She starts unbuttoning his shirt as she continues to suck on his neck raking her teeth across his skin. As soon as she has enough buttons removed, she pulls his t-shirt down to bite his collarbone.

"Fuck yeah," he encourages her. He is lifting her dress up to her waist and he spanks her.

She kisses him hard, and he bites her lower lip tugging on it before sucking and releasing it. She helps him out of his collared shirt and undershirt. Her fingernails rake down his chest. He inhales sharply as she does. She sucks on each of his nipples nibbling on the hard nubs, flicking her tongue over each one.

Sam pulls the dress over her head tossing it to the floor. He stops to admire her body. She flushes with embarrassment but the look on his face tells her that he worships her. So, she sits proudly as his eyes feast on her body. She reaches around unclasping her bra allowing her breasts to be appraised as well. His hands slide up her naked back and he presses his face against her chest reveling in the feel of her warm flesh. Sam sits forward on the couch his back no longer on the cushions. She takes the opportunity to run her hands down his smooth back loving every ripple of muscle her hands come across.

He licks her breast, and she throws her head back in desire. One hand touches her neck sliding down her breastbone and down her abdomen. Kinsey steps off his lap and gets down on her knees in front of him. He starts undoing his belt and she unzips his pants. Underwear and pants are removed, and she pushes them out of the way. Her hands are resting on his thigh as she looks at his erection twitching under her admiration. Bending forward his hand slides into her hair holding it off her face.

Her hand encircles his cock, and she peers up at him. He is watching her. Parting her lips, she takes him inside her mouth, and her gaze locks on his. His body jerks in response. Her mouth bobs up and down on him taking him as deep as possible down her throat. His fingers tighten in her hair applying pressure on her scalp.

Reaching down she slips her hand into her panties and strokes herself while she continues to suck on him. "That's so fucking hot," he tells her. "I'm going to cum soon if you don't stop," he warns her.

"Do you want to be deep inside me instead?"

He is nodding, "Desperately, but like I said if you aren't ready, we don't have to."

Kinsey strips out of her panties and straddles him again, "I think we are beyond that now." She slides him into her as she clutches the back of the couch for dear life. He helps her move on him.

Her tits are bouncing up and down. His arms are crushing her to him but then his thumb is there between their joined bodies, and he is rubbing her sensitive nub causing her to cry out in pleasure.

"Sam!"

"Yes, Kinsey? What can I do for you, my love?"

"Make me cum. I want to cum, I need to cum."

He maneuvers her onto her back bending her knees up to her chest, "I can do that for you baby." He pounds into her so hard repeatedly that she feels herself reaching her climax.

"Yes! Yes! Yes!" she cries out.

"Give it to me," he demands, "Give me your orgasm."

"Take it!" she screams as her body convulses around him, one of the biggest orgasms she has ever experienced wracking her body. She whimpers in the pure pleasure of it, and he grunts in satisfaction.

"Yes baby, yes." He coos for her.

He slows down his rhythm kissing her lips. Her arms circle around his neck bringing him closer his chest now rubbing up against hers. His thrusts are slow and deliberate now. She is making little sex noises. She kisses his jaw before biting it playfully she feels him jerk inside her at the gesture. He repays the favor by biting her neck sending tingles through her whole body. "I'm sorry I'm not going to be able to last long this time. It's been too long, and your body is too damn amazing for me to stop."

"It's okay," she reassures him, "I'm ready whenever you are." He watches her as his pace quicken and she holds his gaze. God, she loves the way he looks at her. He finishes inside her before collapsing on top of her.

She cradles his body he is still inside her. "Mmmmm," she runs her hands over his body still unable to get enough of him. He kisses her slowly and sensually. When he is hovering above her, she says, "Oh God, your face."

He laughs, "What about my face?"

"The way you look at me," she pauses her next words come out slow, "does it for me. Every. Single. Time."

Sam grins, "Really?"

"Oh God, yes. You look at me like I'm the only woman in the world. That anything I say or do is the most fascinating thing you have ever encountered. Like I'm the most beautiful woman you've ever met."

He laughs, "That's a pretty accurate description of how I feel about you. As far as I'm concerned you are the only woman in the world. You were made for me. You take my breath away every time I look into your eyes. Do you know how you look at me?"

Kinsey smiles and shakes her head. "No. Tell me."

"First of all, you look at me like you want to strip me naked and have your way with me."

"Ha!" she laughs but doesn't deny it.

He grins at her then sobers, "You look at me like I'm capable of anything, that I'm the most powerful man in the universe and I want to be that person for you. I've spent most of my adult life wanting to live up to the expectations of a girl I once knew."

"I love that."

"I love you."

"Sam?"

"Yes, my love?"

"You know that I've loved you since we were 21 years old right?"

"I've always suspected. Dreamed. Hoped it was true. Do you love me now?"

"I never stopped loving you."

His lips crash down on hers. "I love you, Kinsey," he says again.

"I love you, Sam."

"I want you to listen to something," He reaches for his phone typing something in. He snuggles in next to her on the couch pulling the blanket, draped over the back of the couch, covering their naked bodies.

"What's that?"

"This song. Do you remember the day you first called me when I had my first real job and you had come home from Europe?" At her nod he continues, "I heard this on the radio on my way home and I felt it in my soul. I went out and bought the CD. I would play it continuously singing it at the top of my lungs."

"What song is it?"

"Listen," he presses play and she instantly knows the tune.

"This is Creed."

"Yes. It's called Higher." He holds his phone out to her, "Read the lyrics. He talks about not wanting to wake up from his dream because he doesn't like the life he has. I felt like you were my dream world and I wanted us to be able to live in it forever."

Could this man get any sweeter? They listen to the song their free hands come together palm to palm and they link fingers. He starts singing the song to her and she feels emotional. She hates that they wasted so many years apart yet at the same time she feels like this was how her life was supposed to go. She wouldn't have her kids and he wouldn't have his. Maybe it was to show them perseverance and, in the end, they are together. She just wants to cherish every moment she has with him. If Grayson's death taught her anything it was to do just that.

The song has ended, and he turns her head towards him, "Hey, did I lose you? You seem deep in thought."

"I don't want to waste another minute."

"I feel the same way. Will you spend the night with me? I know you don't have an overnight bag or anything, but you could borrow one of my shirts. Or sleep naked next to me."

"That sounds perfect. Let me just text my dad and let him know I'm not coming home tonight."

"Oh shit, are you going to be in trouble?"

Kinsey giggles, "We are in our 40s I think I'm past getting in trouble." After she finishes texting her dad, he carries her into the bedroom where they make love again. In the morning she wakes before he does, the sun flooding the room.

She watches him sleep and sighs. She can't believe he is back in her life and as far as she is concerned for good this time. Rolling out of bed she uses his restroom. Going to his dresser she pulls open a drawer and finds a t-shirt. Pulling it on over her head, it hangs down to the tops of her thighs, then goes in search of water.

Opening the refrigerator, she finds bottled water. Taking one out she twists open the cap and takes a drink. Before shutting the door, she assesses what he has in the fridge. It's the cleanest inside of a fridge she has ever seen. There are fresh fruits and vegetables cut up and put in separate containers. Bottles of water are lined up, next to sodas. Orange juice and milk are in the door. There are eggs in a container, and cheese in the drawer. There is leftover Chinese food in a takeout box. She shuts the door and looks around.

Seeing the papers, she had abandoned last night, she smiles. Walking to the chair, she vacated hours before, she picks up the blanket that has fallen to the floor and wraps herself in it. Sitting down she picks up where she had left off. She rereads the sexting part and smiles at the memory of what they did last night.

A half-hour later she is finishing the last text written yesterday. "I just ran into you in the park today. I fear you are just a dream. I missed you so God-damned much. I ache. It's a physical pain of being separated from you. I can't wait to see you tonight. I saw you weren't wearing a wedding band when you took the phone call from your son. I am hopeful you are finally free to be with me like I am to be with you. See you soon, my love."

Sam is behind her pulling her hair from in front of her to down her back. Leaning down he kisses her exposed shoulder. Putting down the paper she stands to face him, the blanket staying on the chair.

"My t-shirt has never looked so good. I think you should keep it." He is shirtless and wearing grey sweatpants low on his hips.

Kinsey puts her arms around his neck leaning up on her tiptoes she kisses him. The shirt rides up her body exposing her bare ass. He takes full advantage as his hands grip her exposed buttocks and pull her closer to him. "You look pretty damn sexy yourself." She runs her hands down his chiseled chest, "I just finished your texts."

"What did you think?" he is nuzzling her neck.

"I loved every single one and if I wouldn't have shut off my phone I would have caved. I wanted to be with you that's not why I left."

He pulls back but keeps her in his arms, "I get it. Grayson was sick."

"He needed me. The boys needed me. I needed to be with him. He was the one that picked up the pieces after I couldn't have you."

"I'm sorry there were pieces of you that needed picking up. I wish I were strong enough to leave all those years ago."

"You can't beat yourself up over should have. We had other lives and loved other people. Now it's our turn to be together, start fresh."

"Move in with me," Sam doesn't pose it as a question but as a soft demand. She searches his eyes. This isn't a rash thought, it's something he has contemplated. He knows what he is asking of her.

"Okay." His grin solidifies her response. He kisses her deeply and she tugs on his waistband. He follows her back to the bedroom never breaking the kiss. They make love again.

Afterward, she is laying down on her stomach her head at the foot of the bed trying to catch her breath. As she brushes her hair out of the way he rolls off her onto his back, their shoulders touching, "Are you sure?" Sam is asking if she really wants to move in with him.

"Now that you mention it..." she teases with a grin.

He leans over and bites her shoulder. She giggles, "Of course, I'm sure. I've been dying to be your girlfriend since the day I met you and now I am. I know it's crazy to just jump right into the deep end with you, but I can't picture our relationship going any other way. There is one problem though..."

Worry etches on his face, "What's that?"

"I have a flight home to San Diego tomorrow night."

"How soon can you come back?"

"I'm not sure. I need to talk to the boys and figure out if we should sell the house or if it is something they want to keep in the family." Sam is nodding his head as she speaks. "I have to pack my things. Possibly get movers or a storage container. It's a lot to think about. I want to know what Rosemary thinks."

"Who is Rosemary?"

"My mother-in-law."

"What is she like?" he asks.

"Rosemary is the best. She has really been there for me and the boys through everything. She told me a couple of years ago that she and her husband discussed it, and they wanted me to move on."

"I'm so glad you had that support."

"Yeah, me too." They talk at length about what it was like for her after Grayson died. Sam listens. She had talked to a therapist, but it wasn't the same as telling Sam. They end up napping wrapped in each other's arms during a lull in the conversation.

Chapter Forty-Eight

♥

Kinsey wakes to find Sam has wrapped them up in a comforter. He is snoring softly next to her. She runs her fingers over his face. He has lines etched on his forehead now he didn't as a young man. She likes them, they give him character. His eyelashes are longer than anyone deserves to have. Smiling she runs her thumb over the same freckle on his lower lip she had all those years ago.

Without opening his eyes, he asks, "Are you about done yet?"

"Never," she whispers.

His eyes open, "You make me so happy."

"The feeling is mutual."

"What do you want to do today?" Sam asks.

"Spend all day in bed?"

"I could get on board with that."

Kinsey's stomach growls under the covers they both look down in that direction and laugh. "I'll see what I can scrounge up in the kitchen and bring it back here," she kisses his nose and hops out of bed.

He is propped up on his elbow his head in his hand, "I will never get tired of the sight of you." Sam promises her.

Kinsey laughs as she saunters out of the bedroom, her head turning over her shoulder as she gives him a look that says "ditto." She is walking naked from his bedroom to the kitchen. She hears a key in the front door moments before it is flung open.

"Shit!" Kinsey dives for the safety of the kitchen island hitting the deck as a young woman stands in horror watching the whole thing.

"Hello?" The young woman asks in confusion.

Kinsey starts laughing at the situation. Peeking over the counter Kinsey says, "I'm so sorry, I didn't realize anyone was coming over."

"I didn't realize anyone else was here. Is my dad home?"

Kinsey rests her head in embarrassment on the countertop, "Quinn?" she guesses.

"Yes, and you are?"

"Kinsey? Is someone here?" They hear Sam call out to her. Both women look towards his bedroom door.

"Sam, please bring me some clothes. Quinn is here."

Sam comes out a minute later, but it seems like an eternity. He is grinning like a fool seeing her hiding naked behind his island. "Hi, sweetie. I didn't know you were stopping by," he addresses Quinn.

Sam is wearing jeans and no shirt. He hands her a t-shirt and a pair of his sweatpants. Quinn looks at her watch, "Dad it's one in the afternoon."

Sam hasn't stopped grinning at Kinsey who is as beat red as the shirt she is pulling over her head before wiggling into his grey sweatpants which she has to roll several times at her waist to fit. Jumping up now fully dressed she faces Sam's daughter.

"Quinn I would like to introduce you to my girlfriend, Kinsey Wells."

"Girlfriend! Since when?" Quinn seems floored by the news.

"I don't know," Sam looks to Kinsey then to his watch, "What would you say? 18? 19 hours?"

Kinsey is grinning at him, "About that."

Quinn is looking back and forth between the two of them. "Well, it's nice to meet you, Kinsey. I didn't even know my dad had started dating again. How long have you been seeing each other?"

Kinsey walks around the counter to shake the young woman's hand. "It's nice to finally meet you, Quinn. I've heard a lot about you."

Sam comes over to hug his daughter before answering her question, "We had our first date last night, but we've known each other a long time."

"Wow, the title of girlfriend already? Where do you live Kinsey?"

Kinsey bites her lower lip as she looks to Sam to answer, "I live in San Diego."

"I just asked Kinsey to move in with me here," Sam adds.

"What is happening?" Quinn's hands clutch her head as if her brain is going to explode at all this information.

Kinsey notices the engagement ring on Quinn's finger, "That is a beautiful ring."

Quinn's eyes widen, "Dad that's what I came here to tell you. Robbie proposed last night!"

"Honey, that's so exciting. Congratulations." Sam hugs her again.

"I'm sorry if I ruined your surprise," Kinsey feels bad.

"Don't worry about it. You just took me by surprise."

"What did your mom say?" Sam asks.

Quinn grins at him, "I wanted to tell you first."

The smile Sam has for his firstborn is precious, "Have you eaten? Let's go out for lunch. We were just looking for food. We can call Sadie and see if she wants to join us. Have you told her yet?"

"Nope. I'll text Robbie and have him meet us too."

"I'm going to just go change into something a little more appropriate," Kinsey says as she spots her clothes from last night on the living room floor. If she didn't think she could be more embarrassed than she already was, she is mistaken. She bites her lip as she looks at Sam her eyes pointing to the living room. One of her absolute favorite things about Sam is the non-verbal communication skills he possesses.

"Quinn, sweetie. Why don't you call and make us a reservation? The weather looks nice, maybe you want to hang out on the veranda while we get ready?"

She looks up from her phone suspiciously, but whatever is going on between her dad and this new woman she doesn't want to know all the details, "Sure, dad." She walks to the glass doors and lets herself out.

"You're a lifesaver!" Kinsey runs to the living room scoops up her and Sam's clothes and shoves them inside her baggy t-shirt and looks to the veranda. Quinn is looking out over the skyline uninterested in what is happening inside or more likely trying to avoid what is going on inside. Kinsey sprints for the safety of his bedroom. A thought stops her once she is through the door, Sam slowly meandering behind her. This is their bedroom. It's a weird feeling. He shuts the door, and his arms wrap around her, and the clothes are still shoved up under the t-shirt.

"What are you thinking?" Sam asks her. "Is it lunch?"

"No," She turns in his arms, "I was just thinking that this is our bedroom when just last night it was your bedroom. It just kind of hit me."

"Are you still okay with moving in? I know this is fast and if you need to slow down, I don't want to scare you off."

"I'm not scared. I take that back. I'm scared that I'm not that scared. Are you scared?"

He is shaking his head, "I'm not scared."

She releases a breath, "Good. What do you think Quinn thinks?"

"Why don't we ask her at lunch? We should get dressed." They separate and she puts on the same outfit from last night. Sam goes to the bathroom to shave.

"I need to brush my teeth," Kinsey says from the door. Sam opens the bottom drawer and pulls out a new toothbrush for her. She comes into the room and takes the toothbrush opening the cardboard and plastic container it's housed in. He cleans the sink out for her before stepping aside to let her use it. He pulls out toothpaste and floss and sets them on the countertop. "Thanks."

"No problem," he taps her bottom before leaving the bathroom.

After she is done, she puts her newly used toothbrush in the holder next to his. "Do you have a hairbrush?" she asks. She walks to the door. He is fully dressed putting on a pair of shoes.

"I have a comb. The girls might have a brush in their bathroom still."

"Okay, thanks." Kinsey leaves the bedroom fully dressed now. She walks to the door that leads outside.

Quinn turns around, "Are you ready?" she asks.

"Almost, your dad thought maybe you might still have a hairbrush here."

"Oh yeah," Quinn moves past her into the apartment. Kinsey follows her to the right past the living room and down the hall to the girl's bedrooms and bathroom. "We have all sorts of stuff in here." She opens the drawers to show her all the goodies. "There's makeup, lotion, hair ties, shampoos, and conditioners. Help yourself."

"Thank you." Kinsey takes the hairbrush out of the drawer and starts to brush out her locks.

Quinn smiles at her in the mirror, "You're welcome." She scoots out of the bathroom. Luckily, her hair is still good with yesterday's wash. Easily she smooths her locks. Shutting off the light she joins Sam and Quinn who are talking in the living room.

Kinsey slips into her shoes and puts her coat on. "Cute shoes," Quinn comments.

Kinsey smiles at her, "Thanks."

"Ready to go?" Sam asks. They leave, locking up the apartment.

Inside the restaurant, Quinn's fiancé and sister are seated on the booth side of the table with three empty chairs across from them. They are speaking in hushed tones when they arrive and jump up as soon as they are spotted. Kinsey would put money on the fact that Quinn had texted ahead to let them both know that dad was bringing his new girlfriend to lunch.

They both slide out of the leather cushioned seats, Robbie, shaking Sam's hand and Sadie coming out from behind the table to hug her dad. "Sadie, Robbie, this is my girlfriend, Kinsey."

Sadie launches herself into Kinsey's arms taking her by surprise, "Oof," escapes her lips before laughing and hugging the young woman back.

"It's so nice to meet you," Sadie says as she pulls away.

"It's really nice to meet you, too." Sadie claps her hands in excitement before going to hug her sister.

Robbie shakes her hand, "Congratulations." Kinsey whispers. Robbie is tall dark and handsome and mouths, thank you to her. You're welcome, she mouths back. Quinn wedges herself between her fiancé and her sister on the booth side and Sam pulls out the middle chair for Kinsey. Once she settles, he slips into the chair on her left across from Robbie.

As soon as the waiter leaves, having taken their drink orders, Quinn puts her hand on the table causing Sadie to gasp, "Shut up!" Sadie picks up her sister's hand. "Robbie, you did so good!" She flings herself towards her sister scooping up her fiancé in the hug too.

"So, tell me how you two met?" Kinsey curiously leans forward.

"Well Robbie is an actor," Quinn starts.

"On Broadway," Sadie interjects proud of her soon-to-be brother-in-law.

"I was invited to an after-party one night with one of my friends and I was introduced to Robbie," Quinn continues.

"It was love at first sight," Robbie tells Kinsey.

"It really was," Quinn looks to Robbie like Kinsey suspects she looks at Sam. "We were inseparable ever since. Last night, after the play, the curtains went down. People were in a standing ovation when the curtain rose it was just Robbie and hundreds of candles lining the stage. He was holding a microphone as he asked the audience's forgiveness, but said he had an important question to ask the love of his life. The audience is like awww and they start clapping louder. He asks me to join him on stage. I was practically pushed out there in front of all those people. I was a nervous wreck but it was as if it was just the two of us. I walk to center stage, and he drops to one knee and proposes. I said yes of course. He stands, puts on the ring, and kisses me. The rest of the cast comes out for a final bow and the curtains close as the thunderous applause continues. Well, that's what I'm told happened after I said yes. I only had eyes for him."

"That is so sweet," Kinsey's hand pressed to her chest over her heart. "I love stories like that."

"What about you and dad?" Sadie asks. "How did you two meet?"

Kinsey turns to Sam smiling at the memory. "We met on the first day of our senior year of college. We were doing an internship. We got in trouble talking while we were supposed to be paying attention to our mentor. He gave us an assignment and said if we screwed it up, we would be fired by the end of the week."

The girls gasp, "So I take it you weren't fired?" Quinn asks.

Sam continues, "Nope. Kinsey's brilliant mind put together a presentation that blew the company away."

"Stop it," Kinsey playfully touches his arm, "Your dad is a genius with numbers he did all the calculations. Anyway, we got to keep our jobs and we got asked back with six other students for the spring semester out of twenty of us."

"That's good," Robbie chimes in.

"So, you went to NYU too? That's where I'm going." Sadie asks.

"Yes, your dad told me. My boys are going there now too."

"Oh really? What year are they?"

"Freshmen. I have twins."

"What are they studying?" Quinn asks.

"Aidan is going into business and Ethan is pre-med."

"That's ambitious." Robbie says, "Good for them."

"Is your ex a doctor?" Quinn asks.

Sam sits forward, "Kinsey isn't divorced."

"You're still married?" Sadie and Quinn say in unison, appalled.

Sam starts to react indignantly on her behalf, but Kinsey puts her hand on his, stopping him from exploding, "I'm a widow. My husband passed away three years ago." The girls sit back in their seats.

"I'm sorry to hear that," Robbie offers.

"Thank you."

"We didn't know," Sadie tells her.

"How did he die?" Quinn wants to know.

"Quinn," her father's voice warns her she is treading on thin ice.

"It's okay. He had stage four pancreatic cancer. That's why Ethan wants to go into medicine. He wants to cure cancer."

"That's very noble of him," Robbie says. The girls are silent for a minute.

"I'm sorry," Quinn says.

"You didn't know. It's okay." Kinsey assures them. Changing the subject she asks, "So, Robbie you sing I take it?"

"Yes ma'am."

"He is an incredible singer," Quinn praises him.

"Your dad is a really good singer, but I'm sure you guys know that," Kinsey says as Sam clears his throat next to her. The looks in his daughter's eyes say otherwise.

"Um, no," Sadie says.

"Dad, you can sing?" Quinn asks.

"Just recreationally," Sam admits, "It's been a really long time since I did it in front of people."

"Seriously?" Kinsey asks.

"I would like to hear you sing," Sadie demands.

"Me too," Robbie adds.

"Let's go to a karaoke bar," Kinsey suggests.

Quinn claps her hands together her face lighting up, "Yes! We should."

Sam raises his eyebrow at Kinsey his arm around the back of her chair silently telling her, see what you started? She grins at him, "Come on it'll be fun."

"Oh, alright," he agrees and is rewarded with shouts of excitement. Their drinks arrive and they order their food. After lunch, they make plans to meet later that night at a karaoke bar across town Sadie has been to.

After lunch, Kinsey asks Sam if he would like to go see her dad. "I'd love to." They drive to her dad's apartment. Pierce is over the moon excited for his daughter. He shakes Sam's hand vigorously and displays zero judgment of her moving in with him. They agree to finally have their raincheck dinner when Kinsey moves back officially.

Chapter Forty-Nine

♥

Later that night, the karaoke bar is packed, and she is surprised when they are shown to a booth. She suspects Robbie has something to do with it and his possible connections in the city. They pile into a plush leather circular booth that faces the stage. The server brings them a song list to go through and takes their drink order.

Sam walks up to the bar without looking at the book and puts in his request. He saunters back to the table everyone's face expectant. "What?" he asks.

"Are you going to keep us in suspense?" Sadie asks.

"It appears that way," he smiles.

An hour later and several cocktails later his name is announced for the stage. The table hoots and hollers for him as he stands and weaves his way to the stage. She has flashbacks to the night they had done a duet together. The alleyway afterward...the music begins. The crowd around them is talking and laughing no one besides their table is paying attention.

Music intro over, Sam starts singing "You Raise Me Up" by Josh Groban. Her heart starts to speed up as she watches him on stage. The audience begins to hush around them, entranced by his vocals. The song picks up and he hits every note bringing claps and whistles from the crowd. He is singing directly to her, but he is also showing off to the crowd. The song brings literal tears to her eyes. Swiping them away she looks at his girls. They are also tearing up at the beautifulness of the moment. Quinn looks at her and they share a smile before their gazes return to Sam.

When he finishes the applause is deafening, standing ovations all around them. Kinsey is grinning at him as he jumps down from the stage and heads for her. Her palms hurt with how hard she is clapping for him. Random strangers are clapping him on the back as he makes his way to her. Standing to greet him, he surprises her by taking her in his arms and kissing her in front of his kids. He pulls away from her smiling, "Thank you for making me do that. I forgot how much fun that is."

"You're welcome."

"So, when are you going to get up there?" he asks.

They separate and slide into the booth. "Oh, no, not me."

"Dad, you were so good!" Sadie shouts across the table, the noise level picking back up around them.

"I'm impressed," Robbie says.

"Me too," Quinn adds, "I had no idea you could sing like that."

"I used to sing to you girls all the time."

"Yeah, lullabies. And we were little how were we supposed to know that you had such range with your voice? Did mom know you could sing?"

Sam is shaking his head, "I don't think so."

"So how did you know?" Sadie asks Kinsey.

"We went out to celebrate one night with our coworkers after we got invited to stay for the spring semester."

"Kinsey and I sang a duet," Sam offers up.

"You should sing it!" Quinn suggests.

Kinsey glares at Sam and he laughs throwing his hand up in surrender, "Hey you started this."

"It's going to take at least another hour to get back on the list," she uses as an excuse.

The waitress takes that moment to appear, "That's okay. Another round for the table." Sadie requests and the server leaves to fulfill their drink order. Sam gets up to go put the song in even as she protests after him.

Kinsey is having so much fun. More fun than she has had in ages. A wave of guilt washes over her and Sam sees it and feels it before she can fully register what is happening. He is leaning toward her, his arm around her back, "You okay," he whispers.

She nods turning into him, her hand resting on his thigh, "I just had a moment of survivor's guilt that's all. I'll be okay."

"Are you sure? Do you want to leave?"

She thinks seriously about leaving before they have to sing but she thinks better of it, "No, but I think maybe we should do a shot of Tequila before going on stage. You know a little liquid courage."

"You got it," he flags down their waitress and puts in the order. The five of them down the shots as Kinsey and Sam are being called on stage. He stands and offers his hand out to her. The alcohol helps, she is feeling looser as he guides her to the stage. Some earlier patrons recognize Sam and begin clapping.

She is handed a microphone and she takes a deep breath. He hasn't picked the song they did forever ago. He chose Bradley Cooper and Lady Gaga's "Shallow" song. He starts his part, and she looks at the screen waiting for her section to begin. This is a more difficult song and really showcases her voice. She opens her mouth and belts out the notes. Sam grins at her encouraging her to put her all into it. She does, she wants to give this to him. She belts it out at the top of her lungs and the crowd responds. Then he is joining her in the chorus. When they finish, he picks her up and they are laughing. The experience is exhilarating.

Back at the table, they are just as impressed with her even though she still believes Sam has the better voice out of the two of them. They wrap the night up a couple of rounds later. Everyone giving hugs. She can tell she has won the girls over and it makes her heart sing. Robbie has a car waiting at the curb, "Do you want a ride?" he asks as the girls pile in.

"No thanks, I think we are going to walk. I'm not that far from here."

"Okay, have a goodnight." He shakes Sam's hand again.

"It was really nice to meet you," He hugs Kinsey.

"It was so nice to meet you. Congratulations again," she tells him.

"Thank you."

They are gone. "Do you seriously want to walk?" she asks.

"Not really but I kind of wanted to have my way with you in a dark alley."

"Do you now?" There is no alley like there was at the previous establishment, so they start to walk toward his apartment crossing the street and turning right. They are holding hands recounting the events of the night when he pulls her into a quiet alley. There is a bump out of brick from the building that partially hides them from the empty street.

He is kissing her, and she wants him so badly. He picks her up. She is still wearing the same cream-colored sweater dress from the night before. Her legs wrap around him and his warm body presses against her. His fingers find her ready for him, so he fumbles with his belt pulling his erection out of his pants. He is inside her. Her eyes lock with his as he pumps into her. Kinsey's fist tightens on the back of his sweater, her thighs clench his hips. The leather of his belt bites into the flesh of her inner thighs. The rough brick she is sure is ruining her dress, but she doesn't care.

"Do you love her?" Kinsey asks.

"No. I only love you."

"Will you leave her?"

"Yes, I want to be with you."

Kinsey cries out. These were the words she had wanted. And now she is sure those are the words he had really wanted to say but couldn't all those years ago. Crying out his name in orgasm, "I love you, Sam."

"I love you, Kinsey," his voice is raw with emotion. His thrust gets more intense pushing her hard into the wall and she welcomes it. Welcomes him. He buries his head into her neck as he releases inside her.

They remain like that holding onto each other as their breathing returns to normal. She runs her fingers through his hair and kisses his neck. "I'm so lucky," he tells her, "I get to take you home with me tonight."

"I'm the lucky one," she tells him. He sets her down gently and she digs through her purse pulling out a tissue while he re-zips himself. She cleans herself up and throws it away in a dumpster on their way out of the alley.

The walk home seems effortless as they hold hands. They shower when they get back to the apartment. Crawling into bed Sam asks her, "Do you mind if I turn on the TV? I like to watch a little news before going to bed."

"Sure," Kinsey snuggles in next to him. He is sitting up propped up on some pillows, he puts his arm around her shoulders as he turns on the screen. The darkened room is illuminated by the light blue color of the commercial before returning to the news.

"Tomorrow's weather is going to be unseasonably warm reaching a high of 78 degrees. But be prepared for a cold front that will be moving in Monday morning so make the most of it."

Sam turns to Kinsey, "Do you want to take the boat out tomorrow?" Kinsey moves away from him to have the conversation. He had told her through his texts that he had been able to keep his business and sailboat if he didn't go after Diane's pharmaceutical money or the house.

"I would love to, but I have plans to hang out with the boys tomorrow."

"Invite them to come along. I want to meet them, but only if you are ready for me too."

She chews on her lower lip. Kinsey reaches for her cell phone which is now on the nightstand on her side of the bed, plugged into her charger. She sends a text to the boys in a group chat. "Hey guys I have a friend with a sailboat and tomorrow is supposed to be nice outside. Would you want to go out on the boat and then maybe do lunch after? Let me know what you think." Send.

Seconds later Ethan texts her, "Sure, sounds fun."

"Ethan's in," Kinsey tells Sam. "What's the address of the dock?" Sam gives her the name of the harbor and she looks it up on her phone.

Aidan's response comes in, "What friend?" She grins, oh boy.

"I'm not sure how to respond to Aidan," Kinsey tells Sam. He sits up straighter.

"What's he saying?"

"He wants to know what friend I have with a sailboat."

"You told him I was a friend?"

Kinsey puts her phone down as she looks at him, "I'm going to tell the boys about you, but I don't want to do it over text."

"How do you think they will take it?" Sam seems worried now.

She places a hand on his forearm. "I'm sure they will be fine with it. It just might take some adjustment."

"Tell him I'm an old friend from college," he suggests. She sends a text to the boys.

"Boy or girl?" Ethan jumps in now suspicious of this new friend his mom has.

Kinsey laughs, "They are on to us."

She texts the address instead. "See you guys tomorrow. I love you."

"It's definitely a boy," Aidan responds.

"Should we interrogate him for you mom? Ask him what his intentions are with you?" Ethan asks.

Laughing Kinsey shows her phone to Sam, and he smiles. "Tell them to ask away."

Smiling she texts, "He says ask away."

"Wait you are with him right now?" Ethan asks.

Aidan texts, "It's past your bedtime."

"Goodnight boys." She puts the phone back on her nightstand as it continues to buzz with questions. She throws herself down on the bed and groans, but she is smiling. "You invited this."

He leans over her, "It's going to be great. I'll charm them like I did their mother."

She wiggles her eyebrows at him, "Let's hope it's not exactly how you charmed me."

"Minx," he kisses her, the boys are forgotten, and the TV is ignored.

Chapter Fifty

Sunday morning Sam and Kinsey are waiting on the docks when Aidan and Ethan show up. She hugs them both as they size up Sam behind her. "Guys, I would like you to meet Sam Anderson."

"Hi, Sam, nice to meet you," Ethan is the first to step forward and shake his hand.

"Pleasure is all mine. I've heard so much about you," Sam shakes his hand before offering it to Aidan.

Aidan shakes it but says, "That's funny we've heard nothing about you." Ethan starts to chuckle but covers it quickly with a cough.

"I'm sure you have tons of questions and your mom, and I would like to answer them all but first can I give you a tour of my boat?" The boy's heads turn to Kinsey when he mentions her. She is doing her best to keep her expression neutral.

Aidan puts his hands in his pockets, "Sure."

"Lead the way," Ethan's hand outstretches towards the boats. Sam turns and they follow. The boat is beautiful, with sleek hardwood floors and a tall white sail that is currently wrapped around the pole. Sam takes them below deck and there is a small kitchen, dining area, bedroom, and bathroom.

"Nothing fancy," Sam says once they are back on deck.

Aidan raises an eyebrow, "I would say owning a sailboat in itself is pretty fancy."

"Aidan!" Kinsey admonishes her son.

Sam laughs good-naturedly. "You're right about that. Do you boys want to help me with getting her out onto the open water?"

"Sure," Ethan says easily, and Aidan shrugs his shoulders. Sam gives Kinsey a look over the boys' heads and she raises an eyebrow at him and cocks her head to the side asking where the charm he had promised was.

"Great, Ethan can you untie the rope attaching us to the dock?"

"I'm Aidan," Ethan says. Aidan chuckles.

"I'm sorry," Sam is quick to apologize.

"Ethan, what is wrong with you?" Kinsey asks.

Ethan smiles sheepishly at Sam, "Sorry man, just giving you a hard time."

Aidan starts laughing, "You guys are too easy. Grandpa already called us and told us you were dating someone before you texted us. We just thought it should have come from you first."

Kinsey's eyes narrow at her father being such a traitor. "We really don't mind," Ethan chimes in. "We don't like to think of you being alone. We know you loved dad and if you have found someone that makes you happy then we are fully on board."

Tears prick Kinsey's eyes not wanting to cry in front of her sons or Sam and the boys instantly recognizing her plight scoop her up into a group hug. "You guys are the best!" she hugs them fiercely and kisses each of them on the cheek.

When they separate, she tells them the rest, "I'm going to be moving back to New York."

"That's great, mom!" Aidan tells her and Ethan nods.

"Into Sam's apartment."

There is a moment of silence. "Okay..." Ethan says slowly.

"You guys are moving a little fast don't you think?" Aidan asks.

"Yes and no. Sam and I have known each other for a long time. I appreciate you boys, trying to be protective. I get it, I really do but we will be okay."

"I've loved your mom for a very long time," Sam adds behind them. The boys turn to face him. "She means the world to me, and I would never do anything to hurt her. You have my word, man to man."

Kinsey watches as her boys nod their heads at his words. "We really aren't trying to give you guys a hard time. It's just coming as a little bit of a shock to us. That's all. We will be fine. Right, Aidan?" Ethan turns to his brother.

"That's right," Aidan levels Sam with his stare.

Sam extends his hand for him to shake. Both boys do. Tensions begin to ease as Sam gently guides the boys around the boat asking for their help. Their afternoon turns blissful out on the water the sun warming their face even though the wind whips through their hair.

Hours later they go to lunch. Sam and Aidan have found some common ground in the business courses he has started taking and Ethan and Sam discuss their passion for old muscle cars. Kinsey smiles as she watches the most important men of her life minus her dad.

Chapter Fifty-One

♥

That evening Sam drives her to the airport. He parks his car rather than dropping her off at the curb. They wait in line together to check her bag and get her boarding pass. They hold hands all the way down to security.

"I'm going to miss you," Sam tells her.

"I know me too. It will probably take me a while though. Wait for me?"

"Forever if I have to."

Kinsey kisses him in the middle of the airport. Neither of them has to hide their love from the world and it is so freeing. It takes them a long time to say their goodbyes as they used to when they were in college.

"I love you," Kinsey says.

"Music to my ears," he kisses her again. His forehead resting on hers, "I love you too. Hurry home."

Smiling she promises, "I will." Walking away, she looks over her shoulder, he is still standing where she had left him, his hands in his pockets watching her go, as others walk around him. He lifts his hand in a wave. Making it to the security counter she hands over her ID and boarding pass. She blows him a kiss before taking her paperwork back from the TSA woman then disappears around the corner.

Rosemary picks her up from the airport. Getting out Rosemary opens her trunk and then gives Kinsey a huge bear hug, "How was it? How are the boys? How's your dad? It must have been nice to catch up with everyone."

"It really was. Everyone is good." Kinsey responds as she picks up her bag, swinging it in the trunk. Horns honk around them as other drivers maneuver into positions that aren't parking spaces and others try to vacate their spots at the curb. Closing the trunk, the women hop in the car. Rosemary gets up onto the highway and Kinsey tries to broach the subject of Sam.

"I'm going to move back to New York," might as well rip the Band-Aid off.

Rosemary looks over her shoulder at her and smiles, "I know dear."

"What do you mean you know? Did my dad call you?" Kinsey is getting indignant at her dad's lack of keeping her news to himself.

"No, nothing like that. More like a mother's intuition. If you want my two cents?"

"Please."

"As much as we are going to miss you, you belong in New York with your family. Grayson told me that it was you that sacrificed your career so he could spend what time he had left with us. I will be forever grateful to you for that. It's the right call. I'm not mad. I just ask that you and the boys come visit us occasionally."

"Of course," Kinsey reaches over to her, and Rosemary takes her hand squeezing her palm. "There's more…" Kinsey releases her hand turning in her seat.

"Oh?"

"I started dating someone."

Rosemary's face lights up, "That's wonderful. Kinsey, I'm so happy for you."

"Really?"

"I really am."

"That's such a relief."

"Why don't you tell me about your young man?" Kinsey does, her face lighting up as she gushes over Sam.

After Rosemary drops her off, Kinsey walks into her big empty house. The silence is deafening, her purse hitting the kitchen countertop startles her. Looking out onto the beach she knows she will miss this beautiful landscape. She also knows that if she were to stay here and not return, she would miss Sam more. Nothing compared to being in his arms. She would be near her boys and her dad.

She calls the real estate company and sets up an appointment for the next day for an evaluation. Things move quickly after that. The agent comes and oohs and aahs over her and Grayson's home. Pictures are scheduled and Kinsey goes through the home deciding what she wants to keep and what she wants to sell.

The realtor had given her the name of a company that will help with an estate sale. The moving company comes and takes everything she has marked to move. She and Sam call and text every day.

The house sells quickly at more than the asking price in this hot market. She waits thirty days to sign the closing papers. Grayson's family hosts a going-away dinner for her.

Sam is at the airport waiting for her when she returns. When she sees him standing holding a cardboard sign with her name on it, she laughs. Up until this minute, she had sometimes thought she had dreamt him up, that her happily ever after may not exist.

Chapter Fifty-Two

♥

"I wish we could have had kids together," Kinsey is stroking his head as they lay in bed on a lazy Sunday morning.

He rolls onto his side his arm going around her waist, "We still could if you want to," he tells her in all seriousness. "I'll get my vasectomy reversed."

Smiling she runs her hand up and down his chiseled arm, "No we are getting too old for that. Besides your vasectomy, I had a really hard time conceiving the boys. It took multiple rounds of IVF. I wouldn't even be a candidate at this stage. It is really tough to go through."

"We could adopt if you want?"

"You would do that? Start all over with a newborn?"

"I would do anything if it was with you."

"You are the sweetest man alive. I swear. I really appreciate the offer, but I don't want to start over with a newborn. I also don't want our kids to be hurt by it. What about a puppy? Didn't you always say you wanted a dog?"

He grins down at her, "Do you want to get a puppy with me? That's a huge commitment. They are like having a newborn."

"I'll have a puppy with you," she sits up throwing off the covers. "Come on let's get dressed."

"Are you serious? Right now?"

"Yes. Right now." She looks over her shoulder at him. "Unless you would like to shower with me before we go?" She wiggles her eyebrows at him as she saunters toward the bathroom. She squeals as he throws off the covers jumping off the bed to race towards her. He catches her in the bathroom, and she is laughing.

"You know I'm not saying no to shower sex, right?"

"Who said anything about sex?" she teases.

He drops to his knees his face burying in her center. Her hand falls to the top of his head her other hand reaching to steady herself on his bathroom sink. "Okay you win," she breathes.

Smiling he begins to lick her. "Mmmm, that feels good. Do you know what I wish?"

"Tell me, baby," he encourages her.

"I wish you would have done this to me when we were in the stairwell at work. Remember when you were punishing me for turning you on at work? Oh, and for fucking you in your car."

"You always fucking turned me on at work. Do you know how hard it was for me not to fuck you in that nap pod?" His fingers slide up inside of her. "I wanted to finger you and when you were good and ready, I wanted to come inside you." He sucks on her clit and her nipples harden. He takes one of her legs and throws it over his shoulder as he uses his fingers and tongue to bring her pleasure.

"Do you remember the last time we kissed in college? We were on the balcony hidden away from the world. I wished you would have bent me over one of the chairs, lifted my gown, and came inside me.

Sam stands turning her around towards the bathroom sink. He bends her over as she described in her fantasy and positions himself at her entrance. "Are you ready?"

"Yes. Please." He is inside her. She closes her eyes and pictures that night as if that was what really happened. It is amazing. They finish, both climaxing and he reaches inside the shower to turn on the water while she uses the toilet.

He grins at her through the mirror. "I'm glad you are so comfortable with me."

"You're my best friend." She wipes and flushes.

"God, you're perfect."

She smiles, "I'm not."

"For me you are."

Sam holds open the shower door for her and she steps inside the glass enclosure with dual showerheads. They are soaping up when he asks. "Hey, I have a question for you."

"Shoot."

"When we were in college, and we got caught by the security guard in my car?"

She giggles, "Having sex? Yeah?"

"Did you really say that you loved me?"

Grinning she confesses, "I did."

"I knew it!" the smile on his face is adorable. "I thought I heard that, but you were making all sorts of excuses about my dick."

"Well, you do have an impressive dick but yes I said I love you."

"Why didn't you say it again when I asked?"

"Would it have helped? Would you have left her for me?"

He sighs, "Probably not. It just always bugged me, and you never said it again so I started to believe I had imagined it."

"Well, I hadn't intended on saying it. I was planning on taking that to my grave." He laughs. "I'm serious," she pretends to twist a key in front of her lip and throw it away.

Kinsey and Sam go to the animal shelter to rescue a puppy. The noise is deafening when they enter, and they still aren't in the room the dogs are being held. "Can I help you?" the woman behind the counter asks.

"We are here to adopt a puppy," Kinsey answers for them.

"Do you have an appointment?"

She looks to Sam knowing they don't then back to the woman, "No, sorry we don't we didn't realize we would need one."

"That's okay," she hands them a clipboard with some paperwork. "Go have a seat over there and come back when you are done." They take a seat in the uncomfortable plastic chairs that squeak on the linoleum when they sit down. There are four pages worth of questions.

"Geez, you would almost think we were adopting a baby," she tells him half-joking.

They fill out the forms as they watch family after family and couple after couple leaving with a dog or puppy. "I hope there are some left," Kinsey bites her lip.

"We can always come back if they run out," Sam tells her. After handing in the paperwork, they are ushered into the back. There were plenty of dogs left. They walk up and down the aisles looking for the perfect addition to their family. Sam calls her over to the end, he is bending over and peering into the stall. When she gets close it appears empty.

"What am I looking at?" Kinsey asks.

Sam squats down on his haunches pointing under the low blue bed. Getting down on her hands and knees on the questionably clean linoleum floor she sees two tiny eyes blinking out at her. One of the volunteers walks by. "Yeah, he's pretty shy. Do you want to see him?"

"Yes please," Kinsey and Sam stand, moving out of the way as she pulls a retractable string from her hip with a cluster of keys on the end. She jiggles the lock before swinging the door wide for them.

"Let me know if you have any questions. What info we have on him is on this paper." She points to a laminated placard. Kinsey ignores the paper as Sam gently picks up the bed and sets it aside. The puppy lays huddled and shaking, tail tucked between his legs, and he backs up into the corner, trying to get away.

"Oh, it's okay little man," Kinsey coos as she steps into the cage getting closer before squatting in front of him.

"It says here he is 12 weeks old. He has four siblings, but they have all been adopted. It's best if he is in a home with no other animals. He was rescued from Tennessee," Sam is reading from the card.

"What kind of dog do they think he is?"

"Uh, a border collie, husky mix. They estimate he will get to be about forty pounds."

"That's pretty good," Kinsey turns to look at Sam. He is smiling down at her. "What?" she asks. Sam nods his chin forward and she turns around. The puppy has made his way over to her and is sniffing her hand.

"Awe," she says in a whisper trying not to scare the little one away. She scoops him up and presses him to her chest. His little body is shaking, and she can feel his heart racing inside his tiny chest. Standing she turns to Sam. He comes over and scratches behind the puppy's ear.

"He is handsome," Sam comments. The puppy is short-haired. Most of his face is white and has one blue eye. The other brown eye is surrounded by a beautiful brindle coloring that goes down his back and his undercarriage is white.

After a couple of minutes of them petting him, he begins to settle down. "How are we doing in here," the volunteer asks.

"Good," they both respond.

"Would you like to take him outside to play?"

Kinsey looks up and Sam and he nods his head, "Yes, please."

"Perfect, follow me," the young girl leads them to a door and pushes on the silver metal bar swinging the door wide. She stays on the inside allowing them access to a fenced-in area. "Take your time and when you're done just come find me."

"Thank you," Sam tells her as Kinsey steps outside onto the crushed stone. There are other people milling about with dogs of different sizes and breeds. She takes the puppy to a quiet corner, so he isn't scared. Setting him down he begins to sniff the ground walking around with a little more pep in his step.

"Oh gosh! Look at his tail," Kinsey exclaims, "It's so cute. I love how it curls."

Sam chuckles. Before the dog's tail had been tucked underneath him now swung upwards back towards the puppy's spine. It was the brindle color all the way to the tip where it looked like it was dipped in white paint. Kinsey calls the puppy, and he bounds over to her showing much more enthusiasm than he had inside.

"Well, that's more like it," Sam said.

"Right?" Kinsey is encouraged by his spunk. The puppy gives a sharp little bark, now wagging his tail and her heart melts, "Awe! I think we need to keep him."

"He's the one?"

Kinsey's head swivels around, "You don't think so?"

"No, I just wanted to make sure you thought so."

Kinsey looks back to the puppy who is now laying down chewing on the tiniest bit of a tree branch he had found. His little white paws are crisscrossed holding down the stick. He stops as he is being scrutinized his head lifting and cocking to the side curiously.

"Do you want to come live with us?" She asks. He jumps up and waddles over to her his head rubbing against her knee. Picking him up again she stands and turns. "He's the one."

"I'll get Sarah."

"Who's Sarah?"

"The girl that's been helping us. Her name is on her shirt."

"Oh," Kinsey wishes she had been that observant. "Yes, let's go find her. I want to bring this little guy home."

After finalizing the paperwork and payment they drive to a pet store and buy all the things they will need and then some for the little guy. Sam fights her hard and loses when she insists on buying the dog collar with a bow tie. "It's just so cute!" Eventually, he rolls his eyes and throws his hand up. The other is holding their puppy in a football hold.

Sam looks down at him and apologizes to the pooch, "Sorry little guy I tried." The dog peers up at him curiously and Kinsey giggles as she throws the collar into the cart.

As they check out with more stuff than they might be able to carry the cashier asks, "What's his name?"

Kinsey looks to Sam. They hadn't even discussed names. "Um, we just got him. We haven't figured that part out yet."

The young man laughs good-naturedly his thick blonde curls that take up more diameter than his face bobs up and down with his understanding. "That's okay. It'll come to you. Your total today is 528 dollars and 19 cents." Kinsey looks at the bags full of food, bowls, a collar, leash, poop bags, puppy pads, a bed, a playpen, and a crate, not to mention the obscene number of toys. "What have we done?" she laughs.

In the car after they have shoved everything into the trunk, he presses the ignition button and turns to her instead of pulling out of the parking space, "I think we should call him Hudson."

"Why Hudson?"

"Because that's where we were the day, we talked about getting him." Sam is talking about the day they had played hooky and walked along the Hudson River discussing their future together.

Dawning has her gasping, "That's perfect." She looks down at the puppy, "Your new name is Hudson." The puppy yips as if he approves. "Oh gosh, I love him already." She squeezes him tight, and he licks her chin.

At home, they set up puppy pads, a playpen, and a crate. Kinsey sits on the floor her legs in front of her splayed wide as she dumps the bag of balls and toys out onto the hardwood in between her and Hudson. Hudson who is sniffing Sam's pant leg comes bounding over when he hears the squeak of a toy. Hudson thrust his nose into the pile of toys and wrestles out a stuffed animal almost as big as him. Carrying it away towards the windows he almost trips twice as it slides across the ground. Plopping down onto the floor he begins chewing on his new favorite toy. Within a half-hour, he decapitated the cute turtle and is now pulling out all the stuffing inside.

That night Hudson cries in his crate. They let him out several times onto the veranda. Eventually, Sam drags the whole crate into their room, and he sleeps for the rest of the night being comforted by their presence. All their kids love the puppy and visit to play even taking him out on walks around the block.

Chapter Fifty-Three

♥

Kinsey works for about a month from the apartment. She is using Sadie's room as her office. The company she works for wants her to come back to San Diego for a meeting. She talks to Sam about her having to go back and forth once a month.

"I'm considering going back to work here. My old firm will probably take me back or maybe my dad's firm?"

"Come to work with me," he offers.

"What?"

"I'm serious. I have my own firm. I can bring you in at an upper level. We can set the world on fire like we always planned."

"What kind of salary can I expect? Vacation time? Perks?" She grins, she is only kidding.

"You name it and I'll have my lawyer draw up the paperwork."

"Are you serious?"

"Dead serious, name your price."

"Do you think it's a good idea to work together?"

"We did it before."

"Let me think about it." She does. Kinsey asks her dad for advice. She calls Trish and they meet for lunch to catch up. She ends up confessing what had happened all those years ago with Sam and how it wasn't just a one-time thing like her friend had believed.

Except Trish says, "I knew it!"

"You did?"

"Honey, please. We have known each other for a long time. I knew you didn't have food poisoning"

Kinsey gasps, "And here I thought I was being so sneaky."

"You guys were bound to get caught." She sobers, "I am over the moon happy for you. I know things haven't been easy but I'm glad you found each other."

"Thank you. So, what do you think? Work together or not?"

"Fuck it, life is short, just do it. Normally, I would say no but you guys seem to genuinely like to be together. If it was me and Tom, I would say hell no, but you guys will make it work. Speaking of Tom, we should do a double date sometime."

"I would love to."

Kinsey begins to integrate herself back into life in New York. Reconnecting with old friends and making new ones. She quits her job in San Diego and starts working with Sam. There is an adjustment period, and each agrees to a separate day at home, so Hudson isn't lonely and a four-day in-office work week. They spend a total of three days in the office together and it is a nice balance.

Sam introduces her to his family. His parents are warm and inviting, and they accept her with open arms. She meets his brothers, their wives, and their kids at Thanksgiving. It is unseasonably warm for November in the northeast, so they are outside while his dad fries a turkey. The kids are running around jumping in a leaf pile.

Rosemary had asked if the boys could come out for Thanksgiving, so she had bought them plane tickets. Her Dad had gone upstate to see his family. Sam's girls are having dinner with Diane but will be over for dessert. Kinsey and Sam are sitting in Adirondack chairs when Kinsey leans over and whispers in Sam's ear, "You were right."

Confused he pulls away from her, "About what? I mean, of course, I was. No seriously, tell me about my infinite wisdom."

She laughs, "Oh boy, I don't even know if I want to tell you now."

"You absolutely have to now."

She ponders for a minute then leans over conspiratorially. He moves closer positioning his ear for her to whisper, "I would never date either one of your brothers." His laugh is deep and rich, his head thrown back as he enjoys this tidbit of information.

His laugh is contagious, and she joins in his merriment. "What's so funny?" Sophia one of the wives asks. Kinsey can't remember which brother she is married to.

"Nothing, just an inside joke."

"I love you so much," Sam turns to her pulling her face close. Her hand comes up to hold onto his wrist as he kisses her. He pulls her closer and his younger brother throws a dishtowel at them and tells them to get a room.

Sam jumps up and takes Kinsey's hand, "Good idea."

Sam's mom gasps and all the men chuckle as he hauls a blushing Kinsey through the backyard. Inside he takes her up the back steps leading from the kitchen to a narrow hallway.

Giggling Kinsey says, "Sam? What are you doing?" She had thought he was kidding now she isn't so sure. His childhood bedroom is small, and she doesn't have time to digest all the details of his past because he is kissing her again. What she managed to take in was brown plaid wallpaper, a bunkbed, and sports posters taped to the wall.

He guides her to the bottom bunk of the bed groaning in protest at their combined weight. "I've never had a girl in my bed," he tells her in between kisses.

"Oh no?"

"Mom would have killed us. No female beside her ever came upstairs while we were in school." The thought of this being forbidden even though everyone had witnessed it downstairs sends a thrill through her. "You like that don't you baby?" Sam bites her neck.

Her hand reaches between them stroking him through his khakis, "Yeah, I do. I want you to fuck me right here, right now."

"Your wish is my command," Sam attempts to get to his knees but his form is hunched over her within the small confines of the bunk. He does his best to unbuckle his belt with Kinsey's help they pull his pants and underwear to his thighs. Lifting her skirt up to her waist exposing her pale pink panties he swears under his breath at the sight of her.

"You like what you see?"

"You know I do." Sam pulls her panties off and sticks them in his pocket. His fingers tease her entrance, "You ready for me?"

She nods her head vigorously and he rubs his erection where his fingers had been moments before teasing her. Kinsey bites her lip in anticipation her fingers grasping his wrists her hips lifting begging him to follow through. He leans down on his elbow, his opposite hand guiding himself inside. Kinsey's hands slide up his arms to his shoulders. She bends her knees his hand moving between her ass and the comforter. With every thrust, the bed makes a terrible sound.

Kinsey giggles and he slows down watching her as he moves. She wraps her ankles around his waist. Her right-hand touches his chiseled jaw her thumb resting on his lower lip. He nibbles on the soft pad of her thumb before taking it into his warm mouth sucking. Her inside walls clamp around his cock. Removing her thumb, she places it in her own mouth sucking on it. He growls replacing her thumb with his lips. He is crushing and demanding his thrust intensifying, the bed's headboard rocking against the wall.

"I think we might break the bed," Kinsey warns. Sam pulls out of her, and she cries out at the loss. He is out of the bed, flipping her sideways then onto her hands and knees, her ass in the air. He is kneeling on the floor behind her. His lips explore the wetness between her thighs, and she cries out into the mattress. His face is buried deep, his hands grasping her hips. She rocks against his tongue.

Standing, his dick is back inside her and his first thrust is not gentle, but the bed doesn't protest this time with the sideways motion. Encouraged he continues with hard and quick succession, driving deep to her cervix wall. Kinsey has grown accustomed to being free to be vocal with Sam, but they are in his parent's home. He rubs her clit, his other hand squeezing her breast through her sweater. "Kinsey."

"Yes, Sam?"

"I'm going to cum. Are you close?"

"So close." Three strokes later she is cumming with Sam right behind her.

After, Sam refuses to give her panties back to her, kissing her lips and smacking her ass telling her, "I want to think about you being exposed and the easy access I could have at any minute." They clean up across the hallway in the narrow bathroom with the original tile. Kinsey can see through the window that everyone is still outside. Probably waiting for them to rejoin them.

Dinner is delicious after taking a bite of Sam's mom's homemade mac and cheese her eyes widen and she meets his gaze. Nodding in approval of this being in his top five favorite foods.

Quinn and Robbie's engagement party is the following Saturday night. It's the first time Kinsey and Diane will be in a room together in over three years. A professional photographer is lining up photos of the family. Quinn asks for Kinsey to be in the family photo.

"Oh no," Kinsey protests.

"Come on," Sadie encourages her. Sam is smiling at her his arm around his daughter.

Diane pulls her aside, "I'm happy you are here."

"You are?" Kinsey frowns worried this is a trap.

"I've never seen Sam so happy." Kinsey looks to Sam who is keeping an eye on her from afar. Ready to pounce if his ex-wife says anything to upset her. "Yes, the girls have been telling me for a while now and I can see for myself that it's true."

"Wow. Well, thank you for that."

"Listen, I don't want to be your best friend," Diane says.

Kinsey holds her hands up in self-defense, "Wouldn't dream of it."

"But we are going to be in each other's lives, and I would prefer it if we could get along for the girl's sake."

"I would love that."

"I'm sorry to hear about your husband. The girls told me that he passed away."

"Yes, he did. Thank you. Did you ever remarry?"

Diane laughs, "Yes, to my job."

The rest of the evening goes without a hitch. On the ride home, Sam says, "Do you know who we have to thank for us being together?"

"Who?"

"Grayson."

Kinsey frowns at him, "Care to explain?"

"Yeah, if he hadn't brought up having you sleep with someone else, I wouldn't be back in your life. You would have never reached out and I would probably still be married, and you would have settled on the west coast. I mean maybe we would have run into each other later on, but we would be in different places than we are now. I think the stars have finally aligned for us."

Kinsey smiles, "You're right. Do you think he is happy for me?"

"I'd like to think so."

Chapter Fifty-Four

♥

Kinsey is sitting blindfolded in the front seat of Sam's car. "What are we doing?" she asks her hands touching the fabric covering her eyes again.

"No peeking," he tells her again.

She puts her hands down on her lap, "Sorry. I'm not good with surprises."

"We are almost there," he says, his hand squeezing her thigh. He pulls over and shuts the car off. "Sit tight." He gets out shutting the door behind him. The inside of the car is quiet. The door opens startling her even though she anticipated it happening.

She lets him remove her from the car. He guides her up some steps. "Hold on," he tells her. She hears a car drive by and a dog bark in the distance. In front of her, she hears the jiggling of keys in a lock.

Sam brings her inside and it smells musty, her nose wrinkles before she sneezes on the dust. It's darker and cooler inside than the sun outside provided so she crosses her arms. Sam pulls off her blindfold and she blinks several times before she can see. There are windows in front of her, but they are covered in wooden slats allowing small slivers of light inside. Turning she sees an old fireplace. The front door is open wide allowing the light inside. A large wooden staircase is covered in cobwebs.

"What do you think?"

"What am I supposed to think?" She asks slowly turning in circles.

"Remember when we were talking about our future and what it would look like?" She frowns as she looks around. "You told me that you wanted to rescue a brownstone." Laughter bubbles up inside her. "We don't have to," he continues, "If that isn't your dream anymore that's fine. We can stay where we are or look for somewhere else if you would like. Or if this isn't the one, we can keep looking."

"Let's take a look around," she suggests. The first floor is a living room that they are standing in. In the back are a dining room and kitchen. A half bath is under the stairs. The next level is two bedrooms and a bathroom the stairs continue leading them to two more rooms and a bathroom.

"I thought we could each have an office, then a spare bedroom."

She doesn't respond just wanders through the home. She walks back out of the house and assesses the exterior. It's an end unit. The detailing is magnificent just needs a good power wash. There is a patch of grass on the left of the home separating the next set of brownstones. She walks down the path to check out the potential backyard seeing as she couldn't see it from the inside. There is no fence, but it is a decent-sized lot.

"It's a big project," she says finally.

"Too big?" he wonders.

She looks to the back of the house. "It will take a lot of money."

"I have it," he assures her.

"An undertaking of this magnitude takes a lot of time. It can break some couples."

"It won't break us."

"How do you know?"

"I just do. We have already weathered so much and come out on the other side."

"Okay," Kinsey says with a small laugh her arms spreading wide.

Sam grins at her, "Yeah?"

Grinning back and nodding her head she squeals, "Yes!" He opens his arms wide to her and she throws herself into him. He picks her up and twirls her around the overgrown garden. Kissing her he sets her down and she turns to look back at the boarded-up home. It's perfect, she can already see how beautiful it will be and how happy they will be here together.

Turning to tell him just this, the words get stuck in her throat, and she freezes. Sam is down on one knee in front of her. His hand is outstretched a ring box open and a diamond catching the sun sparkles. Gasping her hands fly to cover her mouth in the sheer excitement of the moment.

"Kinsey, I hope you know that I love you more than life itself. I've yearned for you, pined for you, and waited for you for the past two-plus decades. You are my best friend, my confidant, my keeper of secrets, my partner in crime, and the person I want to share all my news with, my one true love. Will you do me the honor of becoming my wife?"

"Yes! A thousand times yes!"

Standing he kisses her their lips pressing together tightly his arms crushing her to him. Pulling away he shows her the ring. It is a princess-cut yellow diamond surrounded by a halo of white diamonds on a diamond-encrusted split-shank band. "When I went to buy this, I couldn't decide on any of the rings. None of them were right. When I saw this one, I knew. It's different just like you, and my mom loves yellow roses they are her favorite. I never knew why she liked them, so I asked her one day. She told me yellow is for friendship and she said most women liked red because it meant love, but she said there is no greater love than one born out of friendship. Seeing as you're my best friend and the love of my life I wanted you to have it. I hope you like it."

Tears well up in her eyes at his story making her love the ring even more than she already did. "It's beautiful," she whispers reverently. "You did great."

Sam beams as he removes it from the box and slips it onto her finger. "I have to call the boys."

"They are expecting your call."

"What?"

"I asked your dad, Ethan, and Aidan for their blessing. They all gave it to me without hesitation. I even talked to the girls about it. They are thrilled by the way. I have dinner reservations for all of us tonight for a little engagement celebration."

"Pretty confident I was going to say yes," she teases.

"I felt good about my odds," he grins at her again and she can't help but give him another kiss.

Chapter Fifty-Five

♥

Seven months later, Sam and Kinsey are painting their new bedroom a pewter grey. Her hair is piled on top of her head in a messy bun. She is dressed in an old pair of jeans, a stain on the thigh from staining the hardwood floors. The soft t-shirt she is wearing is her painting shirt, it has different colors in various spots. There is paint in her hair and on her fingers, her painting skills are not stellar, but she tries. She is envious of Sam who is wearing a pair of new jeans and a white t-shirt and not a spot on him.

"What?" he asks with a smile noticing her gaze.

"Nothing," Kinsey responds with a smile.

"I don't believe you," he comes over and kisses her. Her paintbrush accidentally touches his shoulder blade.

She gasps, "I'm so sorry. You were doing so well!"

"You're right, I was doing so well." Sam tickles her sides, and she squeals her brush touching his forearm. They stare at the area.

Giggling she says, "Oops."

Sam's cell phone starts vibrating in his pocket, "Saved by the bell," he tells her with a smile. "Hello?" The smile freezes on his face and quickly falls away. Kinsey's smile fades immediately, putting her paintbrush down. "How bad? Is she okay? I will be right there…. Yes, I understand."

Hanging up the phone Kinsey asks, "What happened?"

Sam runs his fingers through her hair. "Quinn collapsed at work." Kinsey's hand covers her mouth not wanting to ask the next question. "She is at the hospital with Diane."

"Let's go," Kinsey and Sam rush out of the room and down the stairs. She quickly locks Hudson in his crate so there isn't paint to clean up when they get home. "I'll drive," Kinsey offers, grabbing her keys and purse. The drive to the hospital takes only ten minutes but it's the longest ten minutes of their lives.

"It's going to be okay," she tries to soothe him running her hand over his forearm. Parking the car, they rush inside. Diane meets them just inside the doors.

"What happened?" Sam asks after Diane rushes to him hugging him tightly. Kinsey typically would feel awkward at this exchange but under the circumstances, she feels like hugging Diane to comfort her as well.

"They think it's anemia. I don't know. They are running some tests on her now. They said she may need a transfusion and that we should have our blood tested to see if we are a match."

"Great, let's do that," Sam agrees.

Diane turns to look behind her, "The nurse I was speaking to…is right over there." She walks off and Sam turns to Kinsey.

"I'll be right back."

"Go, go," she shoos him towards his ex-wife. He gives her a quick kiss on the cheek and then rushes off. Kinsey paces the waiting room when she spots Robbie and Sadie rushing through the sliding doors.

She meets them, "What happened?" they both ask breathlessly from their sprint from the parking lot and no doubt fear for their sister and fiancée.

"All I know is that she collapsed at work, and they are testing her for anemia. Your mom and dad already went in to get tested in case she needs a transfusion."

"I want to get tested," Sadie demands.

"Your parents haven't come back yet, and they left with a nurse. I'm sure we will have more news shortly and you can get tested if needed."

"Can we see her?" Robbie is staring unseeing at the doors separating him from the love of his life. His elbow is bent his fingers are working at the hair on top of his head.

"I'm sure you will be able to go back soon. Sadie, maybe you can ask the nurse as you're her family."

Nodding, Sadie marches up to the counter, Robbie close on her heels. "Excuse me but my sister was admitted to the hospital. Is there any way we can see her? Anderson. Quinn Anderson."

The nurse types on the computer. "They haven't assigned her a room yet, but if you will just take a seat over there, I'm sure someone will be with you shortly." Defeated, the trio's shoulders slump and they turn around dejected heading for the seats none of them want to sit in. Twenty minutes later Sam retrieves them and takes them to Quinn's room. She is hooked up to an I.V. Diane is sitting at her bedside holding her finger to her lips as they come in, alerting them to the fact that Quinn is sleeping.

An hour and a half later, the doctor comes into Quinn's room. Diane had sent Robbie and Sadie down to the cafeteria to get food for everyone. Sam, who has been pacing the entire time, stops short. Diane stands from her perch on the chair next to Quinn. Kinsey comes out of the bathroom wiping her hands on a paper towel, she doesn't want to miss any of the conversation.

Dr. Rashid is holding a tablet, logging into Quinn's chart she scrolls through the results as the adults crowd her in a semi-circle. "What can you tell us," Sam asks.

"Quinn is anemic and will need a blood transfusion. Unfortunately, neither one of you is a match."

Kinsey looks to Diane, the color draining from her face when she turns to Sam. He has a deep frown, and his hand is squeezing the back of his neck, "I don't understand," he says slowly. Kinsey feels her chest tighten and her hands start to sweat. She continues to rub her palms on the damp paper towels. "How can neither one of us be a match?"

The doctor's lips purse together, "I'm sorry. I thought you knew." Worriedly she looks to Diane hoping she doesn't have to be the one to explain to him why he isn't a match for his daughter.

"I'm her father of course I thought I could be a match and if not me then her mother." Sam's voice is rising, and Kinsey wants to hold him tight but knows that's not what he needs or wants right now.

Diane looks to Kinsey, "You never told him?"

"Tell me what?" Sam is looking between Diane and Kinsey.

Kinsey is dumbfounded at the news, "You never told me that he wasn't her father. You said you got pregnant on purpose. I assumed you stopped taking your pill or put a hole in his condoms. I had no idea he wasn't Quinn's father! And you told me ages ago I haven't thought about it in years."

Sam's face is destroyed when Kinsey meets his gaze. "How could you keep this from me?" Sam is turning his anger at Kinsey.

"I didn't keep anything from you."

"Dad?" they hear a choked cry from the bed. All eyes turn to Quinn who has tears streaming down her face, having heard the entire conversation. Sam rushes to her bedside. Her arms extend, and the I.V. attached to the top of her hand is dangling. Bending over Sam embraces his oldest daughter. Together they cry. Kinsey has a hard time watching the scene her eyes and nose wanting to leak. She uses the same stupid paper towel to wipe her face.

Diane grips Kinsey's elbow. "We should give them a minute." All the women step out into the hallway.

"If there is anyone else, I can test?" Dr. Rashid asks Diane.

"Her sister and fiancée just did."

"Could I try?" Kinsey asks.

"Absolutely. The likelihood of you being a match isn't great not being family, but it is worth a shot."

"Great, where do I go?"

"Follow me."

Kinsey steps forward to follow the doctor but Diane holds her back. "I'm sorry I threw you under the bus in there. I felt backed into a corner. I never thought it would come out. As far as I'm concerned Sam is Quinn's father. Thank you for testing."

Kinsey nods curtly trying hard not to berate the woman that has caused her so much pain over the years, knowingly and unknowingly. The doctor has stopped to wait for her at the corner of the hallway and she rushes to catch up.

When Kinsey returns, she finds Diane sitting on the floor outside of Quinn's room. She is crying silently, her shoulders shaking. Kinsey sinks on the floor next to this woman she sometimes can't stand, and other times is grateful for.

Diane wipes her tears away avoiding Kinsey's gaze. "She won't see me," her voice is barely a whisper.

"I'm sure she is just mad. It might take some time, but she will be able to move past it."

Diane is shaking her head, "You don't get it. I have no one if I don't have my girls. My parents are both dead, but I didn't even really have them when they were alive. Sam was the first person that was in my corner and when I thought I was going to lose him I lied and told him I was pregnant. When he refused to sleep with me, I knew he was calling my bluff. I'm not proud of what I did but I had a family. I had a good life until you came back into the picture and shattered my world."

Kinsey's heart constricts in her chest. Kinsey and Sam's love had come with a price. It was a price she had been willing to pay but not everyone had gotten a say in the matter. It wasn't fair to Diane but what she had done all those years ago hadn't been fair to Kinsey either.

"I'm sure you haven't lost your girls. I'm sorry you've had a rough life. No child deserves to be neglected. You've been an excellent mother to these girls, and they are lucky to have you in their life."

Diane sniffles and turns to Kinsey, "You think so?"

"Of course, I do."

Kinsey notices Sam as he walks around the corner. He stops abruptly as he takes in the sight of the two women on the floor in front of Quinn's room. "Hey, can I talk to you for a sec?" Sam asks, his eyes locking on hers.

Kinsey squeezes Diane's hand before releasing it, "Sure." Standing she dusts herself off and walks around Diane's outstretched legs. Sam leads her around the corner where he had come from. They aren't touching and it feels foreign to her. They walk all the way down the hallway until they reach a quiet area next to the floor-to-ceiling single-pane window, looking out over the city.

Sam leans his shoulder against the wall facing the window. Turning to face him, her back to the view, she crosses her arms, "How are you holding up?" Kinsey is afraid to ask but does it anyway.

He still isn't looking at her, closing his eyes he drags a hand across his face his fingers digging into his eyelids before pinching the bridge of his nose. "I married her on a lie. I stayed with her based on a lie. Quinn is-" his voice breaks and the tears he had been desperate to hold in, come in a rush. Kinsey steps closer her arms wanting to hold him, but he has more to say, "She didn't deserve any of this. If I would have walked away maybe Diane wouldn't have gone through all that she did. But I feel guilty because then I wouldn't have Quinn or Sadie. Kinsey, I couldn't imagine my life without them. I'm supposed to walk her down the aisle in a couple of weeks!"

Kinsey has no idea how to comfort him. "You still will walk her down the aisle."

"I'm not her dad," he croaks out the words.

"That's not true. You are absolutely her dad. DNA has nothing to do with it. You raised her, cared for her, provided for her, and loved her every second of her life. Nothing can take that away from you. What Diane did is unthinkable, but I also know she was desperate for your love and attention, and she didn't want to lose you. I get it-" Kinsey holds up her hand when he starts to protest, "I didn't fight fair either. I didn't go to those lengths, but I understand her not wanting to lose you. I lost you and it's not a good feeling."

"I'm sorry," Sam's words are softly spoken.

"For what?" Kinsey asks honestly uncertain of what he is sorry for.

He pushes off the wall and stands in front of her, his closeness making her feel warm and tingly, "For getting mad at you. I had no right to take it out on you. I just can't believe it. Quinn looks like me and acts like me. She has been my shadow forever. She is my daughter, no one is ever going to tell me otherwise."

"Of course not. You are her father, and she will always be your daughter. Did you guys talk after we left?"

He is shaking his head no. "Robbie and Sadie came in and saw her crying. I just left as they went to console her. I couldn't bear to hear her tell her sister that they were only half-siblings."

"Did you talk to Diane?"

"I told her I fucking hate her. Not my finest moment. Then I walked away as she tried to talk to me."

"I don't blame you, but you will eventually need to talk to her."

"I can't even stand to look at her."

Kinsey holds her arms out to him, and he takes her up on her offer of comfort. Burying his face into her neck he holds her tight. When Kinsey and Sam return Sadie and Robbie are stepping out of Quinn's hospital room with concern on their faces. Diane scrambles from her spot on the floor where Kinsey had left her. Sadie looks at all of them, "She is really upset." The adults share a look but say nothing. "What is going on?" she asks. "We tried," her arm flails between her and Robbie, "to get her to talk to us but she won't stop crying. When she finally stopped, she asked to talk to you," she waves a finger between Diane and Sam.

They head for the door, Sam's hand is on the nob when Sadie replies, "You too," directed at Kinsey. Her heart begins thumping in her chest. This is a family matter why does she want her in there? Is it because she thinks of her as family now? Sam pushes open the door and holds it for Diane to walk through and he waits for Kinsey to join him.

Inside Diane heads for the bed. Quinn's head is turned towards the window even though she can't see out from her bed. Sam and Kinsey walk to the other side to face her. Her eyes are bloodshot and fresh rounds of tears are on her cheeks. Quinn wipes them away and roots around the bed to find the buttons to make it go up. No one says a word as they wait for her to get comfortable. Taking a deep breath her eyes are transfixed across the room to some unknown spot.

"Start talking," Quinn's voice is raspy but determined.

Diane's eyes look to Sam, then Kinsey before back to her daughter. "I lied to your dad and told him I was pregnant, but I wasn't."

"Did you think you were pregnant?" Quinn asks for clarification.

"No. I knew I wasn't pregnant."

Quinn's lips roll in between her teeth biting down on them, "Why would you lie about that?"

Diane takes her own shaky breath, "I thought he was going to leave me, and I couldn't stand the thought of losing him, so I lied." Kinsey looks at Sam, the muscle in his cheek is working overtime as he clenches his teeth.

"Dad?" Quinn looks at Sam, "Were you going to leave mom?"

Sam is silent for a moment then nods once for confirmation. Diane cries out her hand clutching her throat guessing all those years ago where their relationship was headed but not knowing a hundred percent. Kinsey feels her own gut punch knowing they could have been together.

"Who is my biological father?" Quinn still can't look at her mom. Sam and Kinsey are watching her closely curious.

"A sperm donor."

Quinn's hands come up to hold her face with a new round of tears, this time with audible sobbing. Her body bends in half rocking away the pain. The three adults stand around feeling helpless. Diane takes a step forward her hand out to rub her daughter's back, but she quickly drops it thinking better of it, fearful of rejection. They let her cry it out. When she has exhausted herself, she wipes her face and looks at Sam and Kinsey.

Kinsey grabs a box of tissues from the window and holds them out to her soon-to-be stepdaughter. Quinn takes them gratefully, blowing her nose.

"Why were you going to leave mom?" Sam opens his mouth, but nothing comes out. Quinn holds up her hand, "Let me rephrase that. Were you leaving mom for Kinsey?" The room is silent, no one moves, and no one breathes as they wait for a response.

Fear gnaws in the pit of Kinsey's stomach. Will Quinn hate her now if the truth comes out? "Yes," Sam's voice comes out strong and resolute. Kinsey's heart clenches in her chest and she looks to Quinn who is nodding her head. Quinn is a smart girl and had connected all the dots. Tears are streaming down Diane's face.

Sam kneels by the bed taking his daughter's hand. "Quinn," he waits for her to look at him. "I love you and even though how you got here is not ideal I wouldn't trade having you as my daughter for anything. Do you hear me? You have always been my daughter, and nothing is ever going to change that."

Quinn throws her arms around his neck sobbing into his shoulder. Eventually, Quinn wipes her nose and dries her tears pulling away from Sam. "Can I talk to mom alone please?"

Sam stands and kisses his daughter's forehead, "Yes of course." He offers his hand to Kinsey, and she clasps it for dear life as he pulls her from the room. Quinn and Diane talk for hours while Sam paces the waiting room with Robbie. Kinsey and Sadie flip through old magazines.

A nurse comes into the waiting room flipping through a folder. "Quinn Anderson's family." They huddle around her. "Good news, we have a match."

"Is it me?" Sadie asks.

"No, it says here her brother is."

Sadie looks confused. Sam and Kinsey's eyes lock a feeling of dread creeping down her spine. Robbie laughs, "I'm her fiancé. She doesn't have a brother."

The nurse looks again, "Do you mind stepping out into the hallway with me?"

"No, check it again," Sadie asks, "It must mean sister. I'm her sister. I should be a match."

The nurse is now looking unsure of herself and how to proceed. "Let me go check and I'll be back." She turns and practically runs from the room.

"That was so weird," Robbie's fingers are twisting together.

Sadie is looking at her dad, "What is going on? Does this have something to do with Quinn crying earlier?" Robbie's head whips in her direction.

Diane walks in, "What did I miss?"

They all start talking at once. She hears the blood test, Quinn, her brother, match, Robbie, and the nurse checking now. Her mouth goes dry as she looks at a glaring Sam, a wide-eyed Sadie and Kinsey, and finally a nervous Robbie.

"They have to be wrong, right mom?" Sadie asks her.

"I need to speak to Quinn," turning Diane walks to the door. Robbie beats her out of the room racing down the hallway toward Quinn's room. Everyone rushes closely behind him.

Throwing open the door Robbie burst in, "Quinn!" he bellows when he doesn't see her. Kinsey shuts the door behind them knowing this will most likely be a heated conversation. They hear the toilet flush behind the bathroom door, then running water.

Quinn opens the door and takes in the frantic looks from her family. "What on Earth is going on?"

"We think Robbie might be our brother," Sadie bursts out before Robbie has a chance.

The grip on her I.V. pole tightens, "Mom?"

"This can't be true," Robbie's voice cracks.

Fresh tears are streaming down Diane's face, "I... don't know sweetie," her voice is barely above a whisper, and she clears her throat. Quinn who has been crying for hours now, her wild hair and puffy red eyes turns and is down on her knees retching into the toilet.

Robbie runs to her his hand on her back, "What is going on?"

"Did you have a kid before us?" Sadie asks her parents.

"No," they both respond

Quinn wipes her mouth and pulls on the handle. Her hands cup Robbie's face, "I love you so much."

"I love you too. What is going on? You need to tell me."

"Why don't we all come out here so we can talk," Sam suggests.

Robbie helps Quinn off the floor and to her bed. She crawls in and Robbie sits next to her his arm around her shoulders. Her arms wrap around his waist.

"Will someone please tell me what is going on?" Sadie demands.

"Yes, please," Robbie chimes in.

Quinn wipes her eyes, "Dad isn't my biological father."

"What?" roars Sadie and Robbie.

"How long have you known?" Sadie shouts.

"We just found out today," Sam tells her.

"Mom?" Sadie asks. "Are you, my parents?" The thought just dawning on her has her voice coming out shrill.

"Yes," both Sam and Diane assure her.

"I used a sperm donor for Quinn," Diane tells her and looks at Robbie.

"Wait just a minute," Robbie stands and fishes his phone out of his pocket. "Hey dad," he says, "I need to ask you a question and I need you to answer me honestly," Pause. With his palm plastered to his forehead he says, "No, I'm not fine," Pause. "I can't go into it now. Listen did you ever donate sperm?" Pause. "Just answer the question." Pause. "Fuuuuuck." The tension in the room is palpable as Robbie hangs up the phone.

He throws himself down on a chair away from Quinn. His elbows rest on his knees as he bows his head and cries. Kinsey's hand comes up to cover her mouth, tears rolling down freely across her cheeks. She hasn't left the door her back leaning up against it. There isn't a dry eye in the room.

A knock on the door startles everyone, and Kinsey jumps away. Wiping her tears, she turns the handle. The nurse returns, "I'm so sorry. I'd like to repeat the tests if you don't mind."

Robbie jumps up to follow the nurse and Sadie is right behind him. "Would you mind giving me and Kinsey a minute?" Quinn asks.

Sam's eyes lock on Kinsey asking if it is okay. With an imperceptible nod, Sam says, "Sure, sweetie. We'll be right outside if you need us." Leaning over he kisses her on the temple before ushering Diane out.

Quinn pats the end of the bed inviting Kinsey to take a seat. Moving towards the bed she sits down, and Quinn takes her hand. "What am I going to do?"

"Well, first we aren't going to panic. It doesn't look good, and we have to prepare ourselves for the possibility that Robbie could be related to you. If that happens, we will take it one step at a time."

"I can't just unlove him," Quinn cries.

Kinsey scoops Quinn into her arms, "I know. I'm so sorry. I hope this is all just a big misunderstanding."

"Me too." Wiping her tears for the thousandth time Quinn squeezes Kinsey's hand, "Listen, I'm happy for you and dad."

Surprised Kinsey turns to her, "You are?"

"Absolutely. I can see how much dad loves you. How much you love each other. I'm glad you two are getting your happy ever after."

"Thank you. That means the world to me."

Sadie comes back fifteen minutes later without Robbie. The pain in Quinn's eyes is unmistakable. "He just needs a minute," Sadie explains.

Quinn releases a shaky breath and nods her head. A grueling hour later the nurse returns to the room with Robbie and a woman in a business suit in tow. "She wouldn't tell me anything," he says when they all look at him expectantly.

The woman with the tight bun is clearly in charge. "If everyone could just take a seat?" When everyone has complied, she begins speaking, "My name is June Redmond, I'm an attorney for the hospital. I would like to apologize for the mix-up we had earlier today. The labels between Ms. Anderson and Mr. Zimmerman were accidentally switched." A collective gasp and nervous laughter spread.

Robbie rushes to Quinn's bedside crushing her to him. "Oh thank God. I didn't know how I was going to live without you."

Quinn gets her transfusion from Sadie and it takes two weeks for her to fully recover. Quinn and Robbie's wedding is beautiful, and Sam walks her down the aisle. They dance well into the night. The newlyweds fly to Greece for their honeymoon as a gift from Diane.

Chapter Fifty-Six

♥

Kinsey and Sam complete the renovations on their brownstone, and it is stunning. They decide that they want a modest wedding in the backyard.

On Kinsey's wedding day, Aidan and Ethan knock on her bedroom door. Quinn opens it and lets them in. "Can we talk to our mom for a minute?" Ethan asks.

"Sure." Turning she asks Sadie to step outside with her.

The boys are shuffling their feet, hands clasped behind their backs as they avoid eye contact. "Mom, you look beautiful," Aidan tells her.

"You really do look great, mom," Ethan chimes in.

"Thank you, boys," she pulls them close for a group hug.

"We have something for you." Aidan pulls an envelope out of his tux pocket, and she gasps. It's addressed to her in Grayson's handwriting. She had been sure he hadn't left her one. Tears sting her eyes as she takes it from him.

"We are going to give you a minute with that one," Ethan says, and they step out of the room leaving her alone. Sitting on a chair by the back window overlooking her beautifully landscaped backyard set up for her wedding with an arbor, an abundance of flowers, and tulle. She rips open the envelope.

"My Dearest Kinsey,

I love you more than words can say. You are my heart and my soul. I have treasured every minute with you since the moment I laid eyes on you. You have such good energy around you. You make the darkest bleakest times manageable.

Thank you for staying. Thank you for being my wife. Thank you for our beautiful children. Thank you for giving me the happiest years of my life. Thank you for fighting alongside me while I battled cancer.

I know you were probably disappointed when I didn't leave you a letter. I gave it to Aidan one night while you were sleeping. I told him he wasn't allowed to even tell you I wrote you a letter. I threatened to haunt him from the grave if he broke his promise."

Kinsey laughs at this part knowing Aidan is deathly afraid of ghosts. She continues, "I knew if I had given the letter to Ethan he would have caved and given it to you. We both know I'm right," Kinsey is nodding her head in agreement as she wipes her nose.

"My guess is you are marrying Sam. I want to wish you both all the happiness in the world. If it isn't Sam, you are making some other man the luckiest man in the world. But my heart tells me that you and Sam will find each other once again.

Make a great life. One that is worthy of you. Be happy. Enjoy the little moments and savor the big events. You are my everything and now you are going to be someone else's everything.

All my love, Grayson."

Kinsey clutches the letter to her chest. He hadn't forgotten about her. He predicted she would end up with Sam and he was right. Wiping her eyes, she goes to the mirror to see the damage she has done to her makeup.

She reapplies her makeup and then appraises herself. She is happy about the dress she chose. Kinsey had wanted something simple but still wanted it to look like a wedding dress. She had passed on all the ball gown dresses, the ruffles, and jewels.

The first one she tried on was the one. Kinsey knew the moment she slipped into it. Not wanting to miss out she tried all the other dresses she and the saleswoman had chosen, but this was the one. It's high-necked lace, sheer over her collarbone, and three-quarter sleeves. With a heart-shaped neckline underneath, the satin skirt had a slight poof at the hips ending at midcalf. Kinsey had chosen classic pumps to compliment the outfit.

Sam and Kinsey had discussed having groomsmen and bride's maids at their wedding. They asked their children to stand up with them. They had all been delighted. Hudson is their ring bearer. Because her yellow diamond is so flashy, she wanted a thin wedding band. The jeweler showed her a thin circle of diamonds that fits perfectly with all the grooves of her engagement ring. Sam insists on a non-traditional wedding band and chose black titanium.

At the wedding, Trish's present is the mug Sam had given her so long ago. She had held on to it for her.

After the wedding and reception, they are lying in bed Sam confesses. "The boys dropped off a letter to me before the ceremony."

Kinsey sits up to look at him, "From Grayson? What did it say?"

"Did you get one too?"

Kinsey nods, "So what did yours say?"

"Oh no, he said not to tell you."

She inhales sharply, "He said what?" She storms out of bed to find his letter. Sam is chuckling from their bed as she picks his tux off the floor and reaches inside. She finds the envelope inside his coat pocket. Sam is sitting up in bed watching her with mirth on his face as she pulls the letter from the envelope.

The first sentence reads, "You better let Kinsey read this, or she will never let it go."

"You suck," she tells him as she waves the letter at him in all her naked glory.

"I do suck all sorts of things," Sam tells her seductively. She giggles as she climbs back in bed to read the letter.

"To the Man, Who Has Won Kinsey's heart,

You better let Kinsey read this or she will never let it go."

"Ha! I knew it!" Kinsey jabs her finger at the paper as Sam smiles and puts an arm around her.

Kinsey smiles and returns to the letter, "As I've come to learn, life is short, you must live it to the fullest. This is by far the hardest letter I've ever had to write, and I saved it for last. I wanted to get this right. Take care of my family. My boys are going to need a strong male presence in their lives. This isn't a task to take lightly, so if you are up for the challenge, you have my blessing.

Kinsey, as I'm sure you know, loves fiercely. Once you have her love consider yourself the luckiest man alive as I did. Hold her close and remind her every day how much she means to you. I know you will have your ups and downs. She is a strong competitor in arguments, and I don't envy you in that aspect at all. Just keep in mind that she always wins.

Some helpful hints, always put the toilet seat down, make sure all your laundry is in the hamper, and don't leave the water running even if you are going to be right back. This includes leaving the fridge and/or cabinet doors open."

Kinsey laughs, tears in her eyes, she wipes her nose and eyes with the back of her wrist before reading the rest. "He has no idea you are neater than me," Kinsey tells Sam, and he chuckles.

"Make sure you love her the way she deserves to be loved. I'm trusting you to take care of my girl because I am not there to do so. I wish you both a long and happy life together.
Take care, my friend,
Grayson

The End

COMING SOON...
THE BEE'S KNEES
San Francisco 2008

Chapter One

Yes, my real name is Amethyst. Amethyst, no middle name, Carter. If it were up to my mom, I wouldn't have a last name either but when I started school it was required. My mom is a full-blown hippie, unsure of who my father is. She is a free spirit and didn't bother with names back then. The fact I was born with dark purple eyes that haven't changed color since birth, my mom thought it was a sign from Mother Earth to name her daughter after her favorite stone. I doubt my mom's real name is Wind Chime but that is what she goes by. I've never met my grandparents, so I have no one to ask.

I don't believe in any of the sage-burning bullshit my mom does, but I let her live her life peacefully as she doesn't tend to interfere in mine. Every Sunday, I meet her at the local farmer's market to buy our produce and whatever catches our fancy. It's the only time I can consistently put aside for us. Currently, I'm in the final semester of my master's program, while working full-time remotely as a programmer. My dream job is to work in cyber security for the FBI. I'll have met all my requirements for my application by May. It's been intense but worth it.

I can always pick my mom out of a crowd; she is the brightest one around. Her frizzy blonde hair which she refuses to put any product in, irritates me, as much as it doesn't bother her at all. She is always wearing long flowy skirts and billowy blouses with an overabundance of jewelry, nothing worth much. Today is no different. She has a homemade crocheted bag slung over one shoulder across her body, the strap separating her boobs in an unflattering way. I've tried to warn her, but she just tells me that she is not ruled by vanity. Her smile is 1000 watts bright on the already sunny day. "Amethyst," she is waving her hand enthusiastically in the air as if I don't see her.

"Hi, Wind Chime," I say because she doesn't answer to Mom. We hug, and she compliments me on my aura today. I try not to laugh, I'm such a modern girl living with technology and she is the complete opposite living off the land as much as possible. "Thank you," I reply instead.

We start at the same end as usual and visit the same booths saying hi to familiar vendors, my mom charming them all. We fill our reusable Earth-friendly bags as we make our way through the aisles. My mom stops at a booth I don't recognize as a regular and I'm soon not surprised why. A woman dressed similarly to Wind Chime is running the booth. It looks like an antique/junkyard sale is happening in the confines of the ten-by-ten tent. An old oriental rug warms the space on the asphalt.

"I'm Tabitha," the saleswoman tells them, "Let me know if I can show you lovely ladies anything." A brass and glass case sits on a table surrounded by homemade scarves and Knick knacks on the opposite side. Wind Chime is running her hand over the case looking inside when, she pokes her finger tapping the top, "Amethyst!" she exclaims.

"What?" I ask turning from browsing the other side of the booth.

"There is a beautiful amethyst ring here."

"Isn't it stunning?" Tabitha exclaims. Coming over with a key she opens up the case. "It's from the nineteen twenties in a style called Art Deco. I just acquired it from an estate sale." She pulls it out of the plush black velvet holding it to the light, the dark purple gem sparkling. It's a princess cut stone set in white gold or silver. I'm not convinced it isn't just costume jewelry.

Wind Chime takes the piece and attempts to put it on. It slips easily onto her bony finger but the large stone, top-heavy as it is, keeps rotating on her finger and she is unable to stand it up straight. "Do you feel anything?" the retailer asks. I frown, what is she going on about? Feel something?

Wind Chime looks up with enthusiasm. I'm not falling for this lady. "What should I feel?" she asks. The saleswoman steps closer and lowers her voice, conspiratorially. I hate to admit it, but I take two steps closer to hear what she is going to say.

"Some folks say, that when they put on antique jewelry, they get glimpses into the past lives of the souls that wore it before them," Tabitha explains.

"Really?" Wind Chime is breathless, her hand to her heart. I think a tiny snort of "I smell something fishy" comes out of my nose, but neither woman pays me any attention.

"Anything?" the woman asks.

Wind Chime concentrates, even closing her eyes. One eyebrow raises on her face and again I lean forward wanting to kick myself for getting sucked into the drama. Her eyebrow relaxes as both of us watch her. I almost jump when her other eyebrow shoots up sky-high but I'm proud of myself when I don't. Her eyes pop open. Both of us wait expectantly. Her face crumples, "Nothing," she admits disappointment in her voice.

"Oh, well it doesn't happen to everyone," Tabitha waives it off. Or anyone, I think cynically but keep my thoughts to myself. "Do you want to try it, Dear?" she inquires.

I almost look behind me thinking she has to be asking someone else to participate in this load of horse poop. "Oh, Amethyst you should," Wind Chime begs.

"Sure, why not," I say with a false sense of cheerfulness neither woman detect. I hold out my hand for the ring as my mom places it in my palm. Nothing happens, not that I expected it to, it is just a ring.

I slip it easily onto my ring finger. It fits perfectly and the shape and color are beautiful with my hand's skin tone. I look down at my hand and I feel the ground underneath me shake. Are we having an Earthquake? We live in San Francisco, so it isn't out of the realm of possibilities, but my eyes are starting to go out of focus, and I feel nauseous. My head is swimming and I feel like I'm swaying on my feet. I try to wrestle the ring off my finger as the ground rushes up to meet me.

Dear Readers,

My last book, AMNESIA AT THE ALTAR was released in July 2016. I know, a long time ago! In 2017 I wrote the sequel, HONEY WITHOUT THE MOON. The same year I went to a writer's conference in Boston and met with a literary agent who read the first 20 pages of the book and gave me helpful suggestions for the novel. At the end of our interview, she gave me her card and asked to see the book when I was done. Elated I thought my dreams of being traditionally published were close to coming true.
A job change had me working much farther from home and gone a good portion of the week. With the hour-plus commute, I was able to listen to more audiobooks even if I wasn't able to write as much. On one of those long rides home, I came up with the concept for COUNTRY SONG. I started writing the love triangle novel. I enrolled in the James Patterson masterclass course and worked on two other stories called, SHEPARD'S HOOK and SECRETS OF THE RAVINE. One is an FBI murder mystery and the second is a WWII mystery.
In 2019 I decided to go back to college to get my degree. I only needed five classes. I enrolled in English II on Saturdays while working full-time, then Medical Microbiology on Friday nights in 2020. I aced both classes and got invited to be in the Honors Program. I started writing A LONG LOVE AGO after listening to a radio station that had married couples discussing how they spiced up their marriages. Instantly I thought of all the ways that could possibly go wrong. I wrote the first 20k words on my hiatus from work during the pandemic. I also watched everything Netflix had to offer, tried to get lost on road trips with my daughter, long walks with the family, did several home improvement projects, and worked on a puzzle before returning to work.
One story I had in my brain that would not leave me alone is THE BEE'S KNEES. The concept of this book came when I was 17 and antique shopping with my mom. I had never put it to paper until I told a few of my co-workers and they were intrigued by the idea. So, I started writing that

story. Long story short, I get sidetracked easily. The good news is I have plenty of new projects to keep me busy.

My next job change brought me closer to home and a co-worker that loves my work and keeps me on task. Hence me finishing A LONG LOVE AGO with THE BEE'S KNEE soon to follow.

In my personal life, we lost two family pets at the same time. Navigated my children through junior high, and high school, sports, learning to drive, permits, licenses, proms, homecomings, girlfriends, boyfriends, confirmations, and first jobs for both of them. I naively thought my son's senior year would be a breeze, but it turns out it's like a second job. College tours, applications, Fasfa, Common app., and scholarships are stressful and exhausting. We moved my son into college and our daughter started her senior year this past fall. Our daughter struggles with mental health and in turn, our family takes on her pain. It has been rough the past several years, but we are managing as best as we can. We had numerous medical setbacks including Physical therapy for a broken ankle and several ER visits. My mother-in-law's husband died of Covid, so she moved in with us in July and brought with her a dog and a cat adding to our two dogs, a cat, and several guinea pigs my daughter is collecting, so we have quite the zoo here.

I appreciate everyone's reviews of my work. I do read them all. I have plans to go back and re-edit SEE YOU NEVER and AMNESIA AT THE ALTAR. I listen it's just been difficult to go back when I'm trying to move forward.

You can find me on Facebook and TikTok.

Thank you to everyone that believed in me and didn't give up.

Best Wishes,

Misty Jae Ogert